WHATE♥ER
IT TAKES

KRISTA & BECCA
RITCHIE

Cover Image ©iStock
Cover Design by Twin Cove Designs

ISBN: 978-1-950165-21-6

ALSO BY
KRISTA & BECCA RITCHIE

LIKE US SERIES
Damaged Like Us
Lovers Like Us
Alphas Like Us
Tangled Like Us
Sinful Like Us
Headstrong Like Us

ADDICTED SERIES
Addicted to You
Ricochet
Addicted for Now
Thrive
Addicted After All

CALLOWAY SISTERS SERIES
Kiss the Sky
Hothouse Flower
Fuel the Fire
Long Way Down
Some Kind of Perfect

CIRCUS IS FAMILY SERIES
The Failed Audition
The Secret Ex-Boyfriend

A NOTE FROM THE AUTHORS

Whatever It Takes is a New Adult romance. Even though the characters are 17 for much of the novel, we do not consider this book Young Adult. *Whatever It Takes* contains mature language and graphic sexual content and is recommended for readers 18+.

Also to note: Wakefield University is a fictional school set in London that has a high matriculation of International students and uses a semester-based curriculum. Since Willow is American, she uses many colloquial American terms for university (for example: referring to her room as a dorm) that UK students might not use.

CONTENT WARNING

This book contains graphic scenes of physical abuse from older brothers to a younger brother and verbal abuse that may be upsetting to some readers.

"It's the oldest story in the world.

One day you're 17 and planning for someday.

And then, quietly, and without you ever really noticing,

someday is today.

And then someday is yesterday.

And this is your life."

ONE TREE HILL

(SEASON 9, EPISODE 13)

1

PRESENT DAY - August
London, England

WILLOW HALE
Age 20

Yesterday I was a virgin.

Today, I'm not.

And I know I'm not "supposed" to put this great big importance on my first time and virginity and all of that, but I didn't lose *it* until I was twenty. Having anyone touch me is a big deal. Having someone *inside* of me…is monumental. Like Thor crashing down during the climax of *Avengers: Infinity War*.

It was *that* big of a deal. To me. To him.

And now the guy who took my virginity is thousands of miles away in Philadelphia.

"Over here is the campus bookstore, which I checked does not carry comic books so it's already a complete fail," I say to my cell, video recording.

My head pounds from jetlag. It feels like I just stepped off the plane, and I've only thrown my bags in my dorm. I wanted to check out the campus before it got dark. As the sun begins to set, students meander into dining halls for dinner.

I focus my cell's camera on the campus bookstore sign.

Documenting my college experience at Wakefield University is my first order of business, while Garrison keeps me updated on his life back in Philly.

Long distance is not ideal. It's not my first choice. Or second. But until someone invents teleportation or I'm struck down by lightning and develop super-human speed like The Flash, we're stuck to modern technology.

"And over here…" I rotate my cell to rows of booths. "Are all the potential clubs that I'm probably not going to join—"

"HEADS UP!"

I turn. *No no no.* A frisbee is flying straight towards my face.

Ducking quickly, the frisbee sails over my head and across the quad to another guy's hands. My heart beats wildly, and my jaw slowly drops. Dumbfounded. Did I just outmaneuver a flying frisbee? Okay, my reflexes have definitely improved. I am certified-clumsy. Definitely not by choice. Maybe London is a good luck charm for me.

My lips lift into a bigger smile, and I turn to head back down the cobbled path—*oh shit,* my hip and elbow suddenly collide with a girl and her box, both coming out of nowhere.

She stumbles and manages not to faceplant from my elbow-knock. But the brown cardboard crashes to the ground, flaps opening, and I watch as condoms spill onto the cobblestone.

Shit.

"I'm *so* sorry." I quickly squat and start scooping up the condoms.

PRESENT DAY

"No worries. We're both in one piece." Her English accent is noticeable. It hits me again—I am not in America anymore. Add in the fact that this is my new home. That I'm living here for four years instead of the usual three for UK undergrads because my degree requires blood, sweat, tears, and an extra year apparently.

It's all hardly sunk in.

I'm half expecting someone to pop out of the bushes with a big *Gotcha* sign.

I just…I hope moving here was the right decision.

The twenty-something girl in front of me blows a red curl off her lips and bends down to help with the condom spill. She's white, curvy and wears a Wakefield T-shirt—the letters WFU in a circular dark green and gold emblem.

I toss a huge handful of condoms into her box while I perspire everywhere. I am hot. Baking under embarrassment, and I'm aware that this is the most condoms I've ever touched.

When they lower me into a grave, my funeral eulogy will definitely be: *There was that young, innocent Willow Hale who ran head-first into a giant box of condoms and never revived.*

I must be staring too hard at the condoms because the girl says, "You can take some. That's what they're there for."

"Oh no, I'm a vir—" I stop myself. Because…

Willow, duh, you are a virgin *no* more.

The redhead narrows her eyes. "If you're a virgin, you could still use these." She's tossing a couple foiled packets in my direction. "You're in uni. It's better to be safe."

Except the only person I'd want to have sex with isn't here. But I don't have the energy or the time to explain my complicated relationship. Not that she'd even want to hear about it.

Box now full, we both stand, and I pocket three condoms in my faded jeans. She balances the box in one arm and holds out a free hand. "I'm Karla. The student warden…or I guess, what you'd know as an RA—over at Bishop Hall."

Bishop Hall. That's the name of my dorm building. I'm about to tell her that we live in the same place, thankful for such a serendipitous run-in, but Karla tilts her head and eyes my face more incredulously.

"You look familiar," she muses.

I pale and push up my glasses that slide down the bridge of my nose. Moving thousands of miles away was strategic in multiple ways. I thought, maybe, I could return to the shadows. Just for a bit.

No paparazzi.

Less people recognizing me.

I'm on the periphery of fame, and I'm settled with drifting out of it.

"I get that a lot," I say. "Um…I have to go." I jab a thumb towards nowhere. Technically, it's pointed to the middle of the quad. But without making any further eye contact, I actually just walk off in the opposite direction towards the bookstore.

It's a level 10 awkward departure.

My armpits sweat, and pressure slowly builds on my chest. What happens if I run into her again? It's likely, right? She lives in my hall. And now she thinks I'm probably such a loser with zero social skills, and really I have no choice but to actively avoid her.

Less than an hour into my first day in London and I already have added someone on my *Person to Avoid Because of an Awkward First Impression* list. It's unfortunately a long list back in Philly.

I rehash my awkward departure on a loop like rewinding a car crash scene in a movie. What could I have done differently?

About a million things. A gazillion. Trillion.

PRESENT DAY

My stomach sinks.

Shake it off, Willow. I find an empty bench behind the bookstore and sling my backpack on the wooden slates. After I take a seat, I turn to my phone, which has never stopped recording. *Shit.* I end the video and a notification from Garrison pops up. *New message!*

My breath quickens. Longing swells inside me, and then other unwanted sentiments start to infiltrate their way in. Regret. Guilt.

I wish he were here, but I have to settle with the 2D version of Garrison Abbey, which is better than nothing. The thought of him being completely gone from my life only brings a wave of panic and misery.

I click into his video message. A small pot of water is on screen, long noodles sticking halfway out, not fitting. *"My noodles are defective, Willow."*

I smile and my eyes water a little.

"And I know what you're going to say." He turns the camera to face himself. *"Break the noodles. But there has to be some Chef Boyardee rule against that."* He sighs deeply. His aquamarine eyes carrying a heaviness to them like he hasn't slept much. *"So basically, I'm a mess without you."*

"You're not a mess," I whisper to my phone. But he can't hear me.

He runs a hand through his thick, disheveled hair. The tattoos at his collarbone peek out of his plain black T-shirt. Small stars, shaped into a constellation. He has more tattoos, scattered around his body, while I have none. On paper, maybe it looks like we shouldn't be together.

He grew up in a mansion three times the size of my childhood home in Maine.

He was kicked out of two prep schools.

He was almost arrested for vandalizing, for drugs and for underage drinking, and if it weren't for the top shot lawyer his rich parents hired, he might have faced serious consequences at some time in his life.

Garrison Abbey is the kind of guy that wears a D.A.R.E. shirt ironically and hacks assholes' computers for fun. People flock to him because he's cool in this mysterious way. Like Jess from *Gilmore Girls*.

In Maine, most of the student body didn't even know my name. If it weren't for my connections to the Calloway sisters, I'd be considered painfully normal.

I still can't believe we ended up here. Together.

Okay, not together in the physical sense since he *is* thousands of miles away. But together as in we're boyfriend-girlfriend. It took a lot of cosmic happenings for that to come to fruition.

The video of Garrison attempting to cook spaghetti ends abruptly after he switches the stove off, giving up on it. I glance over my shoulder towards Bishop Hall. I don't think I can venture back to my dorm. I might run into Karla again, and I'm not sure I can take another awkward interaction.

As a last-minute distraction, I click into Tumblr on my cell.

My stomach lurches when I see a new post.

Oh no…

Garrison filled out a questionnaire that I didn't tag him in, and that *rarely* happens. He doesn't love questionnaires, but he does them because he knows I'm kind of obsessed. So it's odd that he did this, right? I don't know what it means.

I hold my breath like I can stop an impending impact and slowly read the post.

Name: Garrison

Zodiac Sign: Scorpio

Average Hours of Sleep: idk used to be about 7-8? It's less, so whatever.

PRESENT DAY

Last Google Search: what time is it in London?
Relationship Status: </3

I…can't…breathe.

He put a broken heart as his relationship status. *Broken.* As in, I broke his heart? Or is it just fractured while I'm in London and he's in Philly?

My glasses suddenly fog and the emotion I've been burying suddenly rises tenfold. *Guilt.*

He took my virginity yesterday.

And I'm the one who left. Boarded a flight at 5 a.m. his time. Flew to a different continent and landed this evening. Put an ocean between us. Literally.

A sudden realization overcomes me…oh no. It was goodbye sex.

I had *goodbye* sex my first time.

Removing my glasses, I wipe them on my cotton shirt. My belly twists uncomfortably. New eulogy: *Here lies Willow Hale, the girl who fucked for the first time and then left.*

Maybe it wasn't even fucking. It was more like…love making. Sweet. Kind. And loving. It was perfect—except for the leaving part.

And I know Garrison doesn't blame me for leaving. Not like I blame myself. He held me after we slept together and told me that he still wanted me to go. Wanted me to pursue my dreams and take the hard path—the challenge.

Since I have such a big safety net in Philadelphia, I don't know if I can really thrive there until I learn to thrive on my own first. *London* is the challenge.

But it's also likely I will fail spectacularly, like a mega belly flop into a crowded pool.

I look back at the broken heart on Tumblr.

His words ring in my head. The ones he said to me before I boarded the plane. "*We're going to make this work. I'm going to text and Skype.*" He cupped my cheeks and both of us were crying. "*We're going to make this work, Willow. Because you're my girl, and that's not going to change.*"

We're going to make this work.

Broken hearts and all.

I try to believe it. Placing my tortoise-shell glasses back on, I keep reading his post.

Siblings: three older brothers. Be happy they're not yours.

Love or Lust: lust doesn't hurt.

He sounds sad, but not his usual sad. I reach for my phone to send him a silly gif from his favorite TV show—*Supernatural.* Just as my fingers slide over the screen, I notice the last question and answer.

Met a Celebrity: I think I might be becoming one...

It chills me for a second. How much my life has changed his.

Three years ago, I was no one. I was living in a sleepy town of Caribou, Maine, and my parents were getting divorced. My little sister Ellie was my only sibling, and I only had one friend.

Then I woke up one morning, and little did I know, but everything just...changed.

I found out that Ellie wasn't my only sibling.

I had a brother miles and miles away.

PRESENT DAY

A *famous* brother.

Loren Hale has the kind of fame where he shows up on magazines and tabloids every week. The kind of fame where I had idolized him long before I even knew we were related. Imagine if someone like Chris Evans—Captain America himself—had a long-lost little sister. That sister being *me*. It was that impactful and unbelievable and really…

Three years later, it's still surreal.

Loren Hale changed everything.

For me and Garrison.

2

GARRISON ABBEY
Age 20

Seven days. Six hours. And three excruciating minutes. But it's not like I'm counting how long it's been since Willow and I put an ocean between us.

I like numbers.

I like to code.

It's what I fucking do.

Even at two in the morning on a Friday night. My headphones are tossed aside on my mattress. Giving my ears a rest from wearing them in the office all day. Did I mention it was Friday?

Which means the asshole in the apartment next door is currently hosting some sort of first semester bash in his place. The walls thump from his shitty EDM music.

I can code with most music.

That's not what's really distracting me. It's the laughter and the high-pitched squeals and the frat-bro cheering that pulls my mind away from work.

"JARED!" a girl shrieks. Someone knocks into a shared wall and my *Silversun Pickups* poster falls off the hook and hits the floor.

Yeah, that's it.

I push away from my keyboard on my rolling chair and slide across the hardwood to my stereo setup. I crank it up. Full blast. And then I scroll through a playlist on my phone.

Fuck their EDM.

I put on my favorite band.

Interpol. The song "Evil" starts out slow and builds up, but it emits from my speaker so fucking loud that it's like I'm in a competition with my neighbor. Whose eardrums can we blast out first? Truth, I'd be fine getting a permanent migraine from listening to *Interpol*. It'd be worth it.

Barely a minute later, a knock slams on my door. "Hey!"

The guy says something else, but I can't make it out. Suddenly, the EDM music cuts off.

"HEY!" he screams, more clearly now. "Turn your shit down, man!" He bangs his fist at my door, and my pulse ratchets up.

She flashes in my head.

If Willow were here, she'd tell me to turn it down. Don't start a confrontation. Don't be that guy.

But she's not here.

I stand up.

The pounding on my door intensifies. "Fuck, can you hear me?!"

Striding over, each second there feels like someone is clenching my heart in their fist. *Pump. Pump.* Trying to wake the cold, lifeless organ.

The chorus starts as I put my hand on the knob. I've listened to this song a million-and-one times, but tonight it sounds different in my head. I should turn it off. But something is wrong with me. I feel it deep inside me like dark ink bleeding into paper, and Willow can't change me.

No one can.

I open the door.

My neighbor's angered brown eyes pierce me. Baseball cap turned backward. Penn shirt and khakis. He looks like he should be at the Alpha Omega Zeta house, not some apartment building in Center City.

"Yeah?" I ask, not needing to raise my voice over the music since we're close enough.

He holds out his hand. "I'm Jared, your neighbor. Sorry, man, I didn't get the chance to introduce myself yet."

I moved into this building the same time Willow left for Wakefield. I wanted a change. But it's been a week, and Jared and I have crossed paths a few times already. He's never said a word to me before. So this pseudo-fake-nice bullshit is just all for show.

"Cool," I say, but I don't shake his hand.

Jared pauses for a second and then drops his arm. "Hey, you think you can turn down your music? I'm kind of having a party. It's my girlfriend's birthday."

I glance towards his apartment and notice three girls and two guys wedged in his doorway, watching our interaction. I'm not even sure how many more people are inside his place.

"Then it looks like I'm giving your girlfriend a birthday present." I swing my head back to Jared. "Being introduced to *Interpol* is probably the best gift she's going to get tonight."

Jared laughs dryly, annoyance flashing in his eyes. "Look, we don't want to listen to your music."

"You're right, yours is so much better," I say, sarcasm on my lips. "It's been nothing but pure bliss for the past hour."

"Dude, I'm sorry." Jared holds up his hands in defense. "We didn't mean to be so loud. Maybe we can come to some sort of understanding." His eyes scan me from my bare feet to my head. "You go to Penn? Come grab a beer with us. We've got plenty in the room."

Three years ago, I might have taken that offer.

Today, I just want to be alone.

"I don't want your beer. Just stop knocking into my walls—"

"Holy shit," a girl from the doorway exclaims loudly. Her friends huddle around her, staring at the cell in her clutch. "You're Garrison Abbey!"

Jared frowns, brows knotting. "Ana, am I supposed to know who that is?"

Ana glides over in heels, her blonde hair in a tight ponytail that looks honest-to-God painful. I don't know how girls do that. She puts a hand to Jared's chest. "Ignore my boyfriend. He isn't well-acquainted with entertainment news or *Celebrity Crush*."

I almost roll my eyes at the trash tabloid. Okay, I have picked up the magazine at the grocery checkout before. But it's certified crap.

Jared shakes his head. "Wait, he's been in *Celebrity Crush*?"

"Yeah, with the Calloway sisters," Ana says, pointing to me like I'm not *right* here.

Jared looks me up and down like he's trying to figure me out now. "So are you dating one of the Calloway sisters then?"

I almost laugh.

They're all married.

None of them to me. And if any of the Calloway sisters heard that question, they would most likely die in their own fit of laughter. Willow—she'd probably wrap her arms around me. I'd wrap mine around her. Just to say *this one is mine.*

"Oh my *God.*" Ana's face roasts a shade of red. "Please stop talking, Jared." To me, she says, "I'm so sorry. The second I have the chance, he's bingeing *Princesses of Philly.*" I haven't heard someone mention PoPhilly in a while. The short-lived reality show happened *years* ago. I wasn't in it. I didn't even know the Calloway sisters back then.

A docuseries featuring the sisters and their men is ongoing and more current, but *We Are Calloway* is critically acclaimed and covers serious topics like addiction and PTSD. Maybe too highbrow for this girl since she doesn't mention it.

I'm not in the mood to explain how I'm connected to the Calloways, but luckily I have Ana here willing to do it for me.

She's focused on her boyfriend. "You do know who Loren Hale is, right? If not, we can no longer date." She crosses her arms over her chest, like she's serious about this.

Jesus.

This is dumb.

It's like watching a fucking train wreck with *Interpol* still blaring in the background. Loren Hale should never be the decider for any relationship. If he were, mine would have ended before it even began.

Jared doesn't blink. "Everyone knows Loren Hale."

That's just not true, but okay.

"Prove it." Ana arches a brow.

"He owns Superheroes & Scones *and* Hale Co. I have his baby oil in my shower." Way too much information from my neighbor. And it's not specifically Loren's bottle of baby oil. The family-owned company manufactures baby products. Hale Co. is one of the most well-known brands in the country.

Jared looks to me. "Loren is also married to the sex addict Calloway sister."

My skin crawls with how Jared just described Lily Calloway. Like that's all she's fucking known for. Not the fact that she's the one who actually owns Superheroes & Scones. At one point in my life, I even worked *for* her.

Jared looks to me and continues on. "But I don't get it. How do you know Loren Hale?"

I open my mouth.

But Ana answers first. "He's dating Loren Hale's little sister."

And there it is.

I shouldn't be famous. I shouldn't be recognizable, especially when I'm not always around Loren or any of the Calloways. But it's happening. And there's only a small comfort in knowing that Ana at least took a few minutes to double check her phone before being able to recognize me.

It wasn't instant recognition.

Good.

"Huh," Jared muses.

"I'm going to turn my music down," I say before either of them can jump in. "Keep the banging to a minimum and we won't have problems."

"Wait, it's my birthday." Ana hooks her arm with Jared's. "Do you think you could like call Loren and have him wish me a *happy birthday*. Just really quick. It doesn't even need to be FaceTime. Hearing his voice would be the literal *best* birthday present ever. I'm a huge fan."

I glance to her boyfriend.

Jared's gaze is pleading. Practically saying, *come on, man, help me out.* Like he wants me to give him points with his girl so he can get a blow job later tonight.

I do have Loren Hale's number.

My gaze settles on Ana. "I already gave you your birthday present," I say. "Ask your boyfriend about it."

I shut the door on them.

Immediately, I go to my stereo, lowering the music to a tolerable level. My ears ring. My head throbs. I collapse on my mattress and stare up at a yellow stain on the ceiling. Seconds later, the EDM starts up next door again. But it's softer and no longer vibrates my walls and desk.

Willow did the right thing—leaving.

She can't make real connections here. Everyone eventually recognizes her as Loren Hale's sister, and in London, she has a chance to fall under the radar.

My phone vibrates.

It's now almost 3 a.m. Which means it's almost 8 a.m. in London.

Excitement thrums my veins, thinking it's her, but when I see the text, it's worse than a balloon pop. It's like someone shot a bullet at a blimp.

The person who texted me… It's my boss.

Connor Cobalt: Meeting tomorrow. 11 a.m. My office.

He attached a screenshot of the drug test I took my first day on the job.

It came back positive.

Fuck.

3

GARRISON ABBEY
Age 20

He shouldn't have given me this job. It's what I know as I face the twenty-nine-year-old business titan. Connor Cobalt is the CEO of Cobalt Inc., a company that has a hand in just about everything you can think of. Magnets. Paints. *Diamonds.* The list goes on and on. One big company owning smaller subsidiaries.

So the day Connor looked at me and said he wanted me to create something for him—I should have rejected the offer. There's no way this is going any other direction than south. *Fast.*

I don't even look like I should be working here.

He fixes the cuffs to his thousand-dollar Armani suit.

I'm wearing black jeans and a hoodie. Though, he did tell me on the first day that I could wear whatever the fuck I wanted. So that's on him.

His blue eyes collide with mine as he reaches for his coffee. Intimidating is probably too delicate a word to describe this guy. He oozes *I'm fucking better than you* charisma. And don't ask me how it's charismatic. It should come across like he's an asshole, but it actually doesn't.

I don't get it.

Supreme confidence. That has to be it.

He sips his coffee. Silence lingering, and his eyes focus on me even harder.

It feels hot in here all of a sudden. I push up the sleeves of my hoodie.

"Garrison," Connor says after a tense beat. "I don't want to waste your time. I don't think you want to waste mine." He sets down the coffee cup and slides a printed piece of paper across the table. I recognize it instantly as the attachment he sent last night.

My *failed* drug test.

Awesome.

I read the small details quickly. The chart has a spike for increased levels of THC. *Marijuana.* I smoked a blunt a couple days before Willow left for London. If I'd known there was going to be a drug test at Cobalt Inc., I wouldn't have smoked—but this is my first corporate job.

The only other place I've worked is Superheroes & Scones, and the employees there were all nerds, geeks, or broken toys needing a home. No one even needs a reference to get hired at S&S.

"You're firing me," I assume.

Connor is a hard book to read. Face impassive. He could bluff his way out of any poker hand. It makes this interaction more uncomfortable. I shift in my seat.

"You really think I'd fire you over marijuana?" Connor asks, voice calm.

"I mean…maybe." I glance around the glass walls and the cubicles outside his office. Women walk around in pantsuits and pencil skirts. Men take phone calls and sit in meetings in boardrooms. Every wall is *glass.*

Like they want you to see how fucking important they are. I can't imagine any of his other employees smoking on their free time.

Connor leans back in his chair. "Garrison." He draws my attention back to him. "I don't care if you smoke, as long as it doesn't hinder your performance here."

My shoulders relax and I release a breath. "It won't," I say, almost hurried. It even surprises me. How much I want to keep this job. *It's the only thing I have right now.* "I don't usually smoke weed. I'm not a pot head or anything. It just helps me mellow out sometimes."

Connor nods like he already assumed this about me. "Company policy is to have you take a confirmation test to make sure the first drug test wasn't a false positive. But I'll take this conversation as proof that it wasn't." He passes another paper to me. "Because you failed the first, you're going to have to undergo random drug tests throughout your first year here."

Sounds fair. Shit, I'm just happy I still have a job.

He glances at the clock on his wall, then back to me. "Make no mistake, Garrison. If I find you're taking harder drugs like opiates or cocaine, you won't have a job here. This isn't *Wolf of Wall Street.* My employees are useless to me if their health is at risk."

"Noted." I don't mention how I've tried most drugs. Most I couldn't care less about. And I'm not around people who'd pressure me to do them anymore.

Connor puts his fingers to his temple. "Let's talk about your project."

I grimace. Honestly, I'd much rather talk about my failed drug test again. "It's going splendidly." My sarcasm is broken because it sure as hell wasn't supposed to come out during a meeting with my boss.

"You don't have an idea of what you're creating yet." Connor assumes correctly again.

"I mean, it's kind of difficult when you said I could create *anything*," I tell him. When it comes to tech development, that's a wide fucking spectrum, and I want to choose the right thing. It's just figuring out what it is.

"Take your time," Connor says. "You don't have a deadline."

That scares me even more. Because Connor Cobalt is the kind of guy where you *don't* want to waste his time. And he's giving me infinite quantities of it.

I'm also really aware that not a lot of people get this kind of opportunity. If it weren't for the fact that he's married to a Calloway sister—therefore has ties to my girlfriend—maybe I wouldn't be in this position right now. It feels like nepotism. But I'm not going to throw it away.

"What if I take years to even come up with an idea?" I ask. I can't believe he'd ignore his bottom line just for me. He's a business guy. They tend to give a shit about money, and I'm currently on an eighty-thousand dollar salary with benefits.

"Then you take years," Connor says like it doesn't bother him. "But I don't think you will. And I'm always right."

He's always right.

A part of me wants to prove him wrong. And I don't know what that says about me.

PRESENT DAY

LATER TONIGHT IN MY STUDIO APARTMENT, I TOSS
a frozen pizza in the oven, sink onto my couch and scroll through
Willow's videos she sent me. Re-watching them for the third time.

She's lounging on her bed in a baggie Superheroes & Scones T-shirt
that has to be at least three years old—I recognize the design from a
line of shirts when we first started working at S&S.

X-Men posters are taped to the walls above her head. She rubs at
her eyes, her glasses already off for the night. Watching her makes me
miss her more, but maybe I'm some sort of masochist because I can't
stop. And I just want more.

"So my classes aren't that bad so far," she tells me. "Except for
Intro to Marketing. *Ugh…*" She buries her face in a pillow. "They're
making us do a *group* project." Her words are muffled, and she pops
back up after a second. "I thought I had abandoned those at Dalton
Academy. But *no*, they're in college too, and they are the literal worst."

"Agreed," I say to the video.

She brushes hair off her cheeks and her hazel eyes drift to the
screen. She holds back tears. "Garrison." She says my name like she's
mourning it. "Could you…could you call me when you get off work?
Even if it's super early my time. It's nothing important. I just want to
hear your voice."

My chest hurts like someone dropped a fifty-pound dumbbell
on it.

I didn't call her. It was midnight by the time I left the office, and
that's 5 a.m. her time. She's got a "hellishly" difficult morning class,
and I promised myself that I wouldn't fuck with her studies. College
isn't easy, and I'd hate myself if I distracted her.

My plan: call her during her break between classes tomorrow
afternoon.

The oven beeps, my pizza done, and just as I rise off the couch, my phone lights up. Vibrates loudly. Her name is big across the screen. *WILLOW.*

I catch myself smiling. Selfishly, the first thing I feel is happiness. Like a tidal wave, it surges through me.

My lips downturn fast. And then worry follows close behind. I stand and click speakerphone. "Hey, Willow, isn't it early there?"

"It's six," she says into a yawn. "Did you watch my video?"

I could lie. But that's not something I ever want to do with her. "Yeah," I admit. "I was planning on calling during lunch, so you could sleep in."

She yawns again. "You're too nice, and also I'd rather talk to you than sleep."

Too nice is not something most people say about me. And the fact that she's willing to go without sleep for me is what I didn't want.

I lean against my kitchen counter, eyes transfixed on the screen, even though I can't see her. "Everything okay?"

"I just miss hearing your voice. In real time. Not like through a video clip. How was work?"

I tell her all about my failed drug test, and how Connor didn't even care that I smoked weed. When I end the story, Willow says, "He's right, you know. You're going to figure out what you want to create faster than you think."

Her confidence in me is like a drug. I close my eyes and grip the edge of the counter. It hurts to be away from someone you love so much. God, it fucking hurts.

"Garrison," Willow breathes. "Are you still there?"

I swallow a lump in my throat. "Yeah."

A beat passes before she says, "You remember the night we had sex."

I stop breathing. It's impossible to forget that night. Everything about it was incredible. And I've spent most nights remembering what it felt like to be inside of her. Afterwards, I always try not to think about when it'll happen again. Because likely—it's not going to be anytime soon.

We agreed I wouldn't fly out to visit until her second semester because if I'm up there *with* her, there's a chance the media will start hovering around Wakefield. *Give it some months. Let her settle in.*

I still believe that.

But the hornier part of me—that thinks with the wrong head—isn't fucking thrilled about it. Of course I want to touch her. I want to physically be with her.

I think about her words right now: *you remember the night we had sex.*

"I remember," I tell her. "It was a good night. The best night."

"So you're not upset about it?" she asks, worry in her voice. "You don't think it's *goodbye* sex, right?"

Jesus. "No, Willow. It wasn't *goodbye* sex." My pulse races. "If it were, we would have broken up. We're still together." *Fuck.* "Aren't we?"

"Yeah, I think so," Willow says, and I imagine her frowning.

We're on separate pages. Separate books. Shit, we're literally on different continents. I don't know how to jump back. "Willow, you're my girl."

"What about the broken heart?" she asks.

I rack my brain for a second, trying to figure out what she's talking about. "What...broken—" *Oh shit.* I pinch the bridge of my nose, remembering. "The questionnaire."

I can barely even explain what overcame me to want to fill one out. I was on Tumblr and scrolled past it, and it just reminded me of her. It was enough to quickly fill in the questions. But why did I have to answer with a broken heart?

I'm an idiot.

Willow says, "I just thought that since I left after we had sex, you were upset about it."

"Fuck no," I say strongly. "Willow, that was the best night of my life. I put the broken heart because we're in this shitty long distance thing and I just miss you."

She lets out a giant sigh of relief. "That makes more sense."

"Good." I pause and sniff the air. I smell something...burning.

Shit fuck shit. I forgot to take the pizza out of the oven. My joints unglue and I race to the oven. As soon as I pull down the oven door, dark gray smoke floods out at my face. I cough into my arm, and seconds later, the smoke detector lets out an angry wail.

"Garrison?" Willow sounds panicked.

"Burnt the pizza!" I yell over the alarm. "Call you later?"

"Yeah, go. I love you," she says quickly.

"Love you, too."

She hangs up, and I switch the oven off and try wafting the smoke away from the alarm with a dish towel. It's not working. I have to find...something that will reach the alarm. Fuck you, eight-foot ceilings.

Seriously.

A knock sounds on my door. "Garrison!" my neighbor yells. "Everything okay?!"

Jared and I haven't bumped into each other since his girlfriend's birthday, but the fact that I haven't deterred him either means he's a good guy or he just *really* wants my connections to Loren Hale so he can score points with Ana.

I can't tell which.

But I do open my door for him.

He glances past my shoulder.

"No problems here, man," I tell him. "Just burnt a pizza. You can go home." I'm about to close the door, but he puts his hand on it, stopping me with unwanted force.

I glare.

He's still looking past me at the oven. "Shit, that looks bad. Hold on a minute and I'll grab my broom." He leaves quickly, and I rub at my eyes. Against better judgment—or maybe worse judgment—I don't shut my door on him.

Jared is back in a flash and instead of passing me the broom, he walks right on into my apartment. I tense considerably. My space is *my* space, and I don't remember giving him an invitation. Oh wait, that's because I didn't.

I cross my arms over my chest and stay near the doorway, watching as Jared jams the end of the broom up at the alarm. It takes two *whacks* before it stops wailing.

"These smoke detectors are ridiculously sensitive in the building," Jared says. "Just a heads up."

"Good to know." I try not to sound pissed off or sarcastic or both.

Jared looks around my place like he's on an apartment tour. "Wow, you've got a sweet setup." He eyes the back wall with the desk and four monitors. Two servers. All the chords are neatly bundled and tucked at the floorboard. It took me days to put everything together and not have it look like a mess.

"You a gamer?" Jared wonders.

Probably not the kind he's thinking of. I don't play Call of Duty or Halo or even League of Legends. My true love is the classics on consoles like Sega and N64. But that's not why I have the computers.

"No," I tell him. "I'm a software engineer at Cobalt Inc."

Jared raises his brows. "Damn." He sounds impressed. "But I thought you said you were at Penn."

Never said that. He assumed it. Because I look my age—twenty. And this building is affordable and a short distance to campus. It adds up, I guess.

I shake my head. "I didn't go to college." I'm not ashamed about that. It's not for everyone. Definitely not for me.

Jared looks me up and down. "So you're like one of those geniuses from *The Social Network*?"

I almost laugh. I'm so far from a genius. I'm just good at what I do.

"Not really." I'm about to make up some excuse about work. Anything to get him out of my apartment, but he's already talking again.

"About the other night with Ana," he says into a cringe. "Sorry if she came on strong. She's just a huge fan of your family's."

"They're not my family," I correct him. They're Willow's. I'm just…adjacent to them.

He scratches the back of his neck. "Right, sorry."

"I have to work," I tell him.

"Oh, yeah. I'll get out of your hair." He picks up his broom. "If you have issues with your smoke detector again, you know where to find me." He leaves quickly. A weird feeling crawls under my skin, and I know it's from his sudden saccharine neighborly friendliness. It seems fake, but I really don't want to judge him.

I lock my door and then assess the kitchen. The smoke is almost all cleared out. Checking the pizza, my stomach grumbles and I let out an irritated breath.

Crispy and inedible. Pizza should be neither of those things.

PRESENT DAY

I end up grabbing a Lightning Bolt! energy drink from the fridge and sink onto my desk chair. My computer is one of the few places I can just get completely lost in. Right now, that's all I want.

WILLOW'S TUMBLR QUESTIONNAIRE
Age 17

Rules: Complete the form by answering each section truthfully. Once you've finished, tag other users to complete the task. Begin by sourcing the person who tagged you.

Have you ever...

Been cheated on: never gave anyone the chance to Kissed someone and regretted it: never been kissed (don't judge)

Drank hard liquor: a couple times. I didn't like the taste

Been drunk and thrown up: nope

Met someone who changed you: I met Loren Hale once (my only celebrity run-in). He was standing on my front doorstep (long story). Loren Hale left within like five minutes—but he actually spoke to me. He noticed my Mutants & Proud pin, and I mentioned liking X-Men Evolution (the cartoons). Then he made a comment about the comics and Lily Calloway. He called her his girlfriend, but they were and are still engaged if Celebrity Crush is right. It made me think that girls could read comics too—and the way he spoke, he presumed I already did. I never tried to read them until that moment, until he left and I thought yeah, I'm allowed to read these too.

I started New X-Men and related so much to Wallflower, a girl I really needed a year ago, when my dad divorced my mom. And I would've never read comic books and fallen in love with them if I didn't meet Loren Hale

Fallen out of love: I've never fallen in love to fall out of it

Found out who your true friends are: this is why I keep my circle small. Maggie is the truest friend there ever could be

Lost glasses: multiple times. My little sis sometimes takes them to be funny

Sex on the first date: ...idk maybe I'd do it? Thinking about it makes me nervous...

Been arrested: in a nightmare

Turned someone down: for what? Like dating?

Fallen for a friend: no. I don't like the guys at my school like that (you wouldn't either if you were me)

What was your...

Last drink: Fizz Life

Last phone call: umm, my Grandma Ida. She wanted to crochet me a scarf for next winter and needed to know what color yarn. I told her blue

Last text message: "I bought it! I bought it!" to

Maggie, in relation to Understanding Comics by Scott McCloud—I've been saving up babysitting money to purchase the comic book. I read ANYTHING that Loren Hale recommends (my comic book guru), and he suggested this one not long ago on social media

More questions...

Do you have any pets: my dad hates pets, but when he moved out a year ago, my mom let Ellie get a hamster. It smells really bad

What did you do for your last birthday party: ate out at the Noodle House with just my mom, sister and Maggie. I don't like big parties, especially not ones about me

Name something you cannot wait for: A REBOOT OF NEW X-MEN (PLEASE HAPPEN!!! I'LL TAKE ANYTHING!!!) Also, for Maggie to meet Scarlet Witch (aka Elizabeth Olsen) one day.

What irritates you: being forced to speak up in large crowds

Nickname(s): none (I'm not that cool)

Relationship status: single

Favorite TV show: tie between Gravity Falls & X-Men: Evolution. I love them

High School: ready for it to expire

College: wish I could go. I'm working on it

Hair Color + Length: light brown, straight, and about to my chest?

Height: 5'5''

Your crush: TOM HIDDLESTON!!! (aka Loki)

Tattoos: my dad says no

Right or left-handed: Right

Any surgeries: nothing that serious

Any piercings: double lobe piercings on both ears, just four little studs, two bats and two stars

Favorite sport: sports? *runs and hides*

First vacation: never left Maine before, but when I was really little, we used to go to the coast, about 4+ hours from Caribou, and we went sailing one time. I can't really remember it, but my mom has pictures. Everyone seems happy

What do you like...

Hugs or kisses: hugs for now

Shorter or taller: taller than me. Even if it's only a little taller. That works too.

Older or younger: older but not too old—I couldn't do what Daisy Calloway does with her boyfriend, who's like seven or eight years older (I can't remember)

4

WILLOW MOORE
Age 17

"We're not having this conversation! It's Ellie's birthday!" my mom shouts, the familiar octave present only when she's around my dad.

"Her birthday ended *twenty* minutes ago!" my dad yells. I haven't seen them endure each other's presence since the divorce. I invited him to my 17th birthday dinner back in March and he said he wouldn't come. His exact words: *not if your mom is there.* Now August, he's willing to stomach my mom for Ellie—his little bundle of princess joy.

I don't think I ever fit into what he wanted me to be. His words over the years have been etched into my head.

If you liked more girl things, you'd have more friends, Willow.

If you actually went to a party like a normal girl, you'd have more friends, Willow.

If you wore more makeup and made an effort, you'd have a boyfriend, Willow.
If you stopped watching superhero cartoons, you'd have a boyfriend, Willow.
Every girl your age has one.

But mostly I hate that he left in the first place. I hate that he just walked out on my mom and broke my little sister's heart and tore through their lives, even if he'd already been tearing through mine.

He just said, "*I can't live with your mother.*" And as a teenager, I'm not privy to the details I guess, but the lack of them has only made hate fester more for him than it has for her.

I *hate* that his leaving caused my mom to cry every night for three months. I *hate* that Ellie asked repeatedly, "*When's daddy coming home?*" I *hate* that I was the one who had to say the truth over and over, and I had to watch tears roll down her cheeks every single time. I *hate* that he wasn't here to stomach their hurt—that he never woke up to it, never went to sleep to it, the way that I did. When I look at my dad, I only see the man who has hurt me by hurting the two people I love most.

"Willow?" Ellie whispers again, tugging on my wrist. I look down at my six-year-old sister, her eyes wide like saucers. And she mutters, "Can you tell them to stop?"

I fix her plastic crown that droops to the left. "Only if you wait here."

"I will. I promise." Then Ellie jumps onto my bed and plops down beside my laptop. I notice a Barbie doll in her hand. It must be new.

I leave her quickly, my bare feet on the old carpet, and I squeeze down the narrow stairs towards the kitchen.

"We're not talking about this here, Rob!"

His tone lowers to a heated growl. "Yes *we are.*"

I stop short of the kitchen, able to peek beside the doorframe. The yellow linoleum floors are half littered with wrapping paper and pink balloons, the trashcan stacked with dirty paper plates. My mom hangs onto the kitchen sink, her knuckles whitening.

BACK THEN

I only spot this much outward emotion from my mom when she's not noticing me or forgets I'm here. Though after the divorce, I've seen this side of her more often. On a normal day, she's sweet and subdued. Rarely heated. Almost never angry. She tries to bottle most dark sentiments, something I've learned to do.

As I creep from the corner, I gain a better view of my mom.

Just forty, she has kind eyes, a smooth pale complexion and rosy cheeks, but her usual put-together persona cracks beneath welling tears. She stands opposite a middle-aged man with light scruff, narrowed eyes, and a Miller Lite shirt. And I mentally take sides—I take *hers*, even if I'm supposed to remain nonpartisan.

I see him.

I see him hurting her.

I see him causing her these tears.

My mom who never asks more of me—when what I am is subsequently less.

I clutch onto the doorframe, watching as my dad crosses his arms over his burly chest.

He says to her, "We'll never finalize this fucking divorce if your lawyer keeps putting this off."

My mom inhales a shaky breath. Her nose flares and she fights tears again, straddling more sadness than rage.

No. Tell him to fuck off, Mom. Tell him you don't want him. I bite my tongue, hoping she'll stand up for herself.

"Please, Rob…" she cries. "Just come back home."

My stomach is queasy. I just want her to kick him out, to grow the strength to rip apart the thing that causes her pain. *Come on, Mom. You can do it.*

I wish I had the bravery to help her, but my feet cement to the floor, weighed like shackles of tar-filled balloons.

Through his teeth, he sneers, "I'd rather burn in fucking *hell* than be with a woman who spent over seventeen years repeatedly lying to me."

A chill races across my arms, and I swallow a lump.

"It has nothing to do with you, Rob." Her voice trembles, and then tears burst forth in a guttural cry. It pierces me through the chest, and I stagger one step. I'm blown back.

Meanwhile, *he* just stands there.

He just watches in disgust.

How could he—

"You abandoned *your son*," he says so passionately, so soulfully and hatefully that his face turns blood-red.

And I go utterly cold.

"Your fucking *son*," he repeats with glassy eyes. "The one that I knew nothing about!" He points a finger at his chest. Vibrating—he's vibrating in anger and pain.

I'm shaking with it too.

I don't understand…

My dad licks his lips and adds, "How does the fact that you saw the father of your son on *twelve* separate occasions for two decades, not affect me?"

No.

I rock back.

He's to blame.

Isn't he?

He has to be.

Tears crest my eyes as I try to block out the truth. No.

Think about it, Willow.

I don't want to. It's easy believing one way for so long, to put all of my emotions in this one drawer that makes the most sense. It *hurts* having someone yank open the drawer and dump out its contents, destroying what I know is real.

She's my ally.

She's my confidant and my friend.

She's my *mom*.

She wouldn't lie. She wouldn't *abandon* anyone. She's my mom… the person who spent five hours helping me with a science fair project in eighth grade—who took me to the midnight showing of *Avengers*, even though she had work early in the morning.

She's kind-hearted and loving. She's sweet-tempered and generous.

I can't imagine her abandoning a puppy, let alone an actual person…*her* person…

It's not real.

And then my mom says, with staggered breath, "I never saw his father after the day the baby was born…" I can't tell whether this is true or not. She plants her eyes on the ground in *shame*, never meeting my dad's gaze.

"You're lying again," he grits.

"I'm not!" she screams at the floor. "Those were checks from him, but it's been twenty-four years since I last saw him. He had his assistant fly out…and give the checks to me. Five years ago was the last one. I've told you this. Please, Rob—" She tries to grab onto his forearm, but he jerks away. She catches air and then grips the sink counter for support again.

I lean my weight on the doorframe, my glasses misted with tears, and I take them off with trembling hands and rub them on my green striped shirt. I try hard not to make a noise, but my nose runs…I wipe that with my arm—shaking.

Stop shaking, Willow. It's okay…

My chin quivers.

You've been on the wrong side of things all along. You fool.

I expected my dad to hurt me.

I never expected her to.

My father silently fumes before he bursts again. "And why'd he just give you checks?" He lets out an anguished laugh, hands on his waist. "You're telling me there was nothing attached to them? No stipulation?" He shakes his head in disbelief.

"I told you, he wanted me to keep quiet, out of pity, I don't know. He just kept sending them, and we needed the money for your car, the house—"

"You've got to be..." He yells at the top of his lungs, pissed and furious. I flinch, and then he grabs a nearby bowl of oranges. He tosses it violently at the wall.

I jump as the ceramic shatters all over the linoleum.

"He paid for *my* car, for *my* house?!" He points a finger at his chest again, a good distance still between him and my mom, as though it sickens him to even be near her.

"Please..."

"Did you cheat on me?" he suddenly asks, veins protruding from his neck. "Tell me the fucking truth, Emily!" He's crying.

I've never seen my dad shed a tear, not even from anger, not even when he said goodbye to me.

My mom rocks back a little, as though his words and voice have shoved her hard. At her extended silence, I want to press my back to the wall and slide down into a tight ball. I want to hide, but I can't unfreeze. I can't move.

"I didn't..." The way her voice trails off, it makes it so hard to believe her—but I still want to. I want to believe she didn't do this.

She didn't cheat on my dad. She didn't.

I believe it. I do. I want to be on her side.

My dad breathes heavily, his chest rising and falling, tears dripping. And then he asks, "Is she even my daughter?"

My throat swells closed. *She didn't cheat on my dad. He has it all wrong.*

Maybe I just really want her to confide in me. To tell me the truth. This force inside pushes me, and I round the corner. "Mom?" I sound small.

As I stare between my mom and dad, their rage and hurt and distress start to cage behind an opaque screen, one that bars me from entry.

I blink, wetness sopping my lashes.

I hate that they won't show me anything real right now—that I have to spy in order to see it.

My mom straightens up and rubs her cheeks with the back of her hand. "Go upstairs, honey." Her voice cracks.

"Who's my father?" I ask.

"Rob Moore is your father, and he's Ellie's too," she says adamantly. "It's not what you think—"

"I'm leaving," my father says, his tears dried up. Another glare plastered on his face.

He hardly acknowledges me.

He passes me to reach the doorway, and our bodies seem to lean away from each other, like pressing the wrong side of two magnets together, unable to near.

He has a clear aversion to me, and now I think I know why. He believes I'm not his child, even when I really am.

I listen to his footsteps all the way to the living room. Not long after, the door bangs closed, and my mom turns her back on me, beginning to clean a few dirtied glasses in the sink. She can't just act like nothing happened.

"Mom!" I shout.

"I'm done talking…" Her arms shake like mine, and maybe a year ago, I would've stayed quiet and just gathered these bare details and created my own horrific conclusion. I don't want to live with this half-picture anymore. I don't want to see through clouds, stained glass and opaque screens. I want transparency for my *own* life, and only she can give that to me.

"I'm not done." My voice is softer than I intend. She doesn't turn around. I take a deep, strong inhale. "Mom," I choke, "I'm *not* done."

She slowly spins around, her hand fisting a dishtowel, eyes bloodshot. She waits for me to speak this time.

I lick my lips and I ask, "Do I have a brother?" She lied about him. I'm not sure if I can trust her, and I'm not sure if I should love her—but I do love her, and I do still trust her. That can't vanish that quickly.

But right now, I resent her. For the first time, I truly do. And I hate it.

"Willow…" She shakes her head at me, struggling to reveal what she's kept secret for so long.

I wipe my burning eyes beneath my glasses. I shift my feet and accidentally step on a balloon. It pops loudly, and we both flinch.

My family tree has been set on fire, and I'm desperately trying to find *one* missing branch so I can make sense of myself again.

I need him.

Whoever he is. I need to know what he's like. How old he is. A name. A place. Maybe he understands things that I don't. Maybe he gets it.

"It was a long time ago," she says. "I was a teenager, about your age, a little younger when I was pregnant." She lets out a weak, broken laugh. "You can't even imagine…"

I watch her lean against the sink and stare off at the half-eaten vanilla cake, lopsided on the counter. "Is he still alive? Does he know—"

"Loren Hale," she says, her voice suddenly stoic and cold. "That's your brother."

My legs want to buckle, but I manage to stay upright, my mind whirling as pieces of a much larger puzzle fit in place. "He knew..." He came to *our* house about four years ago. She told me that she knew his father. And I realize, his visit wasn't random. He came and he left so quickly. "Did you tell him not to tell me?" I wonder.

Her lips press in a line, and I take her silence as affirmation.

"Oh my God," I mutter, my chin trembling again as I restrain a flood of tears. She kept him away from me. Why would she do that?

Loren Hale is my half-brother. All this time...we could've talked, had a relationship, been friends—seen each other. Instead there's just this black hole of *nothingness*, hollow and empty.

I feel empty.

"Can you just forget about it?" my mom asks me.

I shake my head in a daze. "No...I want to meet him." I need to tell him that I know the truth now. I want to regain this piece that I've lost.

"You can't," she says tiredly and brushes strands of her hair off her forehead. "The Hales are famous, Willow. The moment the media learns that Loren's related to you, they're going to harass our family. I've tried *so hard* to give you girls a normal life. You may decide to live in that world later on, but Ellie is young and she's not going to. Okay?"

I try to process this as quickly as I can. Hale Co. is what elevated Jonathan Hale's status to "wealthy billionaire" and his son to the heir. But their fame ultimately came through a salacious scandal that involved Lily Calloway, Loren's fiancée.

Soon after, the Calloway sisters and their men became public interest and fodder. They're all in at least three tabloids every day. Paparazzi follow them around Philadelphia, their hometown.

People love them and hate them.

I understand why my mom would want to protect us from that, but Loren Hale has only been this famous for a few years at most. She could've introduced me to him when he was just a rich kid in Philadelphia.

She never intended for me to meet him, to know him…

How can I believe anything she says?

"Willow," she pleads. "Let this go. Jonathan gave us a lot of money over the years. It's over, okay? No one can know that Loren's my…" Her face suddenly contorts. She can't say it.

My heart palpitates. "Your son," I whisper with burgeoning tears.

She shifts her body until I can't see her face. After a short silence, she says softly, "I was only sixteen, Willow."

She was so young.

And she's right, I can't imagine…

Jonathan Hale must've been so old too. I cringe at the picture—at the twisted, grotesque reality that I never knew I was a part of. I feel bad for her, but I worry that if I wade in grief then I'll never grow the strength to meet my brother. I'll flounder in her sadness and hold onto her hurt like I've done since the divorce.

"I'm leaving," I suddenly say—just realizing that these were my father's exact words minutes ago. She blinks back emotions again, and I'm already determining what I should pack. A duffel bag in my closet, some jeans and shirts, my backpack and my wallet.

I'm leaving.

I've never been this bold. I've never been this courageous. I've never felt this lost, but I know nothing's here in Caribou, Maine except pain, and I want to feel something better than this.

I'm leaving for Philadelphia.

"If he wasn't famous," she says slowly, "you wouldn't even think about meeting him." She throws this in my face.

That's not true, I want to believe wholeheartedly, but she roots doubt in my head.

"If he wasn't famous," I say softly, "then this would be a lot easier." I'd be able to call him on the phone. I'd be able to tell him in advance that I'm going to see him. I could even Skype him instead of travel all the way to Philadelphia.

None of that is possible when Loren Hale is an internationally recognized celebrity.

As I turn my back on my mom, as I head for the staircase, I know it's going to be a challenge even approaching him.

But I have to try.

I need to grab this branch before it burns. So I race upstairs, pack a bag, noticing Ellie sleeping on my bed. Five minutes later, I zip up my duffel and sling my faded JanSport backpack over my shoulder.

I hear my mom downstairs, cleaning, and I wonder if she'll try to convince me to stay. I wonder if she cares enough to keep me here.

Part of me wants her to fight for me out of love and fear.

Part of me wants her to let me go so I can be free.

I hesitate, Ellie's plastic crown halfway off her head, breath parting her lips as she sleeps. I crouch close to her and whisper in her ear, "I love you, little princess." I kiss her cheek lightly enough that she never wakes. I know she can survive just fine without me for a while.

She's the energy that keeps this house alive.

I'm just the shadow in the corner.

When I head down the narrow staircase, squeezing my duffel through, the sink shuts off, and my mom emerges in the living room. I slow down between her and the front door.

She dries her hands with a towel, poker-faced and more resilient. "I'm not paying for this," she says. "You're on your own now."

A tear slips down my cheek. "Okay." I guess she's hoping I'll become afraid, run out of money, and turn around. I want to be brave enough to stick it out, but I'm not sure if I'm wired that way.

She adds, "You're old enough to do what you want, and you're old enough to make your own mistakes."

I think about her around my age, pregnant and making some of the hardest choices she had to make. I suppose she would believe that I'm an adult now if she was forced to be one back then. But I'm scared, and I feel like a plastic doll headed for a toy car, unable to see outside of my Polly Pocket house. What lies beyond—I don't know.

"If you need me," she says, "you have to come home yourself." She works for the post office and has almost no vacation days—definitely not enough to chase me to Philadelphia. And I'm not asking her to.

I wish I could say that I'm full of bittersweet love, but I'm mostly dark and resentful. Most of me *hates*, and I can barely meet her eyes without feeling tricked and fooled and deceived.

I want to meet a different pair of eyes that hold greater truths and sentiments, and they're not hers.

I just nod, turn around, and open the front door, the sun already gone. The street lamps already turned on, and I unlock my gold '90s Honda. I jiggle the handle for it to open. The car used to be my Grandma Ida's, and I'm just grateful I have it, something that I can use to leave.

"Drive safe." I think I hear my mom.

I look back at the front door, but it's already closed. The lights are already off, and I wonder if she's happy that I'm going, if all this time I've been a bad memory for her.

Maybe just like Loren Hale has been.

The Calloway Sisters & Their Men – Fan Page

Back Then | *Followers: 11K*

Are you new here? Welcome! This is the fan page for all things Calloway Sisters & Their Men. It's not an "official" fan page and is in no way associated with the Calloways, Meadows, Cobalts or Hales. It's just run by a dedicated blogger (me, Olive!) who is in love with all things Calloway!

Don't know who they are? Let me give you a crash course...

There are four Calloway Sisters, but only the youngest three sisters have gained notoriety after a huge scandal. Headlines were everywhere. Even national news channels! It leaked that Lily Calloway is a sex addict, for real. It probably would have just breezed through the media if not for the fact that they're all heiresses. Their father owns Fizzle. So the Fizz Life or Diet Fizz you're drinking—yeah, the Calloway Sisters are heiresses of that soda fortune.

The Calloway Sisters (and their current ages):
Poppy Calloway (30)
Rose Calloway (26)
Lily Calloway (24)
Daisy Calloway (19)

That's right, their parents named them after flowers! How cute is that? So the biggest deal is that Rose, Lily, and Daisy all currently live together in a mansion (with their men) in Philadelphia. It's like a real-life episode of *Friends*! And you'll probably find a lot more fan pages about them, but I promise to bring the latest and best news about the Calloway sisters. So let's get to their men...

Dating

Daisy Calloway & Ryke Meadows (25) – the adventurous couple. Daisy is a former model and Ryke is a professional rock climber, but they're often caught riding motorcycles together!

Engaged

Lily Calloway & Loren Hale (24) – the geeky couple. Lily owns Superheroes & Scones, while Loren is the CEO of Hale Co. and Halway Comics.

Married

Rose Calloway & Connor Cobalt (26) – the genius couple. Rose owns Calloway Couture, a fashion company for the everyday working woman, and Connor is the CEO of Cobalt Inc.

Poppy Calloway & Sam Stokes (30) – the private couple. Both Poppy and Sam tend to remain out of the spotlight, but what we know is that Poppy is a stay-at-home mom and Sam works for Fizzle.

Children

Lily & Loren: Maximoff Hale (2 months old)
Rose & Connor: Jane Eleanor Cobalt (3 months old)
Poppy & Sam: Maria Stokes (7)

That's the basic run-down. Another important fact that you might want to know—Loren Hale and Ryke Meadows are half-brothers. They have the same dad: Jonathan Hale. There's been some terrible allegations in the press lately about Jonathan Hale. I'm not going to repeat them here because there has been *zero* proof, and like I said, they're *serious* allegations.

I'll have more information as it breaks. Until then, check out the photos and gifs page!

Love you like Loren loves Lily,
xo Olive

5

BACK THEN – August

Philadelphia, Pennsylvania

GARRISON *ABBEY*
Age 17

Mom: Where are you?? Your brothers are leaving tomorrow, and you need to be here before it's too late. You already missed dinner.

"Garrison, it's your turn." Nathan Patrick nods to me, chewing on a toothpick with a wry smile. His combed red hair might as well be fucking brown from my vantage. Smoke from cigarettes and joints create a filmy haze in his family's den—the door open as people drunkenly pass in and out.

I suck a joint between two fingers before standing up and flipping my cards on the poker table, my two queens losing to Nathan's three kings.

Of ten people, three girls let out short cheers. Another two girls in only bras and panties smile but make no loud exclamation. One of them sits next to me: Rachel Barnes, a brunette with diamond earrings and Zeta Beta Zeta aspirations like her sister in college.

She's prescribing to her family's legacy—something I can't stomach without another crappy joint and bottle of vodka.

After overturning my cards, I lift off my black shirt, revealing whatever muscles lacrosse has granted me and a black skull tattoo on the crease of my forearm and bicep. In small font, my favorite lyrics from the *Interpol* song "Rest My Chemistry" outline the inked design.

I don't make eye contact with anyone. I remain standing and blow gray smoke up at the ceiling, my mind lulling and eyelids slowly closing. I'm almost always surrounded by people—friends and acquaintances from Dalton Academy—and even when I stand in a room with them, even when I'm physically here, I always mentally check out for a few seconds.

More if I can.

I always want to be alone, but then when I'm alone, I want to be with people. It's a fucking curse.

Whoever built my mind needs to redo the wires and find better balance because I'm leaning all over the place. I'm tilted and sideways and so fucked up—this isn't even half of it.

The weed is making you a paranoid shit.

I suck the joint one last time before passing it to Rachel, who hesitates before putting it between her lips. She takes one short drag and then coughs into her fist.

Nathan and two other guys give her a hard time. I don't come to her defense—since she's going to be in a sorority anyway. It's not like she's going to need to know how to smoke a joint.

"Your deal, Abbey," Nathan tells me, stretching over the table to pass me the deck of cards. I begin to shuffle.

A girl clears her throat loudly, sort of adjacent to me. "Hi, um…" She taps Rachel's shoulder. I'm not surprised. Rachel looks the most approachable.

Most of the guys are smoking and drinking, one even wears a gargoyle mask from a Halloween store, more stacked behind him on a leather chair. The other girls here have low-cut tank tops and nose piercings.

Rachel is the only one that looks like someone you'd take home to your parents. Though I've brought them all over to my house before. I don't discriminate.

I barely make out the girl's features among the smoke. All I can tell for certain: she's wearing overalls, like the saggy kind you'd put on to paint a house.

I frown. She can't live around here.

"Hi?" Rachel says uncertainly.

Not surprisingly, Nathan takes over, standing from his chair. "How'd you get in here?" He makes it seem like his party is invitation-only, when in fact most of Dalton Academy has been traipsing in and out all night.

"I…uh, the front door was open?"

"I mean the neighborhood. It's *gated*," he says.

The girl takes a step back, more towards me, but I stay still, as uncertain as her, as uncertain as everyone else. My eyelids are heavy, and it takes more control not to sink into my seat and just finish dealing slowly.

"The gate was open…someone was coming in, and I followed them through," she explains. "I'm just trying to find someone. I know he lives in this neighborhood, and I thought you'd be able to point out his house—"

Nathan snorts, and two of my other friends start snickering. "Let me guess—you want to see Loren Hale."

"Yeah," she says softly.

I grimace and turn my head away from her. *Fuck him*, I think. *Rich bastard.* I swallow spite and something else—because if I look around, I see thousand-dollar paintings, an antique globe that probably costs a fortune; I see Rachel's Cobalt diamond earrings, Henry's Rolex watch—my Balmain designer jeans that purposely appear worn.

We're all loaded.

Rich fucking kids. Fuck me.

I want to be alone right now.

But I want to be with people.

I don't know what I want to be.

"So…" the girl says. "Can you help me?" I have to strain my ears to hear her quiet voice.

Help her. All I have to do is point at the house literally down the street. I know the one. I've been around it with my friends *too* much. But something keeps me quiet. Something keeps me tight-lipped and blank-faced.

"Are you a weirdo stalker?" Carly asks. She lets out a short laugh. "Like, are you going to bring him a locket of your hair?"

"Carly," Rachel whispers and then ends up laughing with her.

The guys start in and laugh again.

They all stare at this girl. They all stare, and I keep my head down. I wish I had my hoodie. I wish I could just block everyone out for a second.

The cards slip from my hands, and I end up crouching to gather them, my reflexes fucking tortoise-slow from the weed.

"So you can't help me then?" the girl asks one last time, sounding meeker than when she first arrived—which is hard considering how shy she seems.

"Are you dumb?" Nathan laughs.

My face heats beneath the table, grabbing a king of clubs. I wonder if I was paying enough attention, if I would've made the same comment, the same way. I hope not—but I'm not a good person either.

I'm just as foul, and I wonder if I'm the only one that knows how cruel we all are. How fucked up we all seem.

If I am—I must be doubly cursed or something.

She's about to leave, but Nathan adds, "You want to play strip poker for the information?"

I glance back at the girl. Her lips part in hesitation, and she seems pallid and sweaty. I can barely make out the color of her hair. Light brown, I think, in a loose braid. These dorky black-rimmed glasses frame her small face, and she leans most of her weight on one foot—a nervous, slightly boyish posture that most cotillion, high society girls don't grow up with around here. Their moms would shit a rock if they did.

And she keeps anxiously reaching for her shoulder, like she's trying to grab a strap to a purse that's not there. Jesus Christ, she looks really out of place.

The more she waits to speak, the more I think she's considering playing strip poker with us.

And the joke would be on her. She'd get naked and Nathan would never give her the information. No one would, whether she won the right to it or not. They'd find that funny.

I collect the last of the cards and rise, my posture more assured than hers but I don't look like I took years of ballet like Rachel or like

I listened in cotillion. I'm definitely not what my parents wanted me to be.

And I say aloud, to Nathan, "I'm not dealing another fucking person in, man. I've already started." And I start. Right now. Looking like a dick as I do so.

Before Nathan protests, the girl leaves, weaving between a sloppy drunken guy who spills beer on her shoulders. It's like watching Bambi lose its mother or something. And I can't help but feel like we were the ones that shot the deer.

What do I do about it? I finish dealing the cards and numbly begin the next hand.

AROUND 2:30 A.M., I FINALLY LEAVE NATHAN'S.

I grab my bike and *slowly* (so fucking slowly) ride down the dim street, lit only by lamps and the few houses that reside here. Instead of houses stacked closely together, each mansion has acres by itself, leaving the neighborhood mostly barren.

I bike past grass and a couple trees.

Not far down, I turn right onto Cider Creek Pass. I live in the same gated neighborhood as Nathan Patrick. As Loren Hale and the Calloway sisters. Ever since they moved in, paparazzi camp outside the gates, waiting for them to leave. It's pitiful—on whose part, I don't really know.

I take my palms off the handlebars and just peddle, trying not to think about those people.

There it is.

Floodlights illuminate my front yard, white rose bushes outlining a gray stone, out-of-place Victorian mansion. Like we're some kind of English royalty.

The minute I see my three older brothers on the stone front stairs—unevenly lounged and leaning against the iron railing—I think about riding away. My problem: I have nowhere else to really go.

"There he is." I hear the muffled voice of my oldest brother, Davis. He rises first, football in hand. "Where've you been?" he asks me straight. It's not concern on his face as much as annoyance.

I peddle onto the yard and then slowly climb off my bike, knocking it down without care. "Out," I say, wanting to climb the steps and bypass them into the house, but I gain five-feet before they all join me in the yard, silently saying *you're not going anywhere.*

We're all two years apart from the next. And somehow they all look the same: short haircut, collared shirts, khaki pants and Sperry boat shoes.

Davis is the twenty-three-year-old college graduate, striving for his MBA and a position at my father's million-dollar tech company. He sucks at computers, by the way. Can't even read code—but he's charismatic and a real "guy's guy" so whatever.

Hunter is the twenty-one-year-old athlete with anger issues that everyone blames on "pent-up testosterone" because he refuses to fuck or masturbate until lacrosse season ends. He's a dick—and I say this with zero brotherly affection. He destroyed that when I was a kid.

Mitchell is the nineteen-year-old pretty boy with less charm than Davis but more brains, so he's fucked. I'd like Mitchell more if he didn't act like Davis and Hunter rode golden chariots.

And me, Garrison Abbey, I'm the seventeen-year-old degenerate who skips class more often than he goes, who's yet to find a meaning in being *here*—in life. If I don't follow their footsteps, then I see nothing else I could do right, but I can't follow them and stomach it.

"Dude," Mitchell starts in. "Mom wanted this to be a *family* dinner." College summer break ended today, so they have to go back to the University of Pennsylvania.

"Sorry," I say dryly, scratching the back of my head with mock regret. "I guess I missed the part where we break bread, hold hands and sing hallelujah—maybe next time." I try to take a step forward, and Hunter puts his hand on my chest to stop me. I slap it off and back up immediately, my stomach knotting. "Don't touch me, man."

"Then don't make Mom cry, dipshit."

I stare at the night sky for a second and feel my eyes roll. I also feel Hunter let out an agitated breath and try to step closer to me, but I back up again, about to head for my bike.

"Hey." Davis grabs my shoulder and spins me around, his fingers digging in. He raises the football near my head like he's going to suggest a quick game. Instead he sniffs, and I turn and try to jerk away from him, my tousled hair falling in my eyes.

He grips harder.

"You smell like weed." His annoyance only grows, probably thinking how badly I'm hassling our parents. I'm not easy like my brothers. I don't know how to be and still retain a fucking *soul*.

"Really?" I feign surprise. My only real defense is dry sarcasm. "I thought I smelled like your girlfriend's p—"

Davis slaps the back of my head, and I almost fall forward. And then he shoves the football in my chest. "Like you'd know what pussy smells like." He messes my hair with a rough, irritated hand.

They treat me like a little kid. Like a little brother. I get that. I am one, but as I stand up and face Davis, Hunter, and Mitchell, I feel more like a toy they play with, one they've constantly broken.

I clutch the football. "You didn't really stay up to play football with me."

"Sure we did," Mitchell says with a shrug and looks to Davis and Hunter for confirmation. Neither says a word in agreement. Their hard gazes just drill into me.

I don't want to be here, so I drop the football and I turn around again and go grab my bike that lies sideways in the yard. Hunter chases after me, and I barely have my bike upright before he pushes me.

I drop the handlebars and stagger back. "What the fuck?" I sneer, my pulse quickening.

"We're playing football. You couldn't be here for dinner—you couldn't do *one* thing for Mom, then you're going to do this for us." And he adds (like Hunter always does), "You motherfucking cocksucker." It's his go-to insult, one I know I might've picked up and used before—and I hate that I have. Because it's lame as shit, among other things.

I grit my teeth and inhale once before I shrug stiffly.

Davis *throws* the football at my face. It hits my cheek before I can block it. The pain wells, but I stifle it by grabbing the football off the grass. The minute I straighten up, Hunter tackles me with his full weight. He's two inches taller, fifty pounds heavier, and the wind immediately escapes my lungs.

I choke and try to push him off, but Hunter grips my hair and whispers in my ear, "You think you're fucking cool? Get up, you pussy." He slaps my face twice and laughs, like it's funny.

When he stands off me with the football in hand, I slowly turn towards the grass, kneeling before I rise, my breath caged.

This is how brothers are, my mom always says. *They tease the youngest one. You just need thicker skin, Garrison.*

I wipe the bottom of my nose with the back of my hand and realize it's bleeding. Hunter is only a few feet from me, and I'm surprised he doesn't chuck the football in my eye.

"What? Are you going to cry?" he laughs.

I roll my eyes and just shake my head. I think this is his way of making me pay for whatever emotional hurt I caused Mom today, yesterday—whenever I became more of a nuisance than all of them.

And I'd like to think if I showed up for dinner, we wouldn't still be "playing football" like this. But they would've found some other reason to go hard. They always do.

"Tackle me," Hunter goads, arms outstretched. "Come on, pussy, let's see what you're made of."

I narrow my gaze, my eyes heated, my nose on fucking fire, and I just think, *I hate you. I really fucking hate you.*

Davis lets out a short laugh. *I hate you too.*

Then Mitchell. *Fuck you, Mitchell. Grow two feet and walk away from them.*

Have I even grown two feet yet? Do I even have a head? I blink slowly, wondering if I'm still blazed.

"What are you, dumb?" Hunter's smile fades, irritated, pissed. It's an ugly ass snarl that I've met all my life. I remember one moment as if it were yesterday. My parents ordered pizza for dinner, and Hunter called "dibs" on the last slice. He was seventeen, and my thirteen-year-old-self didn't know better.

I ate his so-called slice.

And then he wrestled me onto the floor, trying to force my finger down my throat so I'd throw it up. After his knee sat on my ribs for too long, I willfully stuck my finger down and vomited that last slice. He didn't want to eat it. He just wanted to deny me the one piece that should've been his. Because he called dibs.

Brothers, right?

Fucking brothers.

Hunter growls under his breath. "Come on!" I learned about a year ago to stop giving into their games. I'd avoid them or just *not* play whatever they wanted to play.

It doesn't always make things better, but it makes me feel like I stood up for something. Davis stares at me like I'm a little rebellious punk.

"It's football," he reminds me.

"Cool, you two play," I tell them, heading for my bike *again*. "I'm out of—" Hunter tackles me, wrestles me on *top* of my bike, the metal digging into my kidneys. I grimace and thrash beneath him, cursing and trying to throw him off.

He lays his weight into me, his usual insult ringing in my ears. He smacks my face a couple times, the blows harder, and then I gather the strength to shove him off and roll out beneath him. I cough once, digging my soles into the grass, and then I stand up enough to grab my backpack and run.

"Garrison!" Davis yells. "We're just playing!"

Fuck you.

I run faster, almost tripping as I reach the asphalt, and I look back once to see if they're following, but all three of my brothers stay behind in the yard. I gather speed towards the main street, off Cider Creek Pass.

Then I slow down, my pulse never slowing with me.

I rub my hands through my hair. "What the fuck," I whisper, hearing the sound of my shaking voice. *Are you going to cry?* Then I rub my throbbing cheek, the wetness apparent. "Stupid shit," I mumble softly and then rummage in my backpack.

I collect a cigarette and lighter, putting the end in my mouth. I suck in deeply, and then I look up and realize how far I've sprinted and then walked.

I'm at Loren Hale's house. It's a mansion, not as ostentatious as my family's. The lights are off, and the driveway is empty. I pace back and forth by the mailbox, smoking a cigarette.

I don't know why I linger. My friends and I—we've pranked their house since they first moved to this neighborhood, and at first, we were just curious. *Who the fuck are these people?* we all thought.

They're not famous because they did something revolutionary or because they acted, sang, and entertained their way into peoples' hearts.

They're famous because Loren's fiancée is a sex addict. The heiress of Fizzle—a soda empire—sucked a lot of cock.

You know, I *met* him—Loren.

He caught me after I shot paintballs at his house windows, and my friends—they just left me there, racing off with their own paintball guns, thinking he'd turn me into the police. Being loyal, I wouldn't have ratted them out.

But that night, Loren Hale let me go.

I don't get it.

I don't understand why he didn't turn me in. He seems like an ass. He's always glaring in tabloid photographs, not more than his half-brother, but still. He looks like a fucking dick—and he let me go.

I don't know why I do it now, but I reach into my backpack and grab a canister of metallic spray paint. With my heart banging into my ribcage, violently saying *no* with each beat, I spray the side of his mailbox. My nose flares, knowing it's bad.

Knowing I should stop.

But I don't.

The paint wets my fingers as I hold down the nozzle tighter, and on one side I write the word **COCK** and on the other, I write **SUCKER**.

Maybe I should've just written *help* instead.

6

GARRISON ABBEY
Age 17

Superheroes & Scones is packed.

Slouched in a red vinyl booth, I listen to Nathan prattle off reasons why he can't stand this place—how it looks like Captain America took a shit on the walls, a red and blue and gray scheme. It's a dumb complaint. We're in a comic book store for Christ's sake.

I take a swig from a bottle wrapped tightly in a brown bag. *Shit.* Sharp vodka slides down my throat, inexpensive and probably a cousin of rubbing alcohol.

This is the best I could steal from the liquor cabinet. My parents only stock shitty vodka, and they'd notice if I took their prized Scotch and bourbon.

"Hey." Nathan waves a hand at my face, sitting next to me. "You here?"

I flip him off and then chug again, leaning against the window. Our friends John and Kyle are seated on the opposite side. Their faces begin to blur, which means today is better than yesterday.

I'm about to put the bottle back to my lips when noses suddenly press against the window, and girls *scream* bloody-murder outside.

"Christ," I curse before following their gazes across the store. Everyone here seems to freeze, comic books half open but eyes elsewhere. With their slack-jawed, wide-eyed expressions, you'd think an A-list movie star just made an appearance.

I'm not surprised by what I see.

Loren Hale and his half-brother, Ryke Meadows, just entered the main storeroom from the *employees' only* door. Nathan, John, and Kyle purposefully escalate their voices and mess with the sugar packets, tearing them open and spilling white granules all over the table.

I can't focus my gaze enough to make out Loren and Ryke's features. But I've read enough descriptions on Tumblr from *obsessed* girls (and probably guys, to be honest) to have their faces forever imprinted in my fucking head.

Loren Hale is all sharp-edged, his jawline like ice and his amber eyes daggered and so scary. He will murder you with them. He wears a lot of red Vans and V-neck shirts. He's so cool. His hair is shorter on the sides and longer on the top (guys take notes!)

How about no.

Ryke Meadows is all hard-edged, his scruffy jawline like stone and his brown eyes narrowed and so broody. He's an animal. Beware. I wouldn't be surprised if he was a werewolf in another life.

Tumblr girls are so weird.

And yeah, I read all of those in my free time. Internet culture is more entertaining than real life. Like right now, I immediately turn my head away from Loren. Because of what's in his arms.

BACK THEN

A baby—*his* baby. The thing can't be more than two months old, and he's crying hysterically at all the noise and attention.

I glance back, only once, to see Lily Calloway taking her son out of Loren's arms. But he's too busy to really notice. He's glaring at Nathan, at *me,* and my friends, the table littered with sugar packets, their voices causing more havoc.

His amber eyes daggered.

He will murder you with them.

Part of me wants to glare back—to prove that he's not murdering me with anything. But my neck grows hot, my stomach unsettled, and I focus on my vodka instead.

Another swig, I think before taking one.

I can't even remember the last prank we did on Loren's house. We've done so many, even in the past month. Even when they had a fucking newborn in there—*stop.*

Drink.

I do.

Not long after, I feel Nathan press closer to my side. Loren squeezes into my end of the booth while his brother squeezes into the other.

Tumblr is right, I think. Despite both brothers having lean muscles, runner's builds, Ryke Meadows acts like the aggressive brute, his elbows on the table, the strong-hand that could literally drag any of us out of here if Loren Hale said so.

It always seems like Loren calls the shots though. He's the talker—his features murderous and cold.

"Hey there," Loren says with this irritated half-smile. It's iconic, his dry smile that says *you're a piece of shit and you know it.* I can't even replicate it. I don't think anyone can.

I hold his gaze this time. And I take the largest swig from my paper-bagged bottle. *I'm not scared of you,* I want to retort. I want him to feel it.

I'm not scared of you.

He tilts his head a little, unperturbed by me. His amber eyes are full of flashbacks, memories that contain all that I've done. The longer I stare, the more I see the paintballs I fired, blasting against the window—panic and shrieking from inside, from his soon-to-be wife.

Some people say that if you mess with Loren Hale's girlfriend, you're on his "metaphorical" kill list forever. That he has ways and means to do you in, to make life not worth living.

Too bad for him.

Because I'm already there.

He can't do me in. He can't touch me.

I miss a portion of the conversation, only hearing the part where Loren says, "I'm not going to lecture you."

I lean forward, not rolling over. "You can't kick us out. We have a right to be here like everyone else." I watch his narrowed eyes flit over my features. He recognizes me from that night—the night where he grabbed me and let me go.

He let me go. Who would even think to do that sort of thing? Who wouldn't turn someone like me in?

John adds, "Yeah, it's our first amendment right to be here."

Ryke Meadows rolls his eyes. "You all smell like cheap *fucking* vodka."

"Sorry," I retort, leaning back with a glare. "We'll buy better stuff next time."

"That's not what I…" Ryke lets out a frustrated growl, and I guess I'm tempted to provoke this "beast" and see him lash out. So I make a crude gesture with my hand and tongue, the vulgar gesture known to crawl beneath his skin. Less so when it's directed at him. More so when it's directed at a girl.

So I'm not really surprised when he doesn't launch himself at me. He just breathes through his nose and looks to his younger brother to deal with us.

Loren rests his forearms on the table, glancing between each of us with less threat in his eyes. "Come on," he says, "you all look no older than seventeen." He gestures to me. "Drinking underage is illegal, so you're not in a power position here."

I glare at the table. *No shit.* I've never been in a power position before. Not *once* in my life.

"What's your name?" Loren asks me.

"Fuck you," I retort, and I switch my V-shaped fingers to a middle finger. Flashes go off by the window near my head, causing white light to flicker in my vision. I wonder if I'll be in a tabloid like *Celebrity Crush* tomorrow.

Probably.

They'll call me the "unnamed delinquent"—predictable.

"How was that bourbon bath?" Kyle snickers. He high-fives Nathan across the table, and I'm reminded of a recent prank. It was John's idea. We filled a bucket with his family's liquor—stuff I would've rather drunk. His parents froze his bank account for raiding the cabinet, so it's not happening again any time soon.

When we had the liquor in the bucket, we tethered it to Loren's front door.

We heard it doused him *and* Ryke. "Two for one"—Nathan had said.

It's fucked up. Because they're both sober, and Loren Hale is known for his stint in rehab and difficulties recovering from alcohol addiction.

Ryke looks murderous at John. "You think it's funny?"

"Ryke," Loren says and shakes his head like *stand down*.

And I mutter, "Pussy." I think it's easier pushing him away. He keeps thinking he's going to change things with us—but he can't.

Nathan laughs. "Nice, Garrison."

I almost choke on the liquor. "Dude." I gape and nudge his side hard. My hood falls off my head.

They don't know our names, but now they fucking know *mine*. I look up, and Loren Hale is staring straight at me, his eyes full of sympathy—I don't get it.

I've *fucked* with him for months.

Hate me, I think. *Fucking hate me*.

"What are you looking at?" I practically spit. *Help me*.

"You," Loren says with hot malice.

I feel sick, my neck scorching now, and I lower my gaze to the table.

"Here's what's going to happen," Loren begins. "You all have two options." We stay quiet, waiting for him to say, *Jail. Jail. Jail.*

"You can stop the pranks," he continues, "never come around our house again. If you're that bored, I wouldn't mind hiring some of you to work here. If you don't want a job, I get it. You can have a discount on comics if that's your thing."

What?

I stare off in a fucking daze. Who is this guy?

Ryke says, "And I'd be willing to teach all of you to rock climb at the gym. But you can't drink."

"Sounds like so much fun," Nathan says with a dramatic eye roll, grade-F level sarcasm.

I tear a corner off the paper bag. "And the second option?" I ask. *Jail*.

"You vandalize our house again or harass our girls, and we'll press charges," Loren threatens. *There it is*. "The minute we even see your goddamn pinky toe on our lawn, I'm calling the cops. Take it from someone who's been in jail, you don't want to be there. Even for a couple hours."

I let out a short laugh. "When were *you* in jail?" The guy grew up as a rich trust fund kid like the rest of us. His dad could've bailed him out before the cops even put on the cuffs.

He captures my gaze. "I doused some asshole's door with pig's blood." His voice is edged and chilling.

My face begins to fall.

"No way." Nathan gawks.

I straighten in my seat. "Yeah?" I ask, more curious. "Where's that asshole now?" *What'd he do to you?* I really want to ask.

Loren shakes his head and shrugs. "I don't know. That shit is long gone, man." His voice tries to soften, but his tone mostly cuts me inside out. "You're going to leave prep school and you're going to take your mistakes with you." He looks at my bottle. "You can stay here if you hand that over and don't cause any commotion. Otherwise, you have to go."

"We'll go," John says before I can decide. He nods to me. "Let's buy that six-pack and head to the elementary school playground."

I don't think I can drink anymore without puking. Not because I reached my limit—I just feel like I've digested something that doesn't go well with vodka or beer.

But I don't want to be alone right now.

So I rise with all of my friends. As I near Loren to exit, I look him over. I'm so fucking conflicted about everything—about who this guy is. About what he just offered. *Take it.*

And then I lose *all* of my friends. They're never going to back down. They have this stupid prank set up, one that involves gargoyle masks. They're not going to stop in favor of getting free comics or a rock climbing lesson.

I don't want to be alone.

But I don't want to be here either.

What escape do I really have?

I think short-term, and I shove the bottle in Loren's hands. "Here, you won't be such a pussy if you drink." If I push him away, then he'll make my decision for me. He'll revoke his offer.

He doesn't flinch. Doesn't even look mildly pissed. He just says, "If that's what you think." He tosses the bottle in the nearby trash.

I'm stunned for a second. I had my first beer at twelve. *You're a man now, kid,* Davis told me and rubbed my head. My dad laughed.

In this moment, Loren Hale looks and acts more like a man than I do, and I was holding a fucking handle of vodka. I have no fucking clue what's rolling around inside of me.

I can't look at him anymore. Rubbing my mouth with a shaking hand, I pull my hoodie back, and the door chimes as I push through, catching up to Nathan.

When I glance back at the store window, I see that girl—the one with the braid and worn overalls. I see her stand up and approach Loren Hale.

I nod to myself. *Good for her.* She finally found him. And she didn't need me to do it.

" Loren?" I ask in a soft, timid voice. I scoot around Ryke Meadows. Both brothers are so tall that I have to tilt my head back and look *up*. Maybe if they were shorter, I wouldn't be nervous. Maybe if they weren't famous. Maybe if I didn't know more about them than they know about me. Maybe if they weren't the current focus of every teenage girl in Superheroes & Scones.

If all of that changed, maybe it'd be easier.

My heart thuds harder and beats faster—their gazes suddenly zeroed in on me. Looking down while I look up. I can't really unmask their expressions. Ryke is stiff and unmoving while Loren shakes his head a little, his eyes flitting over my awkward frame.

I truly feel seventeen. I truly feel like Loren's *little* sister.

Please let him believe so too. I made it this far—I made it to him. It only took almost a month of scavenging Philadelphia for Loren Hale, and the closest I came before today was a house party that amounted to a beer-stained shirt and mortification.

It took me a solid five-minutes to even climb out of my car and enter that house, my first ever high school party, mind you.

I felt in the way. I never knew where to stand, where to scoot to, and even then, I bumped four or five elbows and shoulders. I left with my stomach twisted like a pretzel. And it solidified what I've always known: *Willow Moore is not meant for high school parties.* I'm just not built to live through them.

Fast forward to today: My bank account is creeping close to just $50, barely enough for another night in a Philadelphia motel. I've already spent five nights in my car to save money, and my last hope was staking out Superheroes & Scones. Which proved to be the winning strategy, even though I always thought it was a long shot.

But I've found *him.*

Loren Hale is standing right in front of me.

Now for the hardest part. I open my mouth and adjust my backpack on my shoulder with a sweaty palm. "Hi," I say. I lick my lips repeatedly. *Hi*—is that really all you have, Willow?

I had more planned, I think. I just—I'm looking at my brother. This is the second time I've met him, and I start to see a greater resemblance between us.

We have the same light brown hair. I subconsciously touch my nose.

We have the same slender nose—

Ryke's rough but sincere voice breaks my concentration. "Do you want an autograph or a picture or something?"

I try to meet his expression, but he raises his eyebrows at me like, *we can get anything for you.* Oh my God. I immediately look away and push my glasses up. "No…thanks." I cough a little to hide my nerves, but maybe that just makes it worse.

I'm used to seeing Ryke in video footage, yelling and throwing out F-bombs at paparazzi, trying to block cameras from his brother and girlfriend's way.

Seeing him now—with an unshaven jawline, crinkled brows, brooding eyes, and overwhelming masculine energy—it's like meeting a scruffy god in the flesh.

I'm surprised I haven't combusted into flames yet.

Ryke turns to Loren, probably wondering what to do with a crazy, awkward fan like me.

Say it, Willow. Tell him that you're his sister. Why is this so hard? I blow out a breath, prepared to let this truth out and desperately hoping Loren Hale will believe it.

I meet his amber eyes, our gazes locked for a strong, tense moment. And I say, "I'm—"

"My sister," he finishes.

The hairs rise on the back of my neck, a chill snaking down my spine and arms. My eyes burn as tears try to well.

Loren barely flinches. "Willow, right?"

My mouth keeps falling. All this time, I thought he's been looking at me like *who is this girl?* But he's been really looking at me in disbelief like *this is my half-sister, standing right here.* He's been piecing me together with the middle school girl he once met, so long ago. In Caribou, Maine.

"You…remember me?" is all I manage to say.

"Yeah." His lips rise, and my heart warms. "The day I met my birth mother is one I really can't forget."

"Oh…" That was the first time he met my mom? I mean, *our* mom. My eyes drop for a second. She really did abandon him then…

I take a quick glance at Ryke. His lips are parted in surprise, eyes a little wide as they go from me to Loren and back to me. I wonder if he knew anything about me. If he knew I existed out there, or if Loren just kept it to himself. Because my mom told him to leave Ellie and me alone.

"Do you want to talk over coffee?" Loren asks. I whip my head back to him, a chill never disappearing. *Coffee.* "Maybe in the break room?"

I nod over and over, and the tears just keep rising. I blow out another breath, my strained shoulders loosening.

He wants to talk. He's not going to kick me out. He's not going to tell me to *get lost, kid.* I feel like I'm reaching out to someone who's not only clasping my hand but drawing me closer, so I don't fall backwards on my own.

For the first time since I left home, I feel safe.

I'M IN THE BREAK ROOM OF SUPERHEROES & SCONES.

I can't believe *I'm* here—and yes, I'm slightly shaking. My arms tremble, and my legs have glued together. I wonder if the jitters are from the coffee Loren handed me, the only thing I've consumed today. Or maybe it's nerves—from being in the presence of a famous person for longer than one minute. Or from being related to *this* human being.

I cup the coffee mug, afraid to drink more and have a panic attack at Loren Hale's feet. *Please don't do that, Willow.*

He sits next to me on the bright blue couch. The break room is pretty typical: a microwave, small kitchenette, tables and chairs, a few racks of comic books, and a single bathroom.

Lily, her son, her bodyguard, and Ryke all disappeared upstairs to—well, I'm not exactly sure what leads upstairs. The point is: we're basically alone except for a couple of employees eating sandwiches at a back table, sitting beneath an *Iron Man* poster.

BACK THEN

I think we can speak freely enough, but if Loren is cautious, I'll follow his lead and be cautious too.

"I…" I begin but realize I'm unsure of where to start.

Loren's confidence radiates and practically dwarfs what little I have in this moment. He keeps an arm on the back of the couch, rotated towards my body. "How'd you find out about me?" he asks, discovering a place to start.

Now I have to figure out how to explain everything. I tuck a piece of hair behind my ear, having trouble holding his gaze. "My parents divorced about a year ago."

"I'm sorry." He sounds a little cross, not towards me really, but maybe that's his normal tone of voice? Everything seems to come out harsh, but it doesn't always match his expression.

I guess if I looked at him, I'd have a better interpretation of this moment. *Willow Moore, that little turd, can't even look her own brother square in the eyes*—will definitely be my eulogy.

I shrug and push up my glasses that keep slipping down my nose. "Ellie had her sixth birthday about a month ago, and it was the first time my parents were together since the divorce."

The fight starts to flood me: the balloons littering the linoleum floor, the way my father passed me coldly and never looked back, the half-eaten cake and my mother gripping the counter. My chest tightens, and my eyes burn again.

"I heard them fighting in the kitchen," I nearly whisper, "about how my mom had a son, and she…abandoned you." I clutch my mug harder and finally look up.

He scratches his neck, appearing a little more uncomfortable than he has been. "I had my father, so it was okay." His throat bobs.

I wonder if Jonathan Hale is nice. Just based off tabloid rumors, I'd say *no*. (They're so awful I really hate to repeat them.) Disregarding those, all I have to go on is the fact that he slept with an underage girl—my mom, *our* mom—and got her pregnant.

He doesn't sound that awesome, but if he raised someone as cool as Loren Hale, then maybe he's not entirely bad.

When he swallows, he asks, "Did you confront her about it?" *Did I confront my mom about her abandoning you?*

I just picture my mom turning her back on me, trying to bury this. I see her never chasing me upstairs. Never chasing me outside. I see her in a new horrible light that I can't shake. It hurts…

"Yeah," I say softly, "right then. I asked her about it, and it took some screaming for her to really tell me the truth."

My voice nearly dies by the last word. I wipe my eyes beneath my glasses, hoping these tears won't overflow.

He angles closer to me, kind of like he wants to comfort me but still wants to give me personal space. I'm not a touchy-feely person. My mom wasn't ever that way, and I wonder—I wonder now if it was because of what happened when she was sixteen. Being kind of taken advantage of by Jonathan Hale… I mean, she didn't say that she said *no* to him. So I have to assume it was consensual.

But is it consent if she was underage? And the product of this event… is right in front of me.

My stomach knots, the coffee not settling well with these thoughts.

Then Loren says, "I'm sorry you had to find out like that."

My eyes *sear* now, tears welling as I realize full-force how much my mom kept him from seeing me. Loren wanted me to know about him.

"I ran away," I suddenly say, my voice cracking and tears leaking with the words. I'm crying in front of one of the most famous people alive in the world, and I don't even care anymore. I hate and resent her more than I ever wanted to, and it all *hurts*.

BACK THEN

"You what?" His mouth drops a little, and concern overtakes the edge in his voice.

"I just...I was so mad." My breath staggers between tears. "I told my mom that I was going to find you, and she couldn't stop me. So...I hopped in my car and drove to Philadelphia."

He pinches the bridges of his nose, his eyes tightening closed. "You've been here for an entire month? Does Emily know—"

"She knows."

His reaction makes me feel like I made a mistake—and it's tearing a hole through me. With my mug between my knees, I cover my face in my hands, embarrassed now and heartbroken all over again and full of combatant emotions that cut.

He stands, and I don't have the heart to watch him walk around the break room. I just keep talking—trying to explain and justify why I'm here.

"She's waiting for me to run out of money," I clarify. "She doesn't have any vacation days left to leave work, so she can't come get me." I sound like the villain. My hard-working mother is left at home while I'm off chasing a long-lost brother, leaving her to worry.

If she worried so much, she would've called. A hot tear rolls down my cheek.

Loren plops back on the couch with a box of tissues. That's what he went to find? "How much money do you have left?" He hands me the box.

I take one tissue. "I'm not going back." It hits me now. I don't want to return home. My dad can't look me in the eyes. I expect after this, my mom will have trouble too.

"Willow," Loren says forcefully, "*how much money?*"

He's worried. My stomach has all but curdled. "Enough for a couple more nights at the motel," I lie.

His nose flares, upset. "I'll pay for a hotel tonight and tomorrow, and I can get you a plane ticket back to Maine."

Tears stream down my cheeks. "No, *no*," I cry. "Please don't make me go back. I just met you, and…" I hiccup and remove my glasses, wiping the fogged lenses with my striped blue and green shirt that peeks from my overalls.

I've never felt more alone or lost, and if I go home, these sentiments will only intensify. I can *see* it—all of it. An unbearable pressure mounts on my chest at this purposed future that may become real.

"Aren't you in high school?" he asks.

I don't speak, afraid that if I say *yes*, he'll grab his computer and book me the next flight to Maine.

He's more closed off towards me than before. He shakes his head a couple times. "Your mom is probably sick over this," he says to me.

"*Our* mom," I say, reminding him why I'm here to begin with. I set my glasses back on.

He's scrutinizing me a little more, his eyes flitting over my features.

I wipe beneath my nose. "And I don't care what she is." She can be sick. She can be angry. I feel just as hurt as her over this, and I'm acknowledging my own feelings for the first time in my life instead of burying them to make room for everyone else's.

He grimaces. "Willow—"

"She *lied* to me." I point to my chest. He has to understand how much this hurts. Doesn't he see? "I don't want to be around her ever again."

"How about I call Emily and see where her head is at?" His muscles seem to flex, and he scratches the back of his neck again. He offers me a single weak smile, but I realize that he's nervous…to talk to her, his mom.

She didn't want him. He should be so angry. He should hate her, shouldn't he? How does someone become a bigger person that way, I wonder. How much time will it take because right now I feel like it'd be centuries before I grew a new pair of eyes, a new brain, and thought differently of my mom.

I just nod to Loren, not sure what other options there are. I tell him my mom's number, and after he types it in his phone, he stands. "I'll be quick. Are you hungry?"

I shake my head, holding the coffee mug again.

"Can you get her a muffin from the front?"

I look up and realize Loren has motioned to the employee underneath the *Iron Man* poster. I quickly wipe my wet cheeks, wondering how much this random person saw me break down. I'm never really that emotional in front of people.

"HEY." THE GRUFF VOICE PULLS MY ATTENTION upwards. Ryke Meadows has entered the Superheroes & Scones breakroom with Maximoff Hale, his infant nephew that swats at his arm with a wide toothless smile.

"Hi…" I stiffen even more, watching him grab a couple comic books from a rack and then take a seat right in front of *me*, on the fuzzy white carpet.

Ryke rests his forearm on his bent knee—his whole demeanor confident and cool. He takes a quick glance at the closed bathroom door, the baby that tries to clutch a comic, and then me. Only as soon as we lock eyes, he doesn't look away.

I'm so nervous I may puke.

"You should eat." He nods to the muffin that's frozen in my anxious hand.

I swallow again and loosen my finger joints to pick at the muffin top and eat a small piece. The blueberry is overly sweet, but it's better than coffee.

It's quiet for a second, only the baby making noise. I'm not sure what to say, and maybe he's lost for words too. The tension here is different than it is with Loren and me.

We're both half-siblings to the same person. It's a common link, but trying to understand how we should be with each other—I think it's just complicated. With Lo, I can simply say, *you're my half-brother.* With Ryke, there's not really an easy definition.

Because Ryke isn't my brother. We just share one.

His brows harden in questioning. "What made you want to find him?"

"I learned the truth," I explain, glancing at my hands and the muffin more than a few times. "And I wanted to know him—not because he's famous or anything…" I pale. What if Ryke thinks I'm here to capitalize off his half-brother's fame and fortune?

Ryke scratches his unshaven jaw and nods to me again. "You know I'm his half-brother, right? We have the same fucking dad, so you and I aren't related."

"Yeah I know about you—or *of* you…or you know, whatever the correct terminology is…" I clear my throat and stare intently at the muffin, grateful that I didn't blurt out how I made a gif of Ryke tossing Daisy Calloway over his shoulder, using footage from the short-lived reality TV show.

He runs a hand through his thick, disheveled dark-brown hair. I really want to know what his palms look like. Which sounds *so weird* and creepy.

He rock climbs though, and Tumblr speculates whether his hands are really callused or cracked—which also sounds weird and creepy, but everyone's curiosities run rampant online. And it's hard not to be sucked into this all-consuming vortex that includes the Calloway sisters and their men.

BACK THEN

"Your name's Willow?"

I nod in reply, but he says nothing more. He's trying to draw my gaze back to him. I sense it, and it takes me a couple long moments to stare into his brown eyes, hazel flecks around his pupils.

A piece of muffin goes down my throat densely, no matter how much I swallow.

He says, "I knew about my brother for a long fucking time—he didn't know about me, and it took me years to actually try to meet him. I could have, at any point in my life, but I just…I didn't."

I frown. "I didn't know that."

He almost smiles. "It's not on the fucking internet."

Right…this isn't public information.

His brows rise at me. "You being here at your age, wanting to turn your life upside down just to get to know your brother, it's fucking…" He shakes his head and lets out a breath. "I did it almost four, five years ago? I was in my twenties, and you here, now—it's just brave."

I wipe my eyes quickly beneath my glasses. "You don't think it's dumb?"

His brows furrow. "Fuck no. Meeting my brother was the best decision I've ever made."

I let this digest, and not long after, I breathe easier and peel the paper off the muffin, able to eat more.

His constant F-bombs remind me of a video compilation I've watched. Someone spliced together a lot of his "fucks"—and the video lasted around three minutes. It has over 16 million views and always makes me laugh when I watch it. Ryke seems badass in every frame.

Silence stretches, and Ryke tickles his nephew's foot. The baby has hold of the comic book and giggles.

"Loren knew about me, you know," I say softly. Ryke looks up at me, and I add, "All these years, he knew about me, and I didn't know about him." I'm not in the exact same situation that Ryke had been in. I was the one in the dark. Loren was the one with the knowledge.

Ryke glances at the bathroom door, then back to me. "I'm not sure how much I'm supposed to fucking tell you—but I don't want you thinking badly of my—*our* brother. I don't know what you've been through in your life, but he's been through a fucking lot. And what I do know…" He checks over his shoulder again and then to me. "…when Lo met his birth mom for the first time, he *wanted* a relationship with you and your sister. But Emily basically told him that she didn't want you two to know that you have a brother, and out of respect for her, Lo left you alone."

My chest tightens again. I figured as much, and then I fixate on something else he said. "So…does everyone call him Lo?" I try to straighten my glasses.

"Mostly." He watches Maximoff shake a comic book—oh, the baby actually slobbers on the corner, trying to gnaw on the pages of *Young Avengers*.

"I've been calling him Loren. Is that bad?"

He almost smiles again. "You're his fucking sister. I don't think he'll care either way."

I hesitate to ask something more, but I just let it out in one breath, "Do you think he's happy I'm here?"

His hardened eyes, like *stone*, nearly soften. "These relationships we have with each other—they're not fucking easy, but I wouldn't want to lose a single one. I think Lo feels the same."

"…is now a good time to be here?" I wonder. "Lily just had a baby—"

"Yes," he says deeply, strongly, full of heart. "Lo's the best I've ever seen him." It reminds me that Loren, or *Lo* (that'll take some getting used to), struggles with alcohol addiction, hereditary, on his father's side.

The worst part: I've actually watched him relapse. The paparazzi never missed a beat.

Suddenly, the bathroom door opens, Lo hugging Lily against his side. She's much shorter than him, and her limbs seem ganglier next to his defined biceps, all lean muscles. They stop at the rug, zeroed in on their baby Maximoff chewing the comic book.

"Close your eyes," Lily says quickly and then nearly jumps on Loren's back to shield his view of their son destroying *Young Avengers* right in sight.

"It's too late, Lil," Lo says. "I've seen it."

I smile as she climbs up his back. Lo holds her like he's going to take her for a piggyback ride, and her hands fit across his eyes.

"You didn't see anything!" Lily says.

I wish I could snapshot this and send it to Maggie. My smile fades…or is that wrong? I shouldn't want to publicize them anymore than they already are. That's not why I'm here.

Maximoff rips a page.

"Ryke," Lo groans. "I blame you for this."

"He's not even crying right now. I'm doing a fantastic fucking job."

"You gave him a comic book, and he can't even read yet."

"He's starting early then," Ryke says. "Maybe you should've given me his diaper bag or something."

I listen to them, but their banter isn't totally registering in my head anymore. I remember that Loren just talked to my mom, which means I could be receiving a one-way ticket to Maine soon.

Lily uncovers Lo's eyes. "We're in a store with *tons* of toys on the walls. You could've taken a Green Goblin action figure."

Lo chimes in, "Or Wolverine, Black Widow, Hulk, Spider-Man—"

"For fuck's sake, okay. I got it." Ryke retrieves the ripped and wet comic from Maximoff and then picks him up. The baby giggles, and both Loren and Lily look like proud parents, their smiles infectious.

I shouldn't be here, I think. They just had a baby. I try to remember what Ryke told me, but my gut is telling me not to impede on their lives too much.

"You should babysit more often," Lo tells his brother.

"Fucking hilarious." He hands the baby to Loren, and Lily slides to the floor.

I crumple the muffin paper, finished eating, and when I look up, Loren is suddenly focused on me. I have trouble reading his features.

"Your mom is going to fly out this weekend to talk with you. Until then, you can either stay with us in a guest room or at a hotel. I'll pay for the expense, no problem."

It's not a terrible verdict. My mom will probably reiterate what she's said this whole time: *if you stay here, you're on your own. You make your own mistakes now.*

"A hotel works," I tell him. "I don't want to impose any more than I already have."

His baby squirms in his arms, so much so that I can't take stock in his expression. Lily ends up taking Maximoff so Loren can continue talking with me.

"If you change your mind, the invite is always open." And then he asks, "How old are you, by the way?"

"Seventeen." It's not like I could hide it much longer.

"That's what I thought." He pauses. "You know, Daisy is pretty close to your age."

Daisy Calloway is nineteen—and Ryke's girlfriend, and also spontaneous, lively, and so much cooler than I'll ever be.

Ryke gives his brother a look that I can't decipher.

Loren adds, "She'd probably love showing you around Philly. Is this your first time here?"

Daisy Calloway? Showing *me* around? I don't think she'd be fond of me. I like books. I like scrolling through Tumblr and surfing the internet. I like *sitting* activities, and Daisy is always seen *moving*. She'd probably try to take me on a wild adventure, and I'd slow her down.

I nod. "Yeah, but..." I stand up since everyone else is, and I find comfort in my backpack, slinging it on my shoulder. "I'm not sure she'd like me. I mean, I don't ride motorcycles and...other stuff like that."

I purposefully evade Ryke Meadows since I'm speaking about *his* girlfriend. And he likes motorcycles. And he likes all that "other" stuff.

"Neither do I," Lily pipes in. "They're terrifying."

Ryke raises his brows at her. "You haven't even ridden one."

"*Because* they're terrifying."

I relax some. "Yeah, same. I've never been on one, but I'm scared too."

Lily smiles and then points a finger at Ryke. "Ha!" Maximoff coos in her arms, almost babbling in agreement with his mom.

Ryke rolls his eyes and then sets them on me. "Daisy won't care if you're not into bikes. She'd honestly do anything you want."

Maybe I don't know her well enough to judge.

"I'll take off work some days this week too," Loren tells me.

I remember what Ryke said again, about Loren wanting to see me, to build a relationship too. He's willing to forgo work, just for me. It's validation that this isn't a mistake. Not yet at least.

I inhale a stronger breath. "Okay then…where do we start?"

"How about lunch?"

Ryke and Lily chime in about how hungry they both are, but my glasses fog, my eyes burning with tears once more.

My chin trembles a little, and beneath my breath, I say, "Thank you."

He smiles, one that escalates with sincerity. "We have a lot of catching up to do."

8

WILLOW HALE
Age 20

"Keep your door open," Lo suggested. "It'll be easier to make friends."

That was my brother's advice before I left Philly. Three weeks into the semester and I still haven't taken it. Laughter grows outside my closed door as students walk down the hallway. The air always buzzes on Friday afternoons, classes ending for the week. Plans for parties springing up.

Not that I've been invited to any.

Pencil midair and textbook layered with scribbles and notes, I almost stand from my desk chair and open the door. Almost.

But the laughter grows even louder. What if I disturb the conversation outside? I could ruin someone's joke, and then I'll be known as the girl in room 301 who's quiet and awkward and ruins fun. I'd be a literal buzzkill.

And what if they're all friends anyway? My experience is that tight-knit friend groups rarely allow interlopers. And if they do, the interloper has to bulldoze their way in.

I am not a bulldozer.

I am more like a slow-moving turtle. The only friend groups that will allow me are the ones with clear vacancies.

Before I can settle on a decision—door open or closed—a bright green flyer zips underneath it and slides across my floor. Curiosity spikes and I abandon my textbook to grab the flyer.

FALL INTO FILM BASH
BYOB. ROOFTOP OF BISHOP HALL.
THERE WILL BE SNACKS AND A SCREENING OF THE GOONIES.
FRIDAY, 10PM

Okay…so I've officially been invited to a party.

But the party is *tonight*. I'd need a good week to work myself up to it, or at least have Garrison to go with. There are a lot of reasons I probably shouldn't go. More reasons why I should. Maybe I just need a pep talk from my best friend. I check the clock and do the mental math to convert time zones. It's not too early in Philly, so I dial her number.

Daisy answers on the second ring. "Hey, I was just about to text you. The last pic you sent looked beyond delicious. It literally made my stomach grumble. So either it was fantastic or your photo-taking skills have become extraordinary. Or both. Probably both, right?" I can hear the smile through her words.

My lips already lift. "Bangers and mash *is* really good." Before moving here, I heard not-great things about the food in England, but so far I'm loving it.

I think it helps that Daisy and I made an agreement that I'd send pictures of each new meal, accompanied by a star-rating and review. Bangers and mash was a solid five-stars. *Yummy yummy yummy* was my official review. So it's a good thing I'm a business student and not a professional food critic.

"Hey wait, let's FaceTime." She hangs up quickly and calls back just as fast. When I click into it, her bright green eyes hit mine. Blonde hair splayed across her shoulders and a wide grin. It looks like she's sitting in her tree house, and her eight-month-old baby is curled up on her lap. Sullivan Meadows sleeps peacefully in a unicorn onesie, the hood complete with a glittery horn and all.

There's something about babies that makes me melt. Maybe it was because I grew up with a sister who was eleven years younger than me. I have fond memories of Ellie, and the fondest were definitely when she was young enough to not completely hate me.

Our relationship has been fractured ever since I left Maine, and the more I try to sew it back together, the more it just rips at the seams.

It's been months the last time my own sister even spoke to me, and her words were, *you chose your famous family. Go be with them.*

She won't let me have a relationship with her without severing ties with Loren, and it's unfair. I never felt like moving to Philadelphia was choosing Loren, my famous brother, over my little sister. I would have been gone in a year for college anyway. Moving to Philly, for me, was always about choosing to discover a part of my world that my mom kept secret from me.

Ellie never understood that. She still doesn't. And even though Loren is related to her too—he's her half-brother—I think there's too much resentment there for it to matter to her. I know I'll keep trying to rebuild what I broke, but I'm not sure if there's even a foundation left.

My dad doesn't speak to me. My mom will answer my texts weeks later, and my phone calls are always cut short on her end. I always think about the day I left Maine and the *what ifs*. What if I stayed? I would have never met Lo. Never would have had a relationship with my brother. But I would have kept one with my mom and little sister.

It's a horrible trade-off. One I can't dwell on because I've already chosen a path. This isn't like a comic book. I can't turn back time and see what the other universe has in store for me.

I stop thinking about Ellie and my mom just to focus on Daisy's baby again. My lips lift, joy replacing hurt because little Sulli is nothing short of a miracle.

My best friend went through hurdles and roadblocks and mountains just to have her baby girl, and so seeing Sulli is like a dream come to life.

"How is she doing?" I ask.

"Amazing," Daisy says, eyes lighting up. "She's a certified mermaid. It's officially official, she *loves* the water. I've never seen anything like it. She gets so excited when we take her to swim lessons. The trouble is pulling her *away* from the pool." Daisy crinkles her nose at the thought. "It's like destroying her favorite teddy bear."

I smile, loving these stories. Daisy and I are close in age. I'm twenty. She's just twenty-two, but we're on different trajectories. I'm starting college, and she's starting a family. Still, we make an effort to stay close and catch up. This is a friendship I don't want to lose, no matter how far away I am.

I've already lost one that I thought would never end. Maggie—my only friend from Maine—was supposed to be my forever-friend. But she stopped texting me. Stopped answering my calls. All because I refused to give her information about the Calloways and Loren.

You're related to him, she'd tell me. *Why can't you talk about him to your best friend?*

Because it never felt right. Because the closer I got to them, the more I didn't trust her to not spread it all over the internet.

So maybe I am to blame for that friendship ending. I couldn't give her trust. And she couldn't accept the fact that our friendship wouldn't include discussing Loren and the Calloway sisters.

"How's Ryke handling it?" I ask Daisy. The last time I saw him, he was having a nervous breakdown trying to get Sulli to stop crying. I've never seen someone *so* concerned over a baby's tears. Like he thought he might have broken her. All she needed was a good burp.

Daisy laughs. "I think he'd let her prune into a wrinkly baby just to avoid making her cry," she says. "Which is fine. I'm willing to play the not-so-nice cop role for my peanut butter cupcake." She kisses Sulli's forehead. The baby barely stirs. "But enough about me, Willow. How's Wakefield? How are your classes?"

I take a breath. "That's why I called."

I explain my dilemma and this party.

Daisy nods slowly. "Do whatever makes you feel comfortable."

"That'd be staying in my dorm for the rest of eternity."

"Then go. Have fun. Don't overthink it."

"What if I sit by myself all night and no one talks to me? There's a good chance I don't gain the courage to approach anyone." I can imagine it now. I'm the girl in the corner, eating popcorn and trying to dissolve into the chair.

"Then you'll have a stupendous, amazing time by yourself," Daisy cuts into my morbid thought. "You're an awesome person. All you need to do is believe it, Willow Hale." She wags her brows.

I touch my ring: a plain silver band with a black square in the middle. It's a friendship ring from one of my favorite superheroes in *The Fourth Degree*, Tilly Stazyor, and Daisy has an identical one.

My phone buzzes and a text pops up on top of the FaceTime screen.

Tess: SOS. Did you guys see the professor's email? We have to choose our product and email it to him by tonight.

Oh no.

Tess is a part of my group for that Intro to Marketing course. Last class, I briefly met my partners and we made plans to meet up next week to start our project. We have to create a print and online advertising strategy for a product, and it's worth half our grade.

"What's wrong?" Daisy asks, seeing the haunted look on my face. Another text pops up.

Salvatore: Emergency meeting. Where can I find you guys?

"I think I have to meet with my group tonight," I say. So there goes the party. "But maybe...maybe I'll invite them over here?"

Daisy nods and bites on the end of a Twizzler. "Yes, I like this idea."

Courage emblazons my bones. I am a Gryffindor for a reason, right? Like Neville Longbottom, I can put myself in situations that seem daunting and out-of-my-element. And I will succeed—if I can try to believe it.

So I text the group: My hall is pretty quiet. You all can meet at my dorm. 301. Bishop Hall.

Tess: Sweet. See you soon.
Sheetal: Brilliant!
Salvatore: I'll be there in twenty

Did I just invite people over? I did. Pride overcomes me, followed by an intense wave of worry. Shit, I don't even have snacks or sodas. How am I supposed to host people here? And my room—oh God. Two bras are on the floor and my hamper overflows. This is about the time I'd love to have some woodland creatures come help me. Yeah, if only my life were a Disney movie.

I CARRY A STACK OF FIZZ LIFE CANS AND REDIAL his number. Garrison just sent me a video and he looked different. He mumbled out words and had dark circles under his eyes.

I heard all about his pizza disaster and how his roommate has been acting oddly friendly. As a result, Garrison has been spending longer hours in the office just to avoid his apartment.

I worry he's not sleeping.

And we're both shitty at confronting insecurities head-on, I realize.

Running away and ignoring them is easier.

But I'm not going to ignore him. "Pick up…" I tell my phone. I only have a five-minute window before my groupmates start arriving. I make it back to my dorm when the call goes to voicemail. *Shit.* Struggling, I pocket my phone and fumble with my key. I lose balance and an aluminum soda can falls off the four-can stack. It rolls down the hall, and before I can chase after it, a guy places his shoe on top of the can, stopping it.

I take a quick note of the person who saved the soda. Dusty brown hair, squared jaw. Deep brown eyes and tanned, olive skin. He wears this navy tweed sports coat on top of a plain burgundy T-shirt, and it shouldn't match. But it does.

I also know this guy.

Salvatore Amadio. AKA one-fourth of my Intro to Marketing group. We only briefly met in class, but he's now five-feet in front of me. Bending down to snatch the Fizz Life off the floor.

"Thanks," I tell him.

He appraises the stack of cans in my arms. "Getting drinks?" His Italian accent is thick on the words.

He's from Naples but came to Wakefield for university. International students make up eighty-percent of the school, one of the main reasons I chose it over other colleges. Most people here are far away from their homes like me.

"Yep, can't have a group meeting without Fizz—*crap*." I drop the key and bend too quickly to pick it up. Another can falls off my tower and rolls down to Salvatore.

Okay, this is not going well.

"Sorry," I say.

He laughs. "Don't worry about it." He picks up the second can. "Here." He walks over and holds out his hand for the key. Am I that pathetic that I can't even open my own door? This is a new low. I must be frozen because Salvatore motions for the key again. "We'll switch. You take these." We somehow swap items. I'm carrying all four cans again.

He has my room key.

In seconds, the door is unlocked. I avoid his eyes as I go to my desk, setting down all the soda cans.

From an earlier assessment, I know that Salvatore is very good looking. The kind that would anoint him Prom King—even if he didn't go to that school—and I wouldn't be surprised if hundreds of girls slide into his DMs a day. While I can acknowledge his outward beauty, he is not my guy.

My guy is back in Philadelphia currently either passed out asleep or ignoring my calls. Both options concern me. But I can't worry about that right now—I'm hosting people in my dorm room. For the first time ever.

And right now I am alone with a boy in my room.

Who is not Garrison.

Before I become uncomfortable by the thought, a voice comes from my door.

"Hey, girl! Thanks for letting us use your place." Tess leans into the doorway with a beaming smile. She has tight black curls, dark brown skin, and wears camo cargo pants with a cute beige crop top.

What I've learned after one introduction to my group: I am the plain one. Tess, Salvatore, and Sheetal have trendy styles, where I look like I shop at Old Navy (because I do) in my faded jeans and worn T-shirt. It's not even a graphic tee because I don't love people reading my chest or abdomen or wherever the words would fall. It's literally *just* green. I'm okay with that though.

"Yeah, thanks, Willow," Salvatore says as he pops a can of Fizz Life.

Tess tosses her backpack on the floor beside my bed. "Not going to lie, when I saw Professor Flynn's email, I almost had a small panic attack. We're *so* far behind." Her American accent, I recognized when we first met, but I still asked where she's from. Atlanta. Born and raised.

Salvatore sits at my desk chair. "Where's Sheetal?"

"Took me ages to get a proper spot in the car park. Gutted, let me tell you." A tall Indian girl saunters into the room, tote on the crook of her arm. She's dressed in Calloway Couture's latest line: black trousers that just barely hover over the floor and an emerald-green silk top.

Tess grins. "I love how you say *proper* and *gutted*." She glides over and kisses Sheetal on the lips in greeting.

I've already gathered that they're a couple, but I don't know much more. On our first meeting, we just exchanged names and numbers and brief "where are you froms."

Salvatore is obviously curious because he asks, "When did you two start dating anyway?" He casually sets the open Fizz Life on my desk. My phone lets out a warning beep. Shit. It's dying. I walk around the bed to find my charger.

"Over the summer." Tess hooks an arm around her girlfriend.

"We met at orientation," Sheetal adds, her English accent thick.

"And you said you're from Liverpool." Salvatore notes like he's trying to remember our introductions from earlier this week.

"Is right." Sheetal smiles.

Salvatore looks to Tess. "You're from Georgia, the state not the country. And you…" He's definitely looking at me—or at least trying to—but I'm on my knees, the bed blocking me as I plug in my phone. "…I can't remember what you said."

I'm not surprised. I am unmemorable, and I never told any of them my last name. I don't think they've recognized me, so they could just not be into tabloids or celebrity gossip. It's a checkmark in the *yay I can still be just Willow* category. A major plus.

I pop up from the floor. "I'm from the States. Specifically, Pennsylvania. But I grew up in Maine."

PRESENT DAY

Salvatore meets my eyes. "Yeah, that's right." He says it like he's suddenly remembered, and I'm not sure how I feel about that. On one hand, I'd like to drift into the sea of forgotten people, but on the other hand, I do want friends in London. Or at least acquaintances. Really, I only need *one* acquaintance. I'm not picky.

Sheetal shuts the door. "Now that your memory is sufficiently jogged, Salvatore. Let's get to work."

We start brainstorming different products that we could advertise for the project. Everything from shampoo to laptops. An hour later, we've made a snack run and have narrowed it down to three options. Whatever we choose will determine exactly *how* we're going to market it and what demographic we'll be marketing to, so it's the most important step.

Though, what's concerning me has nothing to do with this project—Garrison still hasn't texted or called me back. Not that I've been checking. Okay, I have checked. Once or twice. *Maybe* five times.

I send him another quick text: Call me when you get this. I'm worried about you.

Footsteps from students running down the hall cut into our silence, all of us flipping through various magazines to grab more inspiration.

Tess stares longingly at the door. "I can't believe I'm doing this on a Friday night." She sighs. "Please wake me up."

Sheetal pinches her.

"Ouch...but thank you, babe," Tess says.

Sheetal smiles and tosses a pretzel in her mouth. "A third-year fella said that this project is *legendary* for business students. Mostly 'cause whichever student has the worst marketing plan ends up being a total whopper of the Fall semester."

A whopper?

Off my confused face, Tess clarifies, "They look like giant idiots."

Sheetal nods. "Last year, the worst in class created a toothpaste ad. Bright red paste for the holidays."

"Oh no." I grimace.

"It was a bloody disaster," Sheetal says. "Pun intended."

Salvatore crushes his Fizz Life can and stands up to throw it away. "Let's just choose from the three we have, they're not bad options."

I look at my notebook, our current options scribbled down.

An umbrella

Waterproof sandals

Fizz

"Let's eliminate Fizz," Tess suddenly says. "If we choose it, Professor Flynn might dock points because of Willow's connection to it."

Wait… *She knows?*

"Yes, go 'ed," Sheetal agrees. She doesn't seem surprised?

"Um…" I push my glasses up the bridge of my nose. "You all know who I am?"

Tess nods. "Your brother is Loren Hale, so that means your sister-in-law is Lily Calloway. Daughter of the CEO of Fizzle. It's all on Wikipedia." *Damn Wikipedia.*

"We also binged the *We Are Calloway* docuseries, like, a little towards the end of the summer," Sheetal says. "But Tess said not to bring it up to you."

Tess nods. "My mom is a director, and my dad is a location scout. As soon as anyone hears the films they made, I get asked a million questions. It's just kind of annoying. I thought it might be the same for you, so I didn't want to make it a big deal."

That's actually really sweet. I'm smiling, my cheeks hurting.

Besides the Calloway sisters and their men, there aren't many other celebrities in Philadelphia. It's not like LA or Hollywood where you can easily meet other people that go through the same public scrutiny. Paparazzi migrated to Philly *because* of the Calloways. Finding someone who gets it, even just a little, is a breath of fresh air.

"Thanks," I say to Tess.

"Don't worry about it," Tess says like it really is nothing.

I look to Salvatore, who's scrolling on his phone. I think he might be looking me up. When he catches me staring, he says, "You can Google me too. Salvatore Amadio." He spells out his full name.

Sheetal laughs. "Are we about to find out your deep, dark secrets, Salvatore?" But we all brandish our phones.

I do a quick Google search and learn that Salvatore Amadio is the son of two famous Italian actors. He was even in a movie as a baby, but he retired from child acting by the age of four.

Sheetal makes a dejected noise. "Well now I'm proper devoed, like. Me parents are in *finance*. An absolute snore. I have no famous family or long-lost siblings."

"You have *meeee*," Tess sing-songs and hugs her tight. Sheetal tries hard not to smile, but it's a lost cause when Tess kisses her playfully on the nose.

Salvatore pockets his phone. "It's not all great," he says to Sheetal but doesn't elaborate.

My cell suddenly vibrates in my palm, Garrison's name on the screen. *Finally.*

"I have to take this," I say quickly and then leave for the hall. It's empty, but I can hear muffled music coming from some of the dorm rooms.

When I click into the call, my worries just tumble forth. "Garrison, are you okay? Your last video looked like you hadn't slept in days. And I'm just now realizing that if you were sleeping I probably woke you up and you needed that sleep. I'm *so* sorry—"

"Willow," he cuts me off before I spiral. "I'm glad you called and texted and practically shot off a rocket flare."

Tears prick my eyes. "You are?"

"Yeah. And I'm in one piece. Like you said, I just haven't been getting sleep. I'm going to make sure I don't stay in the office past midnight."

"Promise?" I ask.

"Promise. What are you doing?"

"There's this group project thing."

"Right now?" Worry and concern breaches his voice. I know he's been worried about distracting me, but I'm making time for him in my life. That's what you're supposed to do for the people you love.

"Yeah, but I'm taking a break—hold on." My door suddenly opens, Salvatore, Sheetal and Tess slipping out of it.

Salvatore catches my gaze. "Hey, we chose the umbrella. We figured we'd just decide and call it an early night."

"I'm going to email the professor," Tess tells me, slinging her backpack over her shoulder.

"See ya, Willow," Sheetal adds before she leaves with Tess.

Salvatore stays for a second. Hands stuffed in his jacket. "We think we can advertise to the university students. Cool designs. Small and portable for class."

It's simple, but maybe that's the beauty of it. "I like it."

"Great." He walks backwards, eyes still on me. "See you in class, Willow Hale." He spins on his heels and heads toward the stairwell.

I don't understand flirting, but I know rom-coms and that definitely was straight out of the movies. Only it does the opposite of causing butterflies to flap in my belly. More like moths dying a slow and unnatural death.

I put my cell back to my ear. "Garrison, are you still there?"

9

GARRISON ABBEY
Age 20

It was unmistakable. The guy's voice on the other end of the phone. But there were other voices too, and I'm not about to jump to conclusions like some jealous, paranoid boyfriend. I trust Willow, and she's allowed to have guy friends.

"Garrison, are you still there?" she asks me.

I lie on my bed in a black hoodie and jeans, staring up at the ugly, stained ceiling. "Yeah, still here."

"That was just my group for that project I was talking about."

Intro to Marketing. I remember. All the pieces clicking into place. "You can call me back when you're done."

"We just finished." I hear her shut the door. "I'm going to Skype you." She must be really worried about me, more than I even thought. Fuck.

I run my hand through my messy hair that touches my eyelashes. I don't want to scare her. And really, I'm coherent. Fine. I'm just burying myself in work, and that isn't *that* bad, all things considered.

Skype alerts me on my opened laptop, and I sit up, placing my computer on my lap, and click into her call.

I see my girlfriend, and I exhale. Willow is sitting on her bed, dorm room dimly lit, X-Men poster hung up behind her.

Her eyes flit around me quickly. "You're right, you are in one piece."

"It was touch and go there for a minute," I joke. A bad one.

She shakes her head, and so softly, she whispers, "Don't."

"Okay," I say. "You look good." Her olive-green shirt accentuates her warm brown, hazel-ish eyes that practically look like melting chocolate. Willow wore that same shirt on her last day in Philly.

I only remember because I went to the airport with her, and that image of Willow leaving is kind of engrained in my head.

"You're home," she realizes. "Isn't it only—"

"One p.m." I answer for her. "Connor sent me home." I don't mention that I fell asleep at my desk. "He thought the same thing as you. That I looked tired."

"He's looking out for you," Willow says.

I snort. "He's looking out for his company. I'm not his friend, Willow. I'm his employee."

She shakes her head like she doesn't believe that, but instead of carrying on, she asks if I've seen the latest episode of *Supernatural*. We talk about all the things we both love. TV. Pop culture. Video games. I'm suddenly wide-awake, just wanting to extend every second I can.

Willow glances at her clock and grimaces. "Holy—we've been talking for *three* hours, and I've sufficiently ruined your nap and the whole purpose of you getting rest." She buries her face in her palms with a long groan. "I'm the worst. I'm sorry." We're both beating ourselves up.

Her for distracting me.

Me for distracting her.

I don't know how to fix this.

"You're not even close to the worst," I tell her. "I enjoyed tonight— or today—or whatever you call it." Tonight for her. Still today for me.

She unburies her face and slowly braids her hair. "So do you want to… maybe… um…?" She takes a breath, her eyes soaking into me like she wants something. And then timidly, she slips off her overall straps and pulls off her green shirt, just in a blue cotton bra.

God.

Blood pulses in my dick, and my eyes trace her soft skin and the tops of her breasts. *Yeah, I want to.* Times a million.

I yank my hoodie and tee off my head. Tossing both on the floor. I adjust the computer, setting my laptop more on my mattress near my waist. I see myself in the screen—what she can see—and my whole body is almost in full view.

I focus on Willow, and I frown. "Hey, we don't have to do this if you're not into it, Willow."

Her shoulders are bowed in, and she's clutching her elbows. She pushes up her slipping glasses. "No, I want to. I really do. It just feels kind of…" She glances around her dorm room. "It's really quiet here."

"I can put on music."

She nods and rubs her arms.

I play an alternative rock playlist on my computer, so she'll hear the noise. "Better?"

"Yeah." Willow exhales. "I'm nervous." She shakes out her head. "I wish I weren't *this* nervous."

I know her well. I know that she's pretty shy and reserved. Our relationship moved *slow* from the start. Like the slowest I've ever had. And there wasn't one day where I wanted to press fast-forward and speed up. She's also the best I've ever had.

In everything.

"It's okay that you're nervous," I assure. "It's probably because we've never had Skype sex before."

I look her over, wishing I could be at her dorm a billion times more now. To ease her nerves, to make her feel good. Fuck, it'd be easier if I could just touch her…

She speaks so softly this time; I don't catch the next words over the music.

I hit the volume on my keyboard. "Say that again?"

"Does it turn you off?" she asks in the quietest whisper. "How nervous I am?"

I shake my head, almost smiling. "No." Honestly, I'm really smiling.

Her lips start to rise seeing my smile. "What?"

"Your insecurities are pretty cute. You always think you're so lame and meek, but you're like that daytime soap opera title."

Willow leans closer to the screen. "*General Hospital.*"

I push longer pieces of hair out of my face. "The other one."

"*As the World Turns.*" Willow grins a bit, knowing that's not the right one either. We both don't watch soaps, but we know our television.

"Damn, college is making you stupid," I say, sarcastic.

She laughs. "You say it."

I sweep her features. "*The Bold and the Beautiful.*"

Willow bites the corner of her lip, her smile appearing again.

"You're beautiful, Willow." I skim my girlfriend with hot desire that pricks my nerves and blankets my skin. My dick strains against my jeans. "I think you should get under your covers and watch me. You don't have to get naked or show me anything."

Her eyes widen. "You'd be okay with that?"

"Yeah. No question." I'm usually the one who takes the lead whenever we're in bed anyway. She prefers that, and I'd rather be in control.

Willow slips under her sheets, and the screen goes wonky as her computer falls to its side. After a second, she must prop the laptop on her lap—since the screen stabilizes. I have a clear view of her face, her cheeks flushed and glasses a bit smudged.

I stay in my camera frame for Willow, and I unzip my jeans and kick them off my legs. Left in black boxer-briefs, I palm my hard dick above the fabric. All the while, I watch her pleasure mount on-screen.

Her breath hitches. I strip off the last layer of clothing. Left buck-naked, and I spit in my hand and stroke my length.

My muscles contract. *Fuck.* Heat blisters across my body, and I look at my girlfriend, aroused flush creeping up her neck. And I imagine sinking my erection between her legs. I imagine Willow beneath me, trusting me—a girl who's delicate and shy at most touch, and I go slow and rock deep. My hardness filling her tight warmth that clenches around me.

I fist my shaft in an up-and-down motion and buck my hips up into my grip. "Fuck," I groan. I just want inside her. I just want to be in bed with her.

I just want more than this, and I know I have to be happy with the fantasy and our ocean-apart reality. Like maybe it'll be enough in the end.

I arch my hips into my clutch again.

Willow lets out a soft, aroused noise.

Fuckfuck. I watch as she adjusts her laptop. She's slipping further into her bed. Lying down. I think she props the laptop on the pillow next to her. I can't see below her breasts, but her arm seems to shift...

And move. Her lips part in a short breath. Her eyes shut for a beat longer.

Fuck, she's masturbating. My muscles flex, sweat glistening along my body, and pre-cum coats my hand.

Desire pulsates my veins like a coked-up drummer banging and banging. "Willow," I groan. "*Willow.*"

She gasps and squirms. I strain my ears to hear her whisper, "Garrison."

I'm an idiot and I reach out at the computer screen like I can touch her. This fucking 2D version is only half of my girl, and yeah, I'd rather be able to pull her underneath me right now.

She covers her face with her hand, nearing a peak. "I want you," she mumbles into a sharper breath. "I want you in…"

"I'm in you," I say in a tight, deep voice. I quicken the friction on my length. "I'm so fucking deep in you."

Willow moans.

My neck strains, blood bursting my veins, and I tilt my head back. "*Fuuuck,*" I grit down.

She quakes.

I hit a powerful climax, and an involuntary noise breaches her lips, this high-pitched whimper that reminds me she's completely let go. Out of her head, and I release into my palm. My body on fire as I pump out the tension.

Fuck.

She breathes hard with me, and I try to remind myself that even miles away, intimacy is still strung between us.

PRESENT DAY

THE NEXT FEW WEEKS, WILLOW'S CLASSES GET harder, and I back off calling my girlfriend until she can call me. I won't be her distraction. She's got shit going for her, and I've ruined enough. I'm not going to ruin her.

To not think about her, I just bury myself in work. It's the only thing that keeps me relatively sane. I'm averaging four to five hours of sleep. Which isn't too bad, all things considered.

And I haven't burnt another pizza. So improvement, right?

I grab my backpack off the bed. Normally on Saturday I'd be in the office, but Cobalt Inc. is having a party for the diamond division, and I really don't want to run into those pricks. They're the guys who pass me and "cough" out the word *nepotism*. They're not wrong. But it is annoying. Coughing words died in prep school. It's fucking lame— especially when thirty-year-old tools do it.

But I got a call, so I do have somewhere to be.

I'm babysitting.

I lock up my apartment and on the way to the stairwell, I pass the cracked door to the shared "smokers" balcony. I quit smoking a while ago, so I've never ventured out there. Voices are muffled from outside, but I can still clearly distinguish Ana's high-pitched drawl.

"What do you mean he's never around? Doesn't he live here?"

"I mean what I said, Ana. He isn't around much," Jared replies, freezing me cold. "Last time I saw him, I helped with his fire detector." I freeze. *They're talking about me.*

"That was *weeks* ago," Ana whines. "If we want to make headway into the inner-circle, you need to be nicer." I almost snort out a bitter-ass laugh. I knew it was all an act. It actually sucks to be right.

"Baby, I'm being as nice as I can be without getting on my knees and sucking him off."

"Maybe—"

"Ana," he snaps.

"I'm just saying, we have one chance to be *in* with the most famous people in the country. Can you not fuck it up?"

I can't with this shit. I leave, hurrying down the stairwell. I pull my hoodie over my head. My anger surging. I'm babysitting, I remind myself. I can't go into it with this type of anger. *Calm down.*

Breathe.

Breathe.

Fucking breathe.

SUPERHEROES & SCONES IS HARD TO WALK INTO

these days. Part coffee shop, part comic book store—it'll always remind me of Willow and all the time we spent working here. Stocking the shelves and serving coffees.

I was shit at the espresso machine. Shit at recommending comics. Shit at shelving the "popular" collectibles in the front and the older ones in the back.

But somehow, I was never fired, and that's kind of a success.

Lily walks out from the back, hearing the chimes of the front door. Her bodyguard lets me in and then locks the door behind me. After-hours, only soft lights illuminate the store, and it's eerily quiet. Like walking into a fucking morgue.

I hate being here.

It's the first time I've felt that in a really, *really* long time.

I hate thinking it.

"Garrison, thankyouthankyou for coming." Lily bounces a three-year-old in her arms and then sets him down. "I'm *so* sorry this is such late notice." I agreed to babysitting her toddler. It's something Willow used to do when she was here.

"It's not a problem." I nod to Maximoff Hale. "We're going to have a lot of fun, right?"

He stares up at me with big green eyes. "Will you watch Batman with me?"

Shit. I raise my brows at Lily. Her husband owns a comic book company called Halway Comics, but everyone in the world is aware that Loren Hale's true allegiance is to Marvel. He says *fuck DC* on practically every Instagram Live I've seen.

She cringes. "Moffy's love of Batman is not going anywhere, much to his dad's dismay."

"Cool," I say with a smile. It's amusing.

"Will you watch it with me?" Maximoff asks me again. "*Pleeeeeassssee.*"

"Sure—"

He's already grabbing my hand and tugging me to the big TV near the collectible toys. Blinds are snapped shut over the windows and glass door for privacy. I'm introduced to a couple extra bodyguards that Lily is leaving with her son and me.

Both men stand near the entrance like silent shadows.

Lily runs around, grabbing keys. She calls out to me. "The fridge is stocked and you remember where the good snacks are?!"

"Break room, bottom cabinet," I mumble under my breath.

Lily doesn't hear me, but she's rushed and glances at the clock. "Thank you! I'll be back soon!"

She exits in a hurry, and her son stares up at me like I'm his total world for the next hour. Maybe because I am.

If Maximoff even knew how I came into his dad's life, would he hate me?

My stomach twists, and I try not to think about that. Moffy is a good kid. He just sits on a yellow beanbag and watches the movie, and when his favorite parts come on, he glances back to make sure I'm paying attention.

One hour and two bowls of popcorn later, the kid is out. Soft snores coming from his mouth. Finding an old *Ant-Man* fleece blanket on a shelf, I rip open the packaging and then cover Maximoff.

Babysitting duties accomplished. Yay me. I lean back against a bookcase, action figures on the shelves, and I scroll through Tumblr.

Willow hasn't answered a questionnaire since she left for Wakefield. Either she doesn't have time to do one or she's just not into them anymore. She reblogged a couple gif sets of that guy from *Gilmore Girls* that she says I remind her of, so that's a good thing, right? She's still thinking about me.

Shit, I need to stop dwelling on this. I run a hand through my hair and bury my head on my knees. I should be working and avoiding all thoughts about Willow. Seconds away from grabbing my backpack and fishing out my laptop, my cell rings.

She's Skyping.

My chest lightens, my lips lift. It's like someone switching on the lights in a dark room, and I know I need to figure out how to find that switch when she's not around. But it's just hard.

"Hey," she says, beaming when she sees me. Christmas morning can't even beat getting to talk to her.

Underneath my happiness is a gnawing sensation. Like something eating me from the inside-out. Termites in my basement, eroding the foundation. I don't know how to shake the feeling.

Focusing on Willow, I notice that she's sitting at her organized wooden desk. Pens and pencils stashed in a cup.

She must be Skyping from her computer, since I have view of most of her room, including her opened door. Students pass by in the hallway.

In another life, could that have been me? College. A dorm. Friends. In another life, I would have lived there and hated every second of it. But I hate being away, too.

I feel like I'm seventeen again, hating two polarizing things and not being able to find peace within the middle. Split apart. Trying to be sewn back together. It hurts. I hate that it hurts.

I meet Willow's eyes.

"Hey," I whisper back, trying not to wake Moffy. "You look pretty cheerful."

"So do you," she replies. "Or at least, more than last weekend."

Last weekend, I had two hours of sleep and downed four Lightning Bolts!—Willow told me that if I drank any more energy drinks she was sending Daisy to come check on me.

She scans my surroundings. "Are you at Superheroes & Scones?"

I nod and then flash the phone toward the sleeping toddler and then back to me.

She looks surprised. "You're babysitting?"

"It's hard to say *no* to Lily." Plus, I genuinely like her kid. Maximoff is sweet and probably the easiest toddler to look after—not that I have a lot of experience babysitting other people's offspring.

Willow nods like she gets it. "Lily has the best puppy dog eyes. They make you crumble."

I pull up the hood of my black jacket. "So hey, I… um, I came up with my project for Cobalt Inc., finally."

Her smile explodes. "Garrison!" she exclaims in a quiet voice, since Maximoff is sleeping. Her enthusiasm emits from the core. "That's amazing. And see, you didn't have anything to worry about."

I shrug. "I'm not going to tell Connor about it yet. He'll probably think it's stupid and pull the plug. I'll ask for forgiveness later or whatever." Which, I know, isn't something you should probably be doing when you're an employee of a multi-billion-dollar corporation.

But I'm too invested in this project to risk losing it. Plus, when I have a prototype, I can better sell the concept to Connor.

I think about not telling Willow the details either. So she doesn't have to keep this secret from her family, but in the end, I can't keep it from her, so I just say, "I want to create a video game based off Sorin-X." He's a character from *The Fourth Degree* comics, the same titles that Loren's company, Halway Comics, publishes.

I need the rights of these comics in order to adapt them into a video game, but I'll jump through that hurdle later.

Willow looks like she could hug me through the screen. But we can't touch, and that realization tunnels through me like a freight train at full speed. It's excruciating. I wish I just told her the news in person—whenever that would be.

"Garrison," she breathes deeply. "That's *perfect*. And you really are the best person to create it. I won't tell anyone, promise."

I nod, knowing she won't, and I quickly change subjects. "How's your project going?" I'd rather talk about Willow because the more I talk about the game, the more I'm probably going to curse the thing to hell. I can already see the project combusting in flames.

She grimaces. "I mean—it's a silly school project. It's not like yours." She pushes up her glasses that have fallen down her nose.

I'm about to tell her she's wrong. That her school is just as important and meaningful than a stupid video game, but someone stops in her doorway.

"Hey, Willow."

My jaw tenses.

It's *that* guy. The one I heard over the phone. I recognize his Italian accent.

He leans against the doorframe. In direct view of her webcam. He grabs her attention, and Willow turns her head to meet his gaze.

I glare. Yeah, I immediately hate this guy for no real reason other than he's showing up unannounced at my girlfriend's door.

Also: he looks like all the assholes in *every* prep school that I've ever attended. Khakis. Fluffy, styled hair. Sports coat. And I'm thoroughly ashamed to say that I attended *three* prep schools because I flunked out of two.

But it's whatever. I can't really read the expression on this guy's face because he's standing too far away from the camera.

That doesn't stop me from squinting at my screen.

"Hey, Salvatore," Willow greets. "Is it six already?"

"On the dot," Salvatore says. My brain starts processing more. This is the guy from Italy that Willow was telling me about. He's in her group for her marketing project. Willow also told me his name is spelled the same as Damon and Stefan Salvatore from *The Vampire Diaries,* even though they're not pronounced the same. She said it was kind of amusing, and at the time, I agreed.

I don't think it's amusing anymore.

"Shit," Willow says. "Time just slipped by. Can you give me a minute?"

"No problem. I'll be on the steps outside."

"Thank you," Willow calls out and then glances back to me. Apologies heavy her eyes. "Garrison—"

"It's not a big deal." I do my best to soften my glare. "Go." I don't even know what I'm telling her to *go* to. My chest is tight.

I don't want to be a possessive asshole. All I know is that I trust her. Don't trust him. Don't know him.

He looks like my brothers. No, he just dresses like a douchebag, like they do. But he's not them.

I swallow hard, my nose flaring. My insides twist, fighting with these feelings. I can't be the paranoid, controlling boyfriend who forbids her from talking to her own goddamn group partner.

I won't do it.

I don't even want to *appear* like I'm jealous or worried about him. She doesn't need that stress. I'm trying to be cool. Everything is cool.

Everything's fine.

She scratches at her arm. "I'm really sorry. This is when I wish I was Hermione and had a Time-Turner. But I am…sadly a mortal."

"A muggle," I rephrase for her, which is something I rarely do for *Harry Potter* references. She's usually correcting me.

She smiles, but it's a sadder, weaker one. "A muggle." She nods and then shakes her head, conflicted. Like she wishes she had time for me and school. Without me asking, she offers more details. "It's a group thing. We're going over to Barnaby's to come up with a slogan for the umbrella ad."

Barnaby's is Wakefield's popular bar. I know because Willow told me about how Tess and Sheetal took her there for an *Avengers* trivia night.

They came in second.

According to Willow, there were some trick questions relating to Captain America that shouldn't have been included. Even coming in second, she had fun and she's making friends. It's a good thing.

She's happy.

I want that for her. That's all that should matter. We say our goodbyes, and just as I pocket my phone, Lily returns from her meeting. She rushes into Superheroes & Scones like she's been away from her child for a decade. Her 24/7 bodyguard stays near the door with the other two, and I can already hear fans coalescing outside.

My stomach knots. I'm going to have to push my way through those crowds. *Great*. I don't love people grabbing at me. I exhale a tense breath.

Lily skids to a stop when she sees her three-year-old curled up on the beanbag, cuddling the *Ant-Man* blanket.

Gathering my backpack, I avoid her gaze and rise to my feet.

"Garrison, thank you," she whispers so she doesn't wake him.

"It was nothing," I say. "See you." I head towards the door.

"Wait, Garrison." Lily catches up with me. "Do you want to come over for dinner? We're having spaghetti. I didn't make it, so it's edible." She smiles softly, and I see those pleading *puppy dog* eyes that Willow was talking about.

To me, it just looks like pity.

Lily knows I'm alone here in the city. My family might live in Philly, but I don't go see them unless it's a holiday and I'm coerced into it. I have no friends. All that's keeping me going is work. I should take her offer, but I don't want to get close to Lily and Loren or any of Willow's family.

I don't know how long our relationship is going to last. And if she breaks up with me, if this all ends, they'll choose her. Like they should. And I don't want to spend time with Lily and Loren just to lose them in the end.

I won't.

I can't.

"I have plans," I lie to Lily. "But thanks."

Without another glance back, I zip up my jacket and leave.

10

PRESENT DAY – October
London, England

WILLOW HALE
Age 20

"Why are you taking photos of the chips, Willow?" Sheetal sips a beer and eyes my cell curiously. It hovers over a bowl of chips—or *fries* as I call them. Barnaby's has great pub food, and it's imperative that I send in my rating to Daisy.

"I promised my friend I'd document the food in London," I explain. "And rate it."

Tess smiles and plucks a fry from the basket. "I'd give these fries a solid two out of five. Needs more salt." She bites into it.

Sheetal reaches for the salt shaker. "You mean, *chips.*"

Tess sticks out her tongue playfully. Sheetal tosses a fry at her, and Tess laughs. Not long after, Sheetal asks, "You need another bevvie?" She eyes her girlfriend's depleting beer.

"Not yet, babe," Tess says, smiling into a bite of fry.

They're an adorable couple, and I'm grateful that they keep asking me to hang out. Even tonight, they could have left after we finished the assignment for our ad, but instead they both ordered a pint.

In my experience, most people don't love the company of quiet people like me. We don't bring enough to the conversation. We take up space at your table when you could have someone louder and more outwardly fun. And maybe that's just my insecurity because Sheetal and Tess don't make me feel like an intruder. They actively *want* me here, even if I'm quiet.

Someone bumps into our high-top table, and with my free hand, I reach for the pitcher of beer before it spills.

"Sorry," the guy mumbles before stumbling over to the bar. Barnaby's is crowded, college students filled to the brim. We're lucky we arrived early and snagged one of the high-top tables.

I return to my phone. "So the *chips* are definitely five out of five." I text Daisy my review: Delicious. Pub food at its finest. My picture kind of sucks though. It's all grainy and the dim lighting doesn't do the chips any favors.

She quickly texts me back.

Daisy: They look superb! Wish you could mail them to me!!

Me too.

"Five out of five?" Tess snorts. "I'm going to need to taste test a few more to see what's up." She digs her hand back into the basket.

I pick up my beer stein and take a small sip, the top mostly foam. It's so strange being in a pub with students as young as eighteen, all legally drinking. "I can't believe I'm twenty and drinking in a bar," I say my thoughts out loud.

PRESENT DAY

"I know, right?" Tess nods. "America needs to get with the program and lower the drinking age." She frowns. "Also, I'm just now realizing that by living here, my twenty-first birthday isn't going to be as epic."

"London has saved you from drinking the night away, getting bladdered, and smelling like a vomitorium," Sheetal notes. "You're welcome."

"Bladdered?" I ask.

"Piss drunk," Sheetal defines.

Tess grins and clinks her glass to Sheetal's.

It's another moment I wish Garrison were here. I don't feel like a third wheel or anything, but I want my new friends to meet him. He's so much a part of my life that it feels like I'm hiding something or omitting this essential thing.

I glance towards the bar. Salvatore leans a hip against it, bodies packed between him, but he's focused on a brunette with skin as pale as mine, wavy brown hair, and a deep blue velvet minidress.

"Speaking of ages," Sheetal says, capturing my attention. "I've been thinking about our little group." She waves around the table, but her eyes are on me. "Tess and I are nineteen. You and Salvatore are twenty. We're all the oldest in the class since we started Wakefield late, and I could see Professor Flynn grouping us off on purpose."

Tess nods. "It'd make sense, right? Our families are all well off, too."

I remember something. "He grouped all the Aussies together."

Sheetal lets out a breath. "Well, that probably confirms the theory. He's giving every group an advantage. Like a commonality somewhere. Being a fresher is hard enough, maybe the fella wants to ease some of the stresses on our first year."

"He *is* my nicest prof," I say.

"Mine, too," Tess agrees.

The music in the pub changes to a popular *Arctic Monkeys* song as I sip my beer. The liquid goes down bitter. Garrison loves this band.

"Oh no," Tess says. "You have that look, Willow."

"What look?" I ask and reach for a fry.

"Relationship trouble," Tess says. "Are you missing your boyfriend?" I only briefly told them about Garrison because the more I talk about him, the more I long for him to be beside me.

I'm waiting for the day where that doesn't happen. Where it doesn't hurt. But I'm also terrified if that day finally comes.

"I wish he were here," I admit. "Garrison and I have been through a lot together."

Salvatore comes back to our table and takes the opened seat beside me. He sets his whiskey down along with a basket of something fried-looking. "What are we talking about?" he asks.

"Willow's boyfriend," Sheetal says.

Salvatore swings his head to me. "The one in Philadelphia?"

"That would be the one." I point to the basket. "What's that?" I whip out my phone to take a pic. New food. New experiences. College success, but why do I feel so badly about it? My stomach twisting.

"Pork scratchings," Salvatore says.

"Or for us Americans, pork *rinds*," Tess adds and takes a couple.

"Do you have a pic of him?" Sheetal asks me.

I nod and scroll through my photos, landing on one where he's in his usual black hoodie. Only the hood is down, so you can see more of his face. Hair brushes his eyelashes. Messy like that. We're standing in front of a Groot cut-out in the movie theater, his arm around my waist.

The sinking in my stomach intensifies.

I understand now.

I'm at a pub. Trying new food. Drinking with new friends. Garrison is alone in Philadelphia. Either working himself to the point of exhaustion or in his apartment trying to fend off Jared, his fame-seeking neighbor. *Guilt*. It assaults me tenfold.

I pass the phone to Sheetal. Tess leans over her shoulder to see the screen, too.

"*Willow*, you like the bad boys," Tess says into a grin.

"What?" I frown. "How can you tell?" It's not like Garrison is wearing a sign that says *I've done some questionable things in my past*…right?

Tess and Sheetal laugh lightly.

"I couldn't tell," Tess admits, "but now we know."

Sheetal hands the cell back and smiles. "You and your lad look like a knockout together, of absolute cuteness."

"Thanks," I mumble and pocket it.

Salvatore looks me over in a slow appraisal like he's trying to figure me out. "How is he bad, exactly?"

"He's not," I counter. "He's a good guy. When he visits next semester, you all can meet him and see for yourselves."

"Looking forward to it." Salvatore takes a sip of whiskey. "He'll love me. I have the best first impressions."

Tess snorts. "Yeah, it's your second and third impressions you need to work on."

Salvatore smiles but nudges my shoulder when he sees I'm not doing the same. He grabs a couple of the pork scratchings and places them on a napkin in front of me. "Give us your Pennsylvania-Maine opinion."

"Whoa! YEAH!" A drunk college student starts screaming at the bar. "Chug! Chug!"

Bodies begin shifting and three people knock into our table. I'm not fast enough this time. The pitcher collapses sideways, and I jump up before beer soaks me.

These assholes don't apologize. Instead they face the bar, their bodies still close enough to ram into the table again.

"Hey! Watch where your arses are bumpin' into." Sheetal snaps at the rowdy guys.

They turn on her in an instant, and I just barely make out one of them say, "Daft twit."

"Hey." Salvatore walks in front of them. "Back off."

Tess tosses napkins on the spill, and I walk around the table to stand beside Salvatore. "Just give us some space," I tell the guys. I'm pretty nice about it, so I don't really expect their response.

"*Just give us some space.*" The taller one with blond curly hair mimics my American accent, only he over-emphasizes it like I'm an airhead.

"We don't want any trouble," Salvatore says.

"Wankers!" Sheetal yells at them.

Salvatore sighs heavily, but he's smiling up at the ceiling.

Tess laughs.

I'm trying my best not to grin. Lips pressed tightly together. Curly Blond pins his glare on me, as though my effort to suppress laughter is the serious crime.

Salvatore slides closer to me, and then puts an arm around my shoulder. It's sudden and all for show, but it still causes me to solidify to utter stone.

"I said *back off*," Salvatore tells him.

Sheetal eagle-eyes the Curly Blond and mumbles into her beer. "What a divvy."

He's about to reply when a server walks over. "We got a problem here, mates?" He looks between our group and the asshole, but unlike the four of us, all of the asshole's friends have left him and migrated back to the bar.

Curly Blond grinds on his teeth. "No. I was just leaving." He steps back.

The server sees the empty pitcher, plus the sopping wet napkins, and he gives us an apologetic look. "I'll grab some towels and bring you lads another round on the house."

He leaves and we all look between each other, seconds away from breaking into laughter.

Barnaby's is our spot. Officially.

And then it hits me. It was a silly, *normal* argument. That guy didn't recognize me. Didn't start a fight because he hated my brother. Didn't call me names because of my relation to the Calloway sisters. London and Wakefield are bringing me this overwhelming sense of normalcy, and I don't want to let it go.

But I don't want to let go of what's back home either.

Garrison.

My family.

I love them more than anyone here can understand.

11

BACK THEN – September
Philadelphia, Pennsylvania

GARRISON ABBEY
Age 17

With a Grouplove song blasting through my headphones, I splice together roughly thirty-four clips on Final Cut, my Mac propped on my legs. I cut and duplicate four-seconds from *Princesses of Philly*.

Right now, I'm looking at Ryke Meadows on pause. He's staring at a mangled motorcycle on the sidewalk. I press play. *"What the f**k? Mother ****ing, piece of sh*t **** **** ******* kidding me."* I pause, trimming one-eighth of a second.

The clip is funnier if it's duplicated and overlayed with a song, so I add music on top of his bleeped out cursing and then add a two-second clip from an interview. *"What the f**k kind of question is that?"* He throws a pillow at the camera.

Nathan suddenly chucks a rubber gargoyle mask at me, hitting my laptop closed.

"Motherfucker," I swear, yanking my headphones to my neck.

"Dude," Hunter says—and no, this isn't my brother. It's one of my friends who pales in comparison to my brother's *greatness* and effervescent *beauty*.

"What?" I glare, lifting my computer screen back up. I set the mask beside me on the desk, the rolling chair squeaking as I shift.

Nathan's den is unusually quiet. No music playing out loud. No poker tournament or multiple conversations happening at once.

It's just a handful of my friends, with rubber masks, black clothes on, and a plan inside their heads. A plan that's put a feverish, crazed look on their faces. The adrenaline high of doing something illegal has already set in.

And I feel sick.

Maybe because Loren has talked to us, not just threatened us, but actually *talked* and it's hard—it's a lot fucking harder to see him as this impenetrable celebrity when he's humanized himself in more ways than one.

My neck heats, and I sweat underneath my hoodie. I can't stop picturing him and his kid, his *baby*.

And the plan tonight: we break into Loren's house. We scare the fuck out of everyone who lives there, and then we run away.

Infants are there. And I know one of the girls…one of the girls is messed up with PTSD or something. When Loren caught me with a paintball gun in hand, I remember one of them—either him or his brother—they said that to me. *My girlfriend has PTSD.* I think it's Ryke's girlfriend, and I'm not sure what this is going to do to her—but it can't be good.

I could voice this to my friends, but I hear their response: *it's only a prank. Grow some fucking balls, Garrison. You pussy.*

My skin crawls, and I'm about to put my headphones back on. The only thing keeping me from puking is this stupid fucking video. *Ryke Meadows and his "Fucks" – Part 2.* The first one I uploaded has over sixteen million views, so I figured a second one is due.

Someone else throws another gargoyle mask at me.

I block it with my arm. "What the fuck?"

"*Dude*," Hunter emphasizes. "We're leaving in a second, and you're playing *Sims*."

Nathan laughs after taking a shot of whiskey. "Did your virtual girlfriend cheat on you with the virtual pool boy?"

I flip them both off. They saw me playing *The Sims* one time, and they've never dropped it. I actually like that game—but if I even tried to admit it, they'd bring it up every minute of the day. And I'm avoiding that headache.

"Let's go." Kyle stands and puts his mask on. He thumps at his chest with his fists.

"You're a gargoyle, not a gorilla," Nathan tells him before sliding his own mask on his face.

"Same family." Kyle's muffled voice comes through. Not long after, everyone begins heading out. I stuff my laptop and headphones into my backpack but leave it and just carry the mask.

Each step I take, I feel worse, and excuses start blazing in my head. To get out of this, to leave. *I'm going to throw up.*

I wipe my forehead with my arm, the mask heavy in my hand. I close Nathan's front door behind me, and they laugh, practically *skipping* down his driveway to the road.

I'm the only one unmasked at this point.

As soon as my feet hit the asphalt, I just tighten up. I freeze in place. They're about five paces ahead of me when Nathan notices I'm missing. He turns around and gestures for me to follow. "Come on."

I shake my head tensely. "I can't," is the only excuse I can purge.

Nathan lifts his mask halfway up his head, tufts of red hair exposed. His eyes narrow at me, and he comes closer, our friends following. If I bail, there's a chance others may bail too—and this was Nathan's plan.

"Why are you being a little baby?" Nathan says loudly, so our friends hear.

"Just go without me," I tell them—the words spilling before I can take them back.

Nathan steps even closer to me. He's shorter and thinner than me, but still, my muscles flex and strain, my pulse accelerating and breath deepening.

"If you ditch us," Nathan sneers, "that's *it*—you know that, right?"

I glare. "Come on—"

"No, we're in this together. That was the *fucking* plan." Nathan gets in my face.

I shove him back, enough to give me space, and he's about to put his hands on me—I lose it and shift out of his path. "Seriously, don't fucking touch me!" I chuck the fucking mask at him.

"You're the one who hit *me*! God, what the hell is wrong with you, Abbey?"

I run a hand through my hair, the strands out of my eyes now. I'm shaking, and I can't say anything. I just walk back to his house, up his driveway, so I can grab my backpack and go home.

"Garrison!" Nathan shouts.

"Forget about him," Hunter says. "He's probably pissed he can't spend time with his fake friends on Tumblr."

I put a cigarette to my lips, shaking way too much to light it. My eyes burn, and I check over my shoulder once. Nathan is glaring at me, as though to say, *if you want to be my friend again, you're going to have a lot of making up to do.* He shakes his head, puts the mask over his face, and turns around, heading down the street with the rest of my friends.

I want to scream.

At myself. At them. At this stupid goddamn place.

But all I do is go inside, grab my backpack, and walk in the opposite direction of them, rounding the street corner to Cider Creek Pass.

12

WILLOW MOORE
Age 17

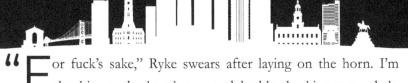

"For fuck's sake," Ryke swears after laying on the horn. I'm clutching my backpack strap and double-checking my seatbelt, secured in the backseat.

Loren glances at me from the passenger seat for the twentieth time, and I nod at him like *I'm okay.*

I've been in the car with them while paparazzi cars and vans tail us, but never this badly. Cameramen caught an "unnamed girl" climbing into the backseat of Ryke's silver Infinity, and the internet has been going crazy with shadowy pictures of me.

I have Tumblr, Twitter, and *Celebrity Crush's* feed popped up on my cellphone, and it's all everyone's talking about.

The number one speculation: *Ryke Meadows is cheating on Daisy Calloway.*

I've seen them together. In person. (I still can't believe it.) I helped Daisy make enchiladas for the house, and Ryke entered the kitchen to help too. I caught him stealing glimpses of his girlfriend, as though just wanting one more mental image of her—and his lips would always begin to rise in a smile.

Sure, I've always been a Raisy shipper, even if I can't relate much to their adventurous spirits, but these small, hidden moments solidify what I've always thought to be true.

Ryke Meadows loves Daisy Calloway.

So no, he'd *never* cheat on her. I don't believe it for a second, and I can only hope the world does too. I don't want to interrupt or ruin their lives by moving to Philly.

At a red light, Ryke angrily rolls down the driver's window and sticks his head out. "Don't cut me off!" he shouts at the nearest SUV, a camera pointing straight at him.

"What kind of precious cargo is in the backseat, Ryke?" the cameraman asks.

"I'm fucking serious. Don't pull out in front of me again like we're playing bumper *fucking* cars."

Loren cocks his head to Ryke. "Want me to drive?"

Ryke says nothing as he rolls the window back up.

"At least I don't have road rage."

"I'm a better driver than you—and don't *fucking* say it."

"You wrecked my car," Loren teases with a half-smile. "I've never been in an accident, so I'm a goddamn *great* driver."

Ryke rolls his eyes but stays quiet and taps the steering wheel, impatient for the light to change.

Loren glances at me again. "You doing okay?"

I tense more. "So is it usually this bad?"

"They're just out for blood today," Loren says. I notice his leg jostling a little, more edged than he's letting on. His phone is also in his hand, so I wonder if he's seen the speculations too. Then I spot the *Celebrity Crush* tabloid site on his screen.

I shift uncomfortably on the leather seat. "Maybe if Ryke kind of…keeps his distance from me, or acts like he doesn't care…" I trail off because Loren is almost near laughter. He has to rub his lips to keep it down.

"You're a fucking ass," Ryke tells Loren, though there seems to be affection in his voice, not hate.

I look cautiously between them. "What is it?"

Loren playfully puts a hand on the back of Ryke's headrest. "Telling Ryke to *not care* is beyond his superhuman capabilities. He's physically and mentally hardwired to *overly* care about people close to him."

I digest this and loosen my grip on my backpack. I'm slowly inching into their world, and I knew there'd be bad parts, like the constant gaze of cameras—but I don't think I ever calculated *these* parts: the loyalty from people who've just met me.

"Funny," Ryke says, hitting the gas pedal as the light turns green. "I don't remember ever being a fucking superhero."

Loren's smile fades, and he stares at his older brother for a long moment, like he wants to say something more. He ends up dropping his hand and swiveling towards me. "Stay close to me when we get out. They'll try to get in your face, and it'll be easier to walk inside the apartment complex if you're near me."

"They're going to ask who I am, right?" I nervously wipe my palms on my jeans.

"I'm going to lie, so you don't have to," Loren tells me. "Okay?"

I notice Ryke going rigid in the driver's seat, his eyes hardening through the rearview mirror. I don't know him well enough to understand why he's pissed. Maybe he's protective of Loren. Maybe he hates lies. Maybe it's the paparazzi in general.

All I know is that I'm about to make my debut in this media-crazed universe. And Loren Hale, my brother, is helping guide me.

"Okay," I nod.

"How many boxes are in the trunk?" Ryke asks.

"Just two. She only shipped my clothes and bedding." I said *she* instead of *Mom* to bypass the awkward tension of releasing her name into the atmosphere. I saw her not long ago. Our conversation at a local restaurant, Lucky's Diner, went something like this:

Mom: *If you stay here, you're on your own. I can't help you in Philadelphia.*

Me: *I know.*

Mom: **looks over her shoulder, expecting Loren Hale to jump out and frighten her by his presence**

Me: *He's not here. (He knew you didn't want to see him, ever.)*

Mom: **silence**

Me: *Can I still talk to Ellie?*

Mom: *When you call, I'll make sure to hand the phone to Ellie. *checks watch**

Me: *…do you want me to come home?*

Mom: *…you would've been out of my house in a year's time anyway for college. Maybe this change now is for the best.*

Then she gave me the faintest of smiles, like a goodbye, like she'd already begun severing me from her mind and she was waiting for me to do the same. She's used to leaving children behind, I realized. Maybe she thought this was the natural course—that she should leave me behind too, in time.

Sometimes I wonder if it was all a ruse, if she just appeared detached so she could let me go more easily. If she spent the night crying on the plane. If she hopes my life will be better here than it was there.

I'd like to believe all of this because it makes me love her a little more and resent her a little less.

Leaving Ellie has turned out to be the hardest part of all. Without constant communication, I can't know how she'll fair. If I fool myself long enough, I can imagine that my absence won't have any real impact on her, but I know it will.

Ryke parks in front of a brick apartment complex, the lot nearly full with cars. I feel out of my element. Not only because four different vehicles park near us, doors opening and cameramen jumping out—but because I'm only seventeen and entering territory that college students step on.

Lo isn't happy about it.

I can see that now as he scans the twenty-something, backpack-clad students, strolling in the apartment complex. His brows pinch, and his eyes darken.

"I'll be okay," I tell him, having to raise my voice as paparazzi gather outside the car doors.

He shakes his head a couple times. "You should really be staying with us."

Six people live in his house: three Calloway sisters and their three significant others, all in their twenties. Along with two newborn babies, one is Loren's son.

There may be extra room in their mansion-sized house, but I don't feel like I'd fit in. In fact, I see myself *always* in the way.

I haven't even met Rose Calloway's husband, Connor Cobalt, yet. He could very well hate me. On the reality show, he came off as a conceited human being. I even made a gif set of him saying (with a straight face), *"Most people never reach the pinnacle of perfection. But I'm not most people, so think of it as an honor to meet me."*

He's a genius. A billionaire. And living in a bedroom down the hall from him sounds like a fantasyland not created for me.

"I don't want to complicate your life," I tell him honestly.

His brows rise at me, and he motions to a bearded cameraman by my window. "And I'm not complicating yours?"

The man meets Lo's gaze, and Lo flashes his iconic dry smile at him. Seeing that smile in person is more powerful than in photograph.

On impulse, I almost take a picture, but I control myself, flipping my phone in my hand. It's so easy to become part of the paparazzi without really knowing.

"I'm going to grab a fucking box and head inside. Do you have your keycard?" Ryke asks me.

I nod.

Loren seems reluctant to do this.

Ryke gives him a look that I can't read. "You can't force her to live with us," he reminds him.

"She's only *seventeen*," he whispers, running a frustrated hand through his hair, thicker on top, shorter on the sides. "She should be closer to the high school she's going to attend, not to Penn."

"I'm closer to UPenn," I say softly, "not Penn."

Both of the brothers swing their heads to the backseat, and I swear camera flashes go off like crazy. The windows are only slightly tinted, so I wonder how much the paparazzi catch.

I feel my cheeks heat, but the color drains, their eye contact more and more intimidating. "Do I have…something on my face?" My voice dies, and by their rising smiles, I immediately regret speaking. I shrink into place.

Ryke tells me, "The only people I've ever heard say UPenn are people who never attended the University of Pennsylvania." He pockets his car keys. "We all call it Penn. At least when we went there that's how it was. Who the fuck knows what students are calling it now."

He acts like he graduated decades ago, but he just turned twenty-six. I'm not that great at math, but I can subtract well enough to figure out that it's been four years since he graced *Penn's* campus.

Lo adds, "Most of the older faculty prefer calling it Penn over UPenn. It's just tradition and it sticks with some people when you're there."

"But Penn State..."

"Is called Penn State," Lo explains. "If you say, 'I go to Penn' around here, most people will assume it's not Penn State."

"And if they don't, who the fuck cares," Ryke finishes. He also flashes the middle finger to the cameraman outside my window. "He's too close to her."

"I'll get out and go around to her door," Lo tells him. "You pop the trunk and grab the first box." At this, both of them open their car doors and climb out. Flashes bombard them, along with a barrage of voices.

I unbuckle and scoot towards the door that Loren nears.

"Back up," Loren tells them before opening my door and letting me out. I squeeze between him and a camera lens.

"What's your name?!"

"How do you know Loren and Ryke?!"

"Who are you dating?!"

My shoulders curve forward at each incoming question, and I clutch my backpack strap, pulling it closer to my body.

Loren leaves my side to grab my second cardboard box, and I follow close by, as instructed. I trip a little over my feet and barely catch myself, avoiding a collision into Lo.

Do not fall, especially on your brother that you recently met.

Unfortunately, I'm most clumsy when I'm nervous.

It's a horrible attribute. I wouldn't wish it on my enemy, but then again, I doubt my enemies would ever feel nervous enough to be clumsy.

Ryke slams the trunk closed, and then we head towards the sidewalk. A cameraman sprints in front of me and walks backwards as he films. "What's your name?!" he asks over the other paparazzi.

"She's my cousin," Loren lies with a dark glare. "So watch what you say and do." He stuffs a hand in his pocket, the action casual but somehow threatening.

About this time, we reach the sidewalk, a direct shot to the glass double doors of the apartment complex. Lo said they can't follow us inside. So I practically hold my breath in anticipation of ditching the eight—no, *twelve* cameramen that flank us.

And then, the weight on my shoulder goes from slightly heavy to very, very light—followed by a *crash* and a *crack!* I freeze in place and look down at the cement, wide-eyed at my backpack's contents.

Shit. The bottom of my backpack ripped.

And my laptop… I'm about to bend down to check it, but I notice other items that litter the sidewalk.

Like an extra T-shirt and shorts for overnight "crashing in my car" purposes. An extra pair of *panties*—these really childish looking blue pair with purple hearts.

Lots of highlighters, sticky notes, and pens.

What's most abundant: *tampons.* And not just one or two. There is an entire *box* of pink plastic-wrapped applicators. I know this because

I bought a box recently, dumped it into my backpack, and thought nothing of it.

I tense up, locked in a shell-shocked state, most likely ghostly pale.

My heart plummets, leaving a hollow hole in its place. My brother—a *new* brother—and his intimidating half-brother plant their gazes on me. And to make it worse: I'm surrounded by men with cameras who will no doubt post this on the internet.

I'm not ready to be a meme. Oh my God.

I can't move. I can't squat. I just stare like maybe this moment will rewind itself, and my jean backpack won't rip apart.

"Oh shit," one of the cameramen laughs.

I barely register Loren's murderous glare, plastered on the camera guy. He shrinks back a little and holds up a hand in surrender.

And then Ryke sets down his box. *What is he doing*—

No!

He starts collecting my tampons like they're pencils and not feminine products. I dazedly animate, like my legs belong to another girl—a higher force pulling the strings attached to my limbs. I kneel and quickly gather all the items, frantically stuffing them in my backpack's side pocket that's still intact.

Not a lot can fit there, so I bundle everything else in my arms. I decide to check the state of my laptop later, but upon glance, it seems okay.

"I can get that," I practically whisper to Ryke, gesturing to the tampons and two comic books in his clutch. I'm not sure he hears me, but I outstretch my free hand, showing him that I'll take it.

I struggle holding everything else, and I almost drop my laptop again.

"I'll carry this," he tells me. "You take that." He pockets the tampons and sets the comics on his cardboard box.

How can he be okay with pocketing my tampons? I'm about to refreeze and solidify all over again.

"Put your backpack on mine," Loren says, drawing my attention up to him. He pats the top of his box, and I rise, reluctantly letting go of my possessions, too afraid I'll spill them all.

"Thanks," I mutter, having trouble even *looking* at Ryke now.

"Does your cousin have a name?!" a camera guy shouts, his words dizzying me.

"Yeah." Loren uses one hand to hold the cardboard box, and the other sets on my shoulder, guiding me forward. "Her name is Willow Hale." He gives them one lasting dry smile before we enter the glass double doors.

As we ride up to the fourth floor in silence, I regain some consciousness that I typically lose in embarrassing moments. It's like a blackout, a fog, an out-of-body experience—my mind so stunned that it decides to abandon my body for a quick second.

I inhale, first and foremost. And then I look up. Ryke and Loren stand on either side of me, so tall that they make my 5'5" height feel short. I catch Ryke *glaring* at the space above my head, eyes narrowed on his brother.

Lo never looks towards Ryke as he says, "I had to lie. So you can stop glaring at me now. And in case you've forgotten, bro, I have the heart of Hades, so you shouldn't be surprised anyway."

"She's not a Hale, Lo."

Loren lets out a short, frustrated breath and meets his brother's darkened gaze. "Yeah? But I couldn't say she's a Moore and have press digging up her little sister's name. This is the better option for more than one reason. You know why?"

Ryke stays quiet and shakes his head, more like *this is wrong*.

"Now they think you're related too," Lo explains. "No tabloids are going to start rumors that you're hooking up…or whatever." Lo cringes at the idea.

I block out everything, internally dying and too overcome to concentrate on any other words or details. The elevator slows and beeps, and I nearly race off down the hall to my room: 458. I unlock the door with my keys—well, almost.

I drop them. I pick them up. And then I clumsily drop them again. It takes four tries before my joints work properly, and I turn the lock.

I have a very neat roommate, the tiny kitchen clean and pretty bare of appliances and food. Maya mentioned how she has a dining hall meal plan at Penn. The living room has a couple *Avengers* posters, *Battlestar Galactica* and *Final Fantasy*—plus stacks of anime on the coffee table.

Maya Ahn is cool. The Superheroes & Scones store manager had a roommate opening after her friend left for California, and it worked out in my favor.

I definitely can't afford the whole rent by myself, and I start working at Superheroes & Scones soon, thanks to Lily's kindness. Hopefully I'll be able to pay off the first month's rent that Lo loaned me.

The apartment splits off into two hallways; the left is hers, claimed by a Darth Vader poster on the door that says:

I WANT YOU FOR THE IMPERIAL FORCES!

The right is mine, unclaimed and bare. I open the door to a dorm-sized room, a simple built-in desk, a wooden dresser, a half-window, and a short single bed.

I take a seat on the slightly stained mattress, the wooden frame creaking. I hear footsteps as Ryke and Loren follow my shadow. I toss my phone from palm to palm, and it suddenly buzzes.

Maggie: Are you with Loren Hale right now?!?!?!

I balk. There's only one way my best friend from Maine could know this *that* quickly. I log onto the *Celebrity Crush* website.

"Oh my God," I mutter. A giant photograph of me snatching tampons off the sidewalk fills the landing page. Ryke has my panties on top of his box, and they've drawn a circle around them.

The headline:

Loren Hale's Cousin Has an Accident
in a Parking Lot!

I type back to Maggie: it's me...unfortunately.

Maggie: YOU'RE WITH LOREN HALE & RYKE MEADOWS!!!! WHAT IS UNFORTUNATE ABOUT THAT??? Also... why didn't you tell me you're his cousin? HELLO!

I knew that she might notice, but I doubt anyone else in Caribou will put two-and-two together and stir trouble for me. So I just text back: I just found out... please don't tell anyone. My mom doesn't want Ellie caught up in this.

Maggie: I won't tell a soul. Skype me soon... I need LOTS of details!

After her last text, I dazedly skim over the article, catching the part where they mention how my "visit looks like a permanent one"—and of course, they point out every single item I dropped.

"This place is small." Lo's voice emanates from the living room.

I set my phone on the mattress and stare at my hands, a little more numb and hollow than before the car ride here. I can't discern whether these feelings are from the severe lack of privacy...or just a normal bout of embarrassment.

"My first year dorm room was fucking smaller than this," Ryke retorts.

"She's not in college yet. She shouldn't live in a shoebox until she has to."

Ryke sighs heavily, their footsteps nearer. "I've already said what I've had to..." he trails off, and I sense them towering in the doorway, their hot gazes on my immobile body.

I can't look away from my palms.

A tense moment passes before I hear them set down the two cardboard boxes.

"Thanks," I say softly, unsure of what I'm feeling exactly. It's not every day that you grace the number one gossip site with your comfiest pair of panties and tampons strewn about. What a strange debut.

"Hey...Willow," Lo says, attempting to soften the sharp edge to his voice. "What happened back there—that'll be yesterday's news in an hour." He clears his throat when I don't respond. "You can think of it like an initiation? Welcome to the family..."

I choke on a laugh that twists my face into a cringe. I finally look up, and both Ryke and Loren wear sympathetic expressions.

Ryke more than Lo, which reminds me of the conversation in the car...about Lo's brother being *overly* caring.

I lick my dry lips, trying to form words when I usually keep everything in my head. It's a hard task to master, and I know I'm still very green at it. "I just...kind of hoped I'd be known for something other than the-girl-who-dropped..." *tampons.* I can't even say what they are. I wince at myself and glance at the scrap of worn jean material on top of a cardboard box. I can sew the bottom later.

"Like I said, it'll be yesterday's news," Lo tells me. "You'll be known for something else in a month's time…" My mind tunes him out the minute Ryke unpockets a handful of tampons, setting them on my dresser.

I go pale again.

"Ryke," Lo snaps, noticing where my attention lies. He whispers something to his brother, who's frowning.

Ryke whispers back, "They're just tampons. You're acting like she dropped a fucking dildo."

"Don't," Loren cringes.

Ryke rolls his eyes. "Lily, *your* fiancée, said she had a bad dream about her sex toys falling out of her luggage and paparazzi catching the incident at the airport—so I'm not the fucking weird one here."

Lo groans. "Why are you talking to *my* girlfriend about dildos?"

I don't know if I should find entertainment in this—if that makes me no better than *Celebrity Crush*—but I guiltily *and* eagerly listen along, wanting their back-and-forth to continue.

Ryke groans now. "We're fucking friends."

"*Hey*, can you at least watch how you say that? You're not friends that fuck."

"Why are you busting my balls?"

"You're the one who brought up Lily and goddamn sex toys. What the hell did you expect out of me?"

Ryke sighs and runs another hand through his hair. He meets my gaze as soon as his hand drops. "I hate that you feel embarrassed about this."

I shrug, unsure of what to say in reply. "You know...I'm a girl." It's difficult to say what I mean. I think I always sound more articulate in my head. "None of my friends talk about...periods or anything..."

Lo and Ryke exchange one look of knowing between each other. And then Lo dials a number on his phone and puts it on speaker.

Within the third ring, it clicks.

"Loren." An icy, female voice frosts the room. "This better be quick. I'm getting my nails done for the first time in *three* months." I think she even mutters, "I'm so sorry"—to her nails.

"God forbid I disturb you, your highness," Loren says.

"Wait—aren't you with your sister?" Rose Calloway, Lily's older sister, is one of the few people aware of the truth. I can hear her shift in her chair, as though straightening up. "Is everything okay?"

I've met Rose a few times. She usually does all the talking and I nod a lot. I like people that don't mind if I'm quiet, and since she's so loud, I thought she'd pressure me to be like her, to speak up and attack with confidence. She actually lets me say as much as I want and fills the rest of the silence with her own voice. I even think she likes it that way.

It makes me like her even more.

Ryke talks loudly so his voice is heard through the speakerphone. "She's upset. Her backpack tore while paparazzi were around us, and tampons fell out."

Every time he says *tampons*, so casually, my heart nosedives all over again.

"Willow," Rose says sternly. "Can you hear me?"

"It wasn't just one," I say under my breath. "It was an entire box..."

Lo puts his phone closer to his lips. "Did you get that?"

"Yes," Rose says. "Willow, most women have a period. We buy tampons or pads or other products. I personally like to be overprepared too. And if anyone—a cameraman, a peer, a stranger—makes you feel strange or uncomfortable for having seen you with them, then just know that they're *boys*, not men. They're *infantile*, little human beings that can't appreciate or respect a woman's body. And in no way should they even *touch* one." I begin to smile and she adds, "I have to go—*no* not yellow polish. I'm not a sunflower—"

She hangs up or maybe Lo does, either way—my shoulders have unconsciously lifted, my hands flat on my legs. I feel a little less numb, a little more awake.

I've never been given a motivational, encouraging speech in my life. The best part: knowing someone cares about me enough to give one. I realize that Ryke and Loren must've understood what Rose's response would be in this situation.

It's a bigger indication that they're all really close to each other.

"Thanks for calling Rose," I tell them.

They don't ask if I feel better, but I think they both can see that I am.

I stand up to check my laptop, which rests on a box. "You don't have to stay. I know I've taken up most of your time today already."

"We won't be that much longer," Lo says, "but I just…I need to tell you something. I just want to explain what happened. I know you probably read it online, but I think you should have our details."

I gather my laptop and then plop back down on the mattress. "Okay…" I think I know what this is about.

Someone broke into their house a few nights ago.

And I've been scared to broach the subject with Loren. It seems so personal, and I wasn't sure if I was allowed to bring it up since I lie on the fringes of their lives.

Ryke crosses his arms, casually leaning against the wall, unsurprised that Lo wants to talk about it with me.

Loren drags the desk chair closer to the bed and takes a seat, his elbows resting on his thighs and his hands clasped together. He stares at them for a long moment, just as I've stared at my own in dazed contemplation. The familiar action seems to bind us together, an invisible tether that's strung between siblings, here and there.

He lifts his head a fraction, just so our eyes lock. His gaze carries horrors and tribulations, I see. His gaze carries more than I've met. "Some guys around your age that live in our gated neighborhood," he begins, "they broke into our house. Everyone's fine." He adds that part quickly but his gaze falls back to his hands.

He looks haunted by the incident, and I glance over at Ryke, his brown eyes planted on the carpet with the same disturbed expression.

"This happened on Ryke's birthday?" I know it did. I read it in multiple articles. I push my glasses up, realizing my face is in a permanent wince.

"Yeah. I would've told you sooner, but…we've been trying to deal with a lot."

"It's okay," I say, just grateful he's telling me at all.

On September 19th, Ryke's birthday, I was at Lucky's Diner. Talking to my mom. Afterwards, I texted Lo that I was going to spend the night at a hotel and probably just hang out there the next day. He replied about three hours after I sent the message, a lot slower than normal.

Loren Hale: Okay, let me know if you need anything. I'm always here.

156

"They didn't steal anything," he explains. "They just came inside with masks to scare us, as a prank. It's not going to happen again, so I really don't want you to be afraid of coming around. The guys who did this, they *live* in our neighborhood. They're just rich pricks…or jerks."

My lips faintly rise. It's kind of funny when he tries to "censor" himself around me, like I'm a little kid. I've told him once that I don't mind when he curses, but he just shrugged. I don't know…I like more that he cares enough to try, even if it's not necessary.

And then my smile fades completely and my brows knot. "They live in your neighborhood?"

"Not for fucking long," Ryke says. He thinks I'm frightened by them being there—but that's not what's rolling around in my head.

If they live in that neighborhood, there's a good chance those are the same guys I saw at that party. The same ones causing trouble in Superheroes & Scones. "What do you mean, not for long?"

"We called the cops," Lo tells me. "We've let them off the hook a lot because…I know what a small charge can do to someone's future. I didn't want to get them written up for putting dog shit on our front porch."

Ryke looks at his brother. "You did the right thing by waiting."

Loren nods a couple times, looking as though he's trying to believe it was the right course of action too.

"We fucking warned them," Ryke adds.

"Yeah." Loren nods again. "So we're pressing charges this time around." He motions to me. "I wanted to tell you sooner because I want to include you in my life, as much and as often as I can, okay?"

I smile. *Wow.* My eyes feel glassy, and I take a deep, strong breath and nod. "I'm glad."

BACK THEN

"Good." Lo stands. "And you should know that some of these guys go to your new school. They shouldn't be there anymore, but some of their friends might be. And if they give you shit, you let me know."

I'm about to ask why they would "give me shit"—but then I realize...*I'm Willow Hale* to them. To everyone. To the world.

I'm the only relative of Loren Hale that will be walking the halls of Dalton Academy.

And Loren Hale possibly just sent their friends to jail.

The Calloway Sisters & Their Men — Fan Page

Back Then | *Followers: 18K*

Big news! Loren Hale's cousin has moved into town. There's not much we know about Willow Hale—yet—but it will only be a short time before Redditors and paparazzi gather more information. Here's what we know so far:

She's seventeen.

That's it. Seriously! We don't even know where she came from. It's like she materialized from thin air. Maybe those conspiracy theories are right and Loren Hale's family all have superpowers. LOL!

But for real, Willow Hale is a mystery. Early reports were that she might have been Ryke's new girlfriend but that's been debunked now that we know Willow is a *Hale*. And not to mention Raisy is a ship that is clearly sailing into the sunset.

Until I get more information, check out the gif set of Willow's epic tampon fumble!

Love you like Loren loves Lily,
xo Olive

13

GARRISON ABBEY
Age 17

pace outside of Superheroes & Scones at 6 a.m., my shit feelings causing me to linger. Only a few cars whiz by every minute, Philly beginning to wake—*why am I awake?*

It's Saturday. I should be in bed sleeping off these shit feelings—*I can't sleep.*

I stop and rest my arm on a parking meter for a second. An old gold Honda hugs the curb.

I parked my car a block away from here, needing the walk to think. Now that I'm outside the storefront, I'm still *thinking* apparently, and it's not helping.

Nothing is helping.

I tug my hood over my head, the morning air cold. Everyone at Dalton knows what happened at Loren's house, and most of them know that I was supposed to be there.

My mutual friends with Nathan—ones that weren't there that night—think I'm disloyal and a shit friend for welching. Believing that I could've helped them escape before Loren caught them.

I can't even hang out with the people that think Nathan is scum for what he did. I'm guilty by association. I passed Rachel in the hallway. She bristled at my presence and said, "You could've stopped your friends, you know. Why didn't you do anything?"

Some mornings, I wish I'd just gone ahead and done it with them. Because I know I could never be strong enough to convince all of my friends to turn around with me. No one gets that.

"Why are you here?" I mutter to myself under my breath. And then blinds begin to open from inside the store. I don't believe in signs or astrology or any of that, but this feels like something.

Move.

I walk away from the parking meter. Nearing the door. Why am I here?

Because I literally have nowhere else to go.

I have no friends. I have no life-altering aspirations. Every door feels shut except this one…the one that Loren Hale left open for me.

If this doesn't work out…I don't know what I'm going to do.

I eye the *closed* sign and then knock on the glass door. I lean over and see Lily Calloway through it. She looks startled, her green eyes widened at me.

Shit. I go still, more uncertain now. Her bald-headed bodyguard flanks her side, the burliest guy I've ever seen. His thick left arm could probably crush my windpipe.

She bites her nails, and I knock again, letting her know that I want to enter the store. I keep shifting, like I might bail and go home at any second.

Lily says something to her bodyguard, her gangly body looking even thinner while she stands next to him. She makes me less nervous for some reason.

He replies back, and then she approaches the door.

I tense as soon as she cracks the door and sticks her head out. I pull back my hoodie so she can see my face, and then I look over her shoulder. "Is Loren here?"

"No." That's all she gives me.

I deserve that.

I deserve even less, actually. I look at her bodyguard again. He crosses his arms and actually *glares* at me. I let out a pained noise, meaning it to be a laugh. "Forget it. This was a mistake." I go to turn around.

"Wait," she says quickly.

I hesitate, halfway turned.

"What do you want?"

How do I say this? I grit my teeth and try to purge my feelings, but all I say is, "Your boyfriend or fiancé or whatever… he offered me and my friends a job." I roll my eyes, realizing how this sounds after what happened. "It's fucking stupid anyway. Everything is."

I'm leaving.

The single thought sounds good, and I know how deep it actually goes.

"Lo told me about that." She swings the door wider open. "Do you want to come in?"

I hardly hear her. My lips part in shock, and my eyes burn. "What?" I breathe, looking between her and the opened door. I fully expected her to shut it in my face.

"If you want a job, you have to come into the store," she says nicely and even produces a smile. "Although…" Her eyes light up. "It'd be kinda cool if we had a superhero mascot out front. Do you want to be a mascot?"

"No." I shake my head in fog, barely registering anything she just said. How can she be this nice to me? She waves me in again, and I tentatively walk inside, my fists stuffed in my jean pockets. I don't think I've ever been this nervous.

Don't screw this up. I know. I know.

Her bodyguard blocks me about ten-feet into the store. "I need to pat you down."

Right.

I could have a weapon or some shit, looking for vengeance for them turning in my friends. I understand. I extend my arms, and the big guy pats my pockets and checks my hoodie. I hear some people talking softly by the cash register, but I don't look over there.

I scan the racks of comics, a cardboard cutout of a couple green-clad superheroes close by.

After Lily's bodyguard finds nothing on me, he nods to her in approval.

"So you want a job?" she asks.

My face twists, unable to detect any resentment on her features. She's what…twenty-four? She looks sixteen, to be honest—just really thin with a round face and rosy cheeks. Her brown hair is chopped at her shoulders, and she scratches her arm while she waits for me to speak.

I don't know what I feel, but it's all rising and hitting me fast. "You're not even going to ask me where I was that night? Or what happened?"

It's hard to believe Lily is a sex addict. The way she stares at me like *"oh right"*—slightly aloof but still approachable like a lost turtle—isn't someone I'd think would have a lot of sex.

Then again, one of my friends, Carly, has a tongue piercing and she's a virgin. So I don't know why I draw these conclusions, knowing they never add up anyway.

Lily pulls back her shoulders some and hesitantly asks, "Where were you?"

The question pummels me full-force, even if I was the one who basically asked it to myself. I look up at the ceiling and shake my head.

And it just rips out of me. "I'm not a good guy. I never told them to stop. I knew that they planned to break in and scare everyone, and I didn't do anything. I just let them leave." I choke on a laugh. "And now they're all looking at a year in prison. And I'm standing free."

She never even flinches. I watch her take in more than just my words, her eyes reddening. It's like she gets it. I don't know how... "What made you stay back?"

I stare at the carpet. "Everything your boyfriend said... fuck, I don't know. It just didn't feel right, scaring girls and babies... I know one of you has PTSD..."

She stiffens. "Wha...?"

"I didn't tell anyone," I say quickly, realizing this is private information. "I promise. I can't even remember who let it slip. Either Ryke or Loren shouted it at me. No one else was around." I drop my head, and my bed-head hair falls into my eyelashes. "I think... you should know that I planned to go with my friends."

I swallow a rock, struggling to force *tears* down.

Stop crying. I'm not crying, okay? I'm not. I just... I want to be someone else. I can't live with this anymore. And I don't even know what *this* is. Yeah I do...

This is me.

"I literally could not move my stupid feet," I say, my voice shaking. "And there's a part of me that wishes I was with them. That I got caught too."

She says softly, "You did the right thing."

I don't think I did. I look up at her. "Did I? I can't even say *I'm sorry* because it feels fucking stupid. Like…" I push my hair out of my eyes. "Like it's not enough, you know? It's not at all." It'll never be.

"This was enough," she says. "I promise, it was."

I try to let out a deep breath, and I try to believe what she's telling me. I don't think I can forgive myself, even if she's forgiven me.

I rub my reddened eyes with my arm and exhale again. I scan the store once more, grazing over the shelves and superhero posters along the wall.

I've never had a place that felt safe, but this one does. It feels like more than that.

"Here, I'll introduce you to Maya, the store manager," Lily says. "She'll have a better idea what positions need to be filled." She guides me towards the checkout counter.

I figure Maya must be the one with short black hair since she takes charge and shows the other girl the register.

"Hey," I say, nodding to the girls.

I startle the one with the loose braid. She bangs into the cash tray, overturning the plastic container. It lands on the floor, cash and coins spilling out. She freezes at first, blood rushing out of her skin, ashen and pale.

Shit.

"I'm *so* sorry," the girl says to Lily. She pushes up her black-rimmed glasses, and it hits me all at once.

I know you.

She seems to dodge my gaze, kneeling to gather all the fallen money. Maya stays at the computer, typing on the keyboard.

"I can help." I squat a little closer to this girl, hoping she raises her head and looks at me, just once. I want to know if she recognizes me too. If she knows who I am—if she hates me like almost everyone else.

Or maybe I just want her eyes to finally meet mine.

While I gather dollar bills, I keep glancing at her, watching as she picks up a few quarters and drops them in the same instant.

My lips rise, and I help her pick those up too. I can hear her breath shorten. And my fleeting smile fades.

Maybe she's scared of me.

I remember her from that party over a month ago.

The girl searching for Loren Hale.

I also remember her from a recent article.

The girl who turned out to be Loren Hale's cousin.

I still can't wrap my head around why she was asking which house Loren Hale lived in when she should've had his phone number. Maybe their parents are estranged from each other—I guess it's not an important detail anyway.

"Okay," Lily says hurriedly, "now you've met Willow and Willow you've met Garrison. Meet-and-greet has ended."

I haven't met her yet, not really. She won't look at me.

I rise to my feet at the same time as Willow, helping her fit the cash back into the register. "Are you new here?" I ask, kind of already knowing the answer based on Maya showing her the checkout counter.

Why won't you look at me?

"Yep," Lily says quickly. "Yep, everyone's new. Willow, can you get my purse from the break room?"

Willow shifts slightly, keeping at least two feet between us. "Sure." She tries to smooth down a stack of fives.

"I can do it," Maya says, scooting closer.

Willow abandons the register and heads for the break room. She has on those same faded overalls and a mustard-yellow shirt. When she walks, it's closed-off, tucked into herself—and a part of me understands that.

More than I ever thought I could.

She pauses midway to the door. "My backpack…"

I notice the old JanSport backpack, propped against the counter. "This?" I grab it and make my way to Willow.

She finally meets my gaze.

Her brown, doe-like eyes are inquisitive and nervous. I see re-cognition, her gaze flitting over my features, to place me correctly.

I stop about a foot away, and her chest rises in a large inhale.

Mine collapses in a deeper one.

I pass the backpack to Willow, our fingers brushing, and something tugs inside of me. I can't make sense of it. All I know: we've been bypassing each other for weeks, two separate strands of time—and in this second, we've finally touched.

"Thanks," she says, pulling the backpack over one shoulder. She holds onto the strap.

When she turns around, she trips over her feet, stumbling a bit before she collects herself and trudges forward.

I feel my lips pull up again, remembering the article. Where her backpack ripped open. She looked cute in the photograph—but the actual article was fucking stupid. It made me want to dump out the journalist's backpack or purse or whatever and highlight every item for the world to see.

"Garrison," Lily says as Willow disappears into the break room.

"Yeah?" I rotate to face one of the most famous people in the world. I think it'd dawn on me more if Lily Calloway didn't live in my neighborhood. If I didn't grow up surrounded by a similar kind of familial wealth.

It's just all ordinary for me.

"You can't," she says with a confident nod.

I frown. "I can't what?" I pull off my hoodie and then fix my hair with my hand.

"You can't…with her." She clears her throat. "I expect *professionalism* in my establishment." She comically raises her chin, and I almost can't tell if she's being serious or not.

"Right…" I nod. "Yeah. I won't…with her." I don't really know what I'm agreeing to—my mind is halfway inside that break room.

Lily nods again. "Okay then. I have to go, but Maya will dole out duties and tasks. Please listen to her."

"I will," I say, wanting Lily to trust me. I know I have to prove myself.

She exits through the *employees' only* door. Leaving me alone with Maya.

The store manager pounds on the keyboard and lets out a frustrated breath. She never looks over at me, but she begins talking.

"You're the one who peed all over the tiles in the boys' bathroom."

I wince at the past memory. "No, that was my… friend." I'd like to say John drank too much alcohol and drunkenly missed the toilet, but he purposefully pissed on the floor.

Her lips purse, her glare set on the computer screen. "Then you're the one who rearranged all the action figures on the shelves into an orgy."

"Not me." I shake my head. *Kyle.*

Though her words are a punch to the gut—because I can deflect all day and know that these acts are partially mine to claim.

I never stopped my friends. I couldn't. And I'm not all innocent either.

"You're the one who put porn mags in front of every DC comic."

I shake my head harder. "That wasn't me." *Hunter*, not my brother but my friend.

She tenses and types faster on the keyboard. "Then you're the one who wrote on the bathroom wall with Sharpie: 'stop trying to invent the most revolutionary shit. It's already been done.' And then you drew a slice of pizza."

I rub my lips to keep from laughing. Her eyes flicker to me in my silence, narrowing and narrowing.

My mouth downturns, and I drop my hand. "Yeah, that was me." I gesture to her. "I can go clean it…"

She turns her attention back to the computer and says something in another language. I think Korean. I watch too many foreign YouTube videos that I can just barely detect the language. If I paid more attention, I might've been able to catch one or two words and understand her better.

That's not the point though. She purposefully wants me to *not* understand her right now. It's working. I shift uneasily, realizing how much trouble I've caused the store manager.

"I'm sorry," I finally apologize—what I should've started with. "I'm really sorry, and I'm going to try to make it up to you." I extend my arms. "Put me to work."

I expect her to direct me to the bathrooms, to go clean toilets. "I was going to put Willow on inventory today. You can start in the storage room with her—*blasted piece of technology!*" She bangs the side of the computer, frustrated.

"Hey, let me see." I head over to Maya, setting my hoodie on the counter.

She scoots to the side and points at the blue screen of death, pretty much the worst problem for Windows. "I've restarted it four times."

"It might be a hardware problem."

"How do we fix that?" She drums the counter with two fingers.

"You'd have to buy new equipment."

Her mouth falls. Before she freaks out, I add, "I'm going to reboot it in safe mode and then check the computer's memory. You didn't install any new drivers, did you?"

Maya shakes her head slowly. "No."

"Hey…" Willow emerges from the break room, hesitantly approaching us at the checkout counter. "What should I do?"

Maya is about to respond, but her phone rings, cutting her attention. She looks frazzled. "This is our indie distributor… I'll be back." She answers the phone and sprints into the break room.

I type in a couple commands and then wait for the computer to reboot. "I don't know if you remember me." I turn to look at Willow.

She stands closer to me than before, glancing at the blue screen and keeping her hands on the white countertop. "Sort of," she says softly.

My pulse kicks up a notch, and I motion to the computer. "I'm trying to get it working."

She nods and pushes up her glasses again. "Are you good at computers?"

"Sort of." My lips try to rise.

Hers almost do too, but she stays quiet, just watching the blue screen blink out while I discover the issue. I'm so used to loud, overpowering noises—my friends talking over one another—that the hushed quiet between us is different for me.

It beats the silence of being alone. Because I can feel her here, beside me, thinking.

After a minute or so, I speak. "Do you go to school around here?"

"I start at Dalton Academy on Monday."

Loren Hale's cousin is going to Dalton Academy. The preparatory school that Loren went to as a teenager.

My muscles tense, instantly scared for her—because there are a lot of people that dislike him, based on his reputation with their older brothers or friends-of-friends. Now that he's famous, there's a shit ton of jealousy in the mix too.

"I can show you around school," I offer, though I'm not sure how much this will help. It's not like I'm beloved right now either.

She stiffens. "You go there?"

"Yep." I bend down to check the hard drive after the memory check passes. The fan looks nasty with dust and cobwebs. I blow on it and realize that the thing probably overheated. I tinker with the equipment for another minute and let it cool off.

The front door chimes and about four more employees enter like they own the place, dispersing behind us towards the bakery and coffee makers.

Willow nearly hugs the counter. Like she's in the way, but she's not. She squeezes next to me, and then pauses. Realizing how close she is, she starts to back up. "Sorry."

"No worries," I tell her and gesture to the computer. "It's all fixed." The Windows screen pops up and asks for the administrator's password. I could login as "guest" but I test a few passwords, one being *Scott Summers* since the Cyclops cardboard cutout greets people when they enter the store.

It works. "Weak password," I mutter, opening Chrome.

"How can you tell?" Willow fixes her braid, her arm brushing mine. An electric current runs through my veins—the brief contact more innocent than what I'm used to. More pure. Maybe that's why it feels so different.

"A strong password doesn't duplicate characters and it has numbers." Anything less and an encryption program would take virtually three seconds to crack the password.

She gives me a cautious glance, a coffee machine grumbling to life behind us while feet clap against the floor.

"What?" I pop open Tumblr, about to type in my username.

"Do you break passcodes a lot?" Her cheeks pale again. "I mean, you don't have to answer that if you don't want to."

I want to hug her to my side for some reason. To comfort her maybe. She hangs her head a little and keeps glancing around at the employees, bustling behind us.

I don't wrap my arm around her or pull her closer though. She has that closed-off stance, which I take as a sign that she might not like me touching her at all.

"A few times, yeah," I tell her. "I have software that does it." It's not like I'm hacking into anything important. I've taken over my friends' Twitter accounts as a joke a few times—that's it. I could probably do a lot worse.

She doesn't say anything. She's dazedly staring straight at the Tumblr screen. "You okay?" I ask, typing my username: **ryumastersxx**

"No." She winces. "Yes, I'm good. Just...shocked that you'd like this and *this*." She points at the Tumblr logo and then my username.

My brows knot. "Wait, do *you* like *Street Fighter*?"

"You have a tattoo." She glances at my inked skull between my bicep and forearm.

"I don't know where we're going here."

"And you have a *ton* of friends—" Willow gets cut off as a college-aged employee walks behind her, nearly bumping into her side. I never move, so she ends up right against my waist, tucked close to me now.

"You okay?" I ask.

She nervously takes off her glasses and wipes the lenses. "I just never thought someone like you would like this stuff."

"Well I didn't think someone like you would be into an old video game."

After a short pause, she asks softly, "What's someone like me?"

I think about it for a second. "…a girl." I feel bad even saying it, and I realize that my perception of people isn't what it should be. Maybe no one's really is. We can't really know who people are until we meet them.

"I'm not the only girl who likes video games," she says. "And I'm definitely not the only one that likes Tumblr."

"That I know," I say, more than curious about how she uses Tumblr. Quickly, I reblog a couple gif sets from *Supernatural*. "What's your username?"

She fixes her glasses. "I can't say."

I raise my brows. "What is it, some secret?"

"Sort of."

"Sort of," I repeat with an uncommon, growing smile. "Can I get a hint?"

She gives me a knowing look. "So you can break into my account? No."

"What's your first pet's name?" I quip. "The city you were born in?"

She shakes her head at me like *not working*. I didn't think it would, but she's less nervous to meet my eyes. Hers are pretty: brown but a little hazel near her pupils.

"For the record," I tell her, "I don't have a ton of friends…" *at least not anymore.*

"It looked like you did," she mutters.

My stomach turns. I decide to change the subject back to the lighter one. "We could message each other if you share your username with me."

She thinks hard again. "You really want to know it?"

Do I want to know what she's like online? What kind of things she's into? Yeah, I do. "I wouldn't be asking again if I didn't."

"I'll tell it to you, but only if you fill out a questionnaire on Tumblr first."

I frown in confusion. "Why?"

She tucks a flyaway strand of hair behind her ear. "I've filled one out recently, and I don't like deleting things…"

It hits me. She doesn't want me to see her answers, at least not without jumping into the same boat she's floating in.

A questionnaire.

I try to stifle a laugh that almost escapes. It's probably one of those things you tag your friends in and they tag other people—I don't do those. Ever.

She begins to recoil from me, and I immediately want to punch myself in the face. *Shit.* I set a hand on hers, and she jumps.

"Sorry." I let go. "I'm not trying to be an ass. I just…you really want me to fill out a questionnaire?"

"Only if you want my username."

I give her a weak smile—I'm not good at smiling, to be honest. I can't remember the last time I was happy enough to reveal my teeth in one. Maybe never. I bet I was a morose, assholish baby. "Alright." I commit. "I'll do it."

She shows me a link to the questionnaire. I vaguely skim some of the questions, zoning in on really personal ones. If I end up doing this, it'll mean opening up to Willow…and Willow opening up to me.

What do you say, Garrison?

I say that I've never done that to anyone before.

This will be a first. And I'm surprised I have some of those left.

14

BACK THEN – September
Philadelphia, Pennsylvania

WILLOW MOORE
Age 17

Garrison said he'd fill out the questionnaire later. Maya came in and doled out duties for us before he could even start. Most of the day I spent checking inventory, and she made Garrison clean coffee machines, mop floors, and bus tables.

I don't see him when I exit Superheroes & Scones at 5 p.m.—though I can't stop thinking about him. He seems like trouble, like someone I'd stay a thousand feet away from in Caribou, Maine. If my suspicions are right, his friends were the ones that broke into Lo's house.

He seems characteristically *bad*.

I'm just scared he'd pressure me to do something I wouldn't want to do. I've never had friends like that, but he seems the type, doesn't he?

I approach my gold Honda on the curb, knowing that I'm judging him.

But I'm judging him off prior actions.

I can't make up my mind. In fact, my mind really hurts even trying to place Garrison in a category. Maybe I shouldn't try to place him at all.

I crawl into my car and then start the engine. It lets out a whiney noise. "No…come on." I turn the key again, and smoke suddenly plumes from the hood. "Crap." I climb out, and in haste to check beneath the hood, smoke rushes out, so hot that it burns my arm.

I drop the hood and it clatters down.

"Hey, Willow!" The concerned voice drives nerves throughout my body. Oh my God, Garrison is sprinting over to me, his hoodie wadded up in one hand and his car keys jangling in the other.

"Hey," I say, pressing my reddened arm to my chest, the sting lessening. I'm shifting so awkwardly that I probably look like I have to pee.

He wafts the smoke above the hood. "What happened?"

"I don't know… it's an old car." I cough as another gust of smoke rushes out towards me.

Garrison motions with his head to the curb. I follow him, vehicles speeding by on the city street.

"Do you know anything about cars?" I ask hopefully.

He shakes his head. "Just computers." He glances over at the corner street. "I can give you a ride to wherever you need to go. You can call a tow truck or get your cousin to come look at your car in the meantime."

Cousin? It takes me a moment to register what he means. Loren Hale, *my cousin*. Which means that Garrison read the debut article about me and my tampons.

BACK THEN

I immobilize. *Don't think about it.*

"Willow?"

"Uh, yeah…yeah." I shake my head like I'm trying to rid all the cobwebs. "Thanks. A ride would be great." I'll call the tow truck later. So I end up feeding the meter with a few more quarters and then grab my backpack.

"This way." He nods towards the corner street. We walk a block until he stops by a black Mustang, black leather interior, and black custom rims. It has to be expensive. If it's not, it does a great job pretending to be.

"This is your car?"

He opens the passenger door for me. "Yeah…I live in the same neighborhood as Loren." An unspoken truth strains between us: *my old car is dying and spurting out smoke one block away.* After finding out that we share a few unique similarities, it's this economic difference that creates the most tension, both of us uncomfortable for different reasons.

"Was that your house that night of the party?" I ask before climbing in. Everything is clean, no stray water bottles or takeout wrappers beneath the seat. My car is a mess of receipts and paper napkins from Wendy's and Taco Bell.

I'm the slob, I realize. I sink further in the seat and hold my backpack on my lap, hugging it close to my chest.

He answers me when he's buckled. "Not my house. I live one street over." He turns to me. "Where do you live?"

"I should've told you that it's kind of out of the way—"

"It's fine. I have nowhere to be."

I nod and then give him the address. He plugs it into his phone and docks it on a stand, the GPS alive with directions.

"I thought you'd live with your cousin," he says, probably thinking I'd have Loren's type of wealth too. I guess he's learning differently today.

And I don't know why he keeps saying that—*your cousin*. He knows who Loren is. Maybe he doesn't like bringing up his name, not after the break-in.

"I didn't want to impose on him," I explain. "He has a baby."

"Yeah, I saw Maximoff's first baby picture along with the rest of the world." His voice is dry, not at all impressed with their celebrity status.

"You don't like *Princesses of Philly*, I take it." The reality show didn't make them famous or last long for a huge impact, not beyond some cool gifs, but it's easier mentioning PoPhilly than Lily's sex addiction.

He fixes the air vents, keeping the really cold air off me. Am I shaking?

"I've watched it, but it's not the show that bugs me." Garrison stops at a red light. "Every time I leave my neighborhood, paparazzi start shouting at my car like I might have a Calloway sister in my backseat. And the questions they ask are fucked up." He taps the steering wheel and then sets his aqua-blue eyes on me, a mixture of blue and light green—one of the most unique colors I've ever seen. "If you need a ride on Monday, let me know." He must note the surprise on my face because he adds, "I wake up early."

"It's out of your way," I remind him, though going to a new school with someone sounds a lot less anxiety-ridden than going alone.

But *Garrison?*

What if it's some joke? What if this is like *Never Been Kissed* and it'll end with him driving by and chucking eggs at me?

He says he's not popular, but he has all the makings of a popular high schooler: toned biceps that indicate his athleticism (i.e. he plays a sport), a face that'd be the lead in any CW show—or at least the little brother to the star (i.e. like Jeremy from *The Vampire Diaries*), and messy brown hair that sometimes touches his eyelashes—hair that says *I could be in a boy band, but I'm too cool for that shit.*

Not to mention his tattoo.

And his confident yet dark scowl…

I suddenly draw this conclusion: *I don't know Garrison Abbey.* Not enough to say whether or not he'd chuck eggs at me.

If I really believed he'd do that though, I would've never climbed in his car.

"I know it's out of the way," he says as the light turns green. "I also don't care. I usually try to waste three hours in the morning anyway."

Three hours? "You wake up at five a.m.?"

"Doesn't everyone," he says dryly, his fingers twitching a little. The car smells like citrus, not cigarettes, and there aren't any bottles of alcohol or beer anywhere, but I've seen him smoke and drink before. He switches topics. "Are you a junior?"

"No."

He frowns. "Sophomore?"

"Senior," I reply.

"You look younger."

"It's the braid," I mutter, shifting in my seat a little.

He glances at me once before focusing on the road. "The braid is cute."

I feel my lips lifting. *Do not smile like that.* It's this giddy smile that should never reveal itself to the person who put it there. "Okay," I suddenly say.

"Okay…yeah?" He knows that I'm accepting his offer to pick me up on Monday.

I nod. "How should we communicate?"

He switches lanes easily. "By letters probably," he banters. "I'd say two tin cans, but I don't think the string would reach from me to you."

"What about communicating in ones and zeroes?"

He feigns confusion. "What is that? Ones and zeroes…nah, I don't like those." He almost smiles, because after today, I know he likes the internet, maybe even more than me.

15

PRESENT DAY - October

London, England

WILLOW HALE
Age 20

I haven't spoken to Garrison in weeks.

Days turned into nights. Nights turned into mornings. And time seems to seep like water between my fingers. Losing it all.

Our videos to each other have grown more infrequent and shorter. The ones I send, I'm rushed, frazzled running between classes.

His are more concerning. Heavy-lidded eyes and mumbled words before he dozes off.

I lie in bed, wide-awake. My eyes pin to the ceiling, little glow-in-the-dark stars pasted to the cement.

Call him again, my thoughts pull me. I snatch my phone and dial, but it rings to voicemail. Not surprising really. It's only 9 p.m. in Philly, and Garrison works until midnight. He's the type of person that zones completely into his work, loses time and sense of everything around him.

It's why he's so good at what he does, and I can't blame him for not answering. Not when there were plenty of calls I missed because I was in the library or dining hall or…Barnaby's.

I toss my phone aside.

A tree branch scrapes my window as the wind picks up outside. Rain pelts the glass and tries its best to soothe me to sleep.

But I'm too wired. Too longing.

Too much of a lot of things.

My fingers brush my lips. It's been so long since we've even kissed. Since he's held me. *Touched* me. Since I've run my fingers through his hair. Since he's wrapped his arms around me like I'm the only person he wants to embrace. To protect. To love.

I lean over and turn off my lamp, plunging my dorm room into darkness. Alone, with the sound of the rain shower, images of Garrison pop into my head. His hair that curls a little by his ears and his aquamarine eyes that always stare *through* me. Like he knows.

He knows.

What it's like to have people who are supposed to love you unconditionally but they don't. Who are supposed to protect you. But don't.

He'd touch my cheek and say, "It doesn't matter anymore. We're not seventeen. We don't need them. We always have each other."

I'd stand on my tip-toes and press my lips to his. Warmth underneath his palms as he slid them underneath my shirt. He's the only guy that ever touched me like that. Kissing. Hugging.

Anything.

Everything.

My body hums, pulsing and clenching harder between my legs. Wanting him. Wanting more.

PRESENT DAY

Ever since I moved to London, I dream up this one single memory when I want to get off alone. This one visual is enough to make me wet and come easily. So right now, I start to think about it again.

I think about the night I lost my virginity.

My hand dips down underneath the sheet. Underneath my pajama shorts. Under my panties. My fingers brush between my legs, breath hitching, and I feel the dampness.

Closing my eyes, I try to visualize every piece of that night. As if I'm back in my Philly bedroom.

Garrison thumbed my nipple, his mouth against the nape of my neck. Sucking a sensitive spot that quaked my sweaty limbs.

I remember the room. Bathed in candlelight, smelling of rose petals and vanilla. Soft music played in the background, and each touch between us felt tender, comfortable and wanted.

Our legs intertwined on the plush mattress. Fluffy blankets kicked aside.

He propped himself up on his elbow, and his hand traveled from my breast down the curve of my hip. Drinking in my bare body, and I soaked up his lean muscles that formed actual abs. Showing off his athleticism. I eyed his boxer-briefs, snug on his toned waist, and his dick pushed against the fabric.

Watching him made me calm down. I breathed and tried to stay out of my head.

Right now, I try not to remember how anxious I was. I don't want to warp the best moment into one of total nervous awkwardness.

Back in my London dorm, I rub my clit. *Remember, Willow.*

I remember how Garrison did this thing—something he usually did if we were tangled up and making out. He tried *really* hard (pun intended) not to grind his erection into me. Like he didn't want me to feel his hardness and pressure me to have sex if I wasn't ready.

Even then, when we agreed that night would be *the* night he'd actually enter me—he still hovered over my body. Like it was just instinct at that point.

I trembled, a little anxious. Also hot with temptation and anticipation. I craved him so badly. Arousal ate me up inside, pulsated between my legs. Blazed the back of my neck. Aching, *longing*.

His hand veered over to the soft flesh of my stomach. Shirt and jean shorts already on the floor, his fingers stopped at the hem of my panties.

"Is this okay?" he whispered in my ear.

"Yeah," I replied, voice raspy. He kissed my lips, urging them open slowly. I followed his lead, and his tongue slid sensually against mine.

I didn't know where to put my hands.

Don't remember.

But it's hard to forget how my palms made uncertain, awkward movements. Usually I would hold his shoulders. That night, I wasn't sure if I should touch his dick.

"Do you need me to…?" I started, but I didn't even know what I was offering. A blow job? A hand job? Another sort of job I was unaware of?

We hadn't even run all the bases together before that night. I've touched his dick—but I wouldn't call it a full-on gold-star worthy hand job, and I've never put him in my mouth before.

I'm always in my head. Anxious and nervous like I'm doing things wrong, and Garrison has been sweet in not pressuring me to go further. I'm just more relaxed with him touching me than the other way around, I guess. Usually, we just make out, grinding a lot, and he'll finger me until I come.

Back when we were in bed together, Garrison pressed his lips to mine again. More tenderly. "No, this is for you. Just relax, Willow."

PRESENT DAY

His fingers skated below the fabric of my panties, his touch achingly slow, and when he brushed the sensitive spot, I let out an aroused breath.

I inhaled the vanilla scent around us and held his firm shoulders. He slipped into me, and I gave myself to Garrison. I trusted him.

I loved him—I *love* him.

He pulsed his fingers in me, filling me, and his thumb teased my clit. Torching my body and nerves. *His fingers would be replaced by something bigger and harder*, the thought lit me on fire and brewed excitement.

As I touch myself in London, I imagine he's here just like that night. About to fill me to the brim. His erection inside me. Rocking. Pleasing.

I remember how my breath staggered back. "Garrison," I moaned at the soft pressure of his fingers. Building more arousal.

He pressed his forehead to mine, rocking slightly. He needed friction. He wanted friction. He ached to be in me. I could see all of this in his eyes and shallow breath.

Pleasure mounted.

His bare chest was slick with sweat, and a deep noise rumbled inside his throat. A noise that drove home who he was. Masculine. Man. Mine. And I was his. *I am his.*

How? I wasn't even sure.

I was bookish and quiet.

He was rebellious and misunderstood. Guys like him usually didn't fall for girls like me. But here we were.

His movements grew faster, our lips skimming with hot breath, and he brushed his thumb over my clit. I crumbled against him in a crashing wave.

My toes curled and euphoria spotted my vision. My breath staggered, moans catching in my throat.

In London, I grip the twisted sheets and arch my hips. Wishing he were here, touching me. *He is*, I pretend.

"I've got you," Garrison breathed that night, lips to my ear.

I rolled down the blissful sensation. Eyes heavy lidded, I kissed the closest thing I could find—his forearm. A *very* pretty forearm.

When our eyes met, his overwhelming desire avalanched mine, covering me in so much need that I nearly quivered beneath him.

"You can do it now," I said softly.

He rubbed my thigh and searched my gaze. "You sure you're ready? I can get you off again—"

"I'm sure," I said, confident about this decision. My hands drifted to the ridges of his abs. "I want to feel you inside me."

Arousal pinned against his heady eyes. "Fuck."

We were both smiling. Excitement swelled around us like a ruthless, restless ocean, and we were both happy to let the riptide pull us under.

He rose off the bed and I watched as he made the trek to my dresser—where he knew I kept the emergency condoms. Just in case.

He was buck-naked like me. He was twenty like me. But tattoos inked his toned body and he moved with such ease and confidence. No longer looking like the jock that I pegged him as when I first met him. He was a bad boy. Misunderstood. *Mine*.

I pulsed just watching him, and I relaxed into my pillow. In quick movements, he had the foil packet and returned to me.

As soon as he was back on the bed, Garrison drank me in again, like I was the most beautiful creature to ever grace the universe.

"Willow." He said my name in a way that caused every inch of me to shudder. Like dipping a toe in a cold pool.

I glanced down at his length, his knees on the mattress as he ripped open the condom with his teeth. His dick was larger than anything that had ever been inside of me.

I leaned up, and he cupped my cheek and kissed me. I held his arms for comfort, wanting him close. He broke apart my legs with his knees. My heart beat rapidly.

I thought it might hurt a lot, and that was what I feared the most. Being scared and then making an awkward mess of things. But Garrison knew that already.

I'd told him before.

He whispered against my lips, "If it hurts too much, you tell me and I'll stop, okay? I'm fine with that."

His words were like magic. Vanquishing my nerves.

I nodded, and I rested my shoulders back to the mattress. My legs around him. Vulnerable and ready, *so ready*.

For the first time, I watched him sheath himself in front of me. More confidence radiating off every inch of him. It was contagious, fueling timid parts of me.

He climbed further over my body, his hand beside my cheek. He lowered his head, his lips fusing with my lips. His tongue tangling with mine, his breath melding with mine, his heart beating with mine.

I was swept up into hot sensations. Into the fiery moment, and his hand slid along my hips and then pressure welled between my legs.

A sharp pain came and went, replaced by an overwhelming fullness that dizzied and electrified. Sparking more need. More desire. More want.

"God, Willow," Garrison groaned like this is a very *good* place to be. I trembled underneath him, desiring more friction. His eyes soaked into mine. Concern wrapped in extreme craving. He was already moving his hips.

He was already rocking against me and watching him pump inside me—*oh my God*. I gasped, and he held my hand in his, lacing our fingers on the pillow. "This good?" he breathed.

I nodded, words lost in my throat. *So good.*

With that confirmation, he started thrusting harder. Working me up, sweat glistened on our skin, and a high-pitched noise escaped my lips, something else tickling my throat. "Ahh." I clutched onto his bicep, the one with the inked skull. I was riding a surge of pleasure, the end not even in sight. "*Garrison*...please don't stop."

"*Fuck*," he groaned, placing another kiss on my lips. He drove deeper in me and welled up sentiments pricked my eyes.

He let go of my hand and clutched my cheek. His pace and the fullness absolutely annihilating me. In the best way. Obviously worthy of a mental revisit.

I was lost beneath him.

He was lost above me.

We found each other between every staggered breath. Every racing heartbeat. Every aching need. Until we were both sweaty and overcome by an intense, passionate crash. Nerves firing. Breaths heaving. Bodies colliding with blissful pleasure after all those years of waiting.

In my dorm room, I ride the same wave. I reach a peak.

I cry out his name in a soft, aching whisper. He lights me on fire—even when he's miles away. But there's a difference.

I come down, and I roll on my side. No one else tangled in the sheets with me.

He's not here to pull me in his arms. He's not here to say *I love you.* He's not here so I can say *I love you* back.

He's not here to ask if I'm okay. To push the sweaty pieces of hair off my face. To kiss me one last time before we fall asleep.

So I fumble for my phone. And I try to call him again. "Please answer," I mutter alone in London. "Please answer."

It rings.

PRESENT DAY

And rings.

"Please, Garrison." It stops ringing.

Beep.

"Voice-mailbox full," an automated voice replies.

I roll onto my back and hold my phone to my chest.

16

PRESENT DAY – October

Philadelphia, Pennsylvania

GARRISON ABBEY
Age 20

Halloween.

Also known as Loren Hale's birthday. He already texted me about some "surprise" party he's throwing himself. Only it's a surprise for all his guests, not him—the guy with the birthday. It's so Loren Hale, you really can't make this shit up.

The elevator at Cobalt Inc. is slow as fuck today. Maybe it's broken? It goes down and down and down like the ticking of a clock, and I'm worried that I'm not ditching out of here early enough to avoid the party. I glance at the text again.

Loren Hale: I'm picking you up at 9:45 p.m. for my birthday party. The outing is a surprise. No questions will be answered. Participation is not optional.

He's such an asshole, even in text. He didn't even ask where I'd be, so I assume Connor tells him I work until midnight. But joke is on him because I'm out of here at 9:30 p.m. tonight.

The elevator finally makes it to the lobby, and I pull out my phone to call an Uber. Just as I exit the revolving doors, shoes landing on the sidewalk, a black limo slows at the curb.

Fuck.

Second option: Avoid eye contact. Maybe I can get away with ignoring the limo. I focus on my cell and notice that the nearest Uber is ten minutes away. *Fuck* Halloween.

"Garrison Abbey!" Loren shouts from the limo. "Let's go! My birthday awaits!"

Don't be an asshole. I let out a breath of defeat and glance up. Half of his body hangs out of the limo's opened window. He holds out a hand like *come on.*

Trying not to seem too unenthusiastic, I pocket my phone, adjust my backpack on my shoulder, and approach the limo. Each footstep heavy.

Loren is about to open the limo door, but I grab onto the windowsill and shove it closed. Lo glares almost instantly like I just told his kid that Santa Clause isn't real. And in the next instant, his eyes soften considerably. Like he's trying to be nice—and that act is hard for him.

He opens his mouth, and I cut him off. "Thanks for the invite, but I decided I'm not going."

His amber eyes are really fucking hard to look at. They basically scream a million things. Disappointment. Confusion. I avoid them, preferring his ruthless glares to what he's showering me with right now. Seriously, I stare anywhere but at him.

The street.

The light pole.

PRESENT DAY

The revolving doors I just left.

I can't hang out with them like we're friends.

I can't hang out with *him*. My girlfriend is his little sister. For fuck's sake, I vandalized his house three years ago. Did he suddenly have amnesia? He should be pushing me down on the curb. He should be kicking me and calling me a thousand different names. Not inviting me to *his* birthday party.

Jesus. It doesn't make sense.

I steal one glance back at him, and he's looking over my shoulder like he's trying to find someone. And then he tells me, "Because you have so many friends lined up inviting you places." In mock surprise, he puts his hand to his lips. "*Oh my God,* there's your bestie waving you down. He's so excited to see you."

Fuck him.

I glare.

He glares back, and then I think, *this is stupid.* He's just trying to piss me off to get me to go. He's a button-pusher, and the more I'm around him, the more he's learning mine.

I roll my eyes. "I have *work*, you fucking…" I let out an aggravated noise and scuff the sidewalk with my Converse. What the fuck am I doing?

"If the CEO of the company can take time off for my birthday, then so can his employee." Loren tries to open the car door again, but I lean my bodyweight against it.

His cheekbones sharpen.

"I'm serious." I take a deep breath. "I have to finish what I'm working on and…" I stare off. What else? God, I'm pathetic. I can't even come up with a decent excuse.

"Just let me out for a second. I won't force you in the limo." The edge is still in his voice, but there's no humor attached. He's serious.

I step back and pull the sleeves of my hoodie down over the tops of my hands, the wind picking up. Chillier tonight. Loren opens the door and climbs out of the car. No Halloween costume on, which kind of surprises me. Just a black crewneck T-shirt and dark jeans.

He's taller than me by a few inches, and I pull my hood back just to brush longer strands of my hair out of my face.

"I *want* you to come," Lo emphasizes.

I shake my head. Why? Because I'm Willow's boyfriend? Because he thinks I'm some loser without anyone to hang with on Halloween?

He stares right into me. "Jesus Christ, do I need to drop to my knees and beg?"

I blow out hot breath through my nose, and a bright flash in the distance catches my attention. We both turn our heads.

Paparazzi parallel parked down the street. Loren and the Calloway sisters attract them like moths to a flame, and they burn fucking bright. At least, I can get away from it. I can't even imagine having to *always* deal with the constant cameras.

We only have a minute before we're bombarded, and I don't want to be in *Celebrity Crush* tomorrow.

So I quickly say, "It's different." Loren swings his head to me, confusion lining his eyes. I continue on. "This is a boyfriend-girlfriend, couple thing. I'm the seventh wheel now that Willow is gone, and I see that it's a *pity* invite, man, so just *leave me alone*."

He cocks his head. "Pity? Do you know who I am?" He touches his chest. "I have waded in self-pity too much to ever spare pity for other people. And you can ask Connor and Ryke in there." He points to the limo. "I don't aimlessly throw out invites like I'm a flower girl at a wedding. I have very few friends, and you're one of them."

What? No.

We're not friends. It may have been years since I spray-painted *Cock Sucker* on his mailbox, but it doesn't change the fact that I did those things. I don't deserve his friendship. I definitely don't deserve him trying so fucking hard to get me to go to his party.

I deserve *none* of it.

Me, being alone on Halloween is karma. It's penance for all my shitty deeds. That's where I deserve to be. Friendless and alone.

But he's here spending energy on me, and there's a part of me that wants to just get in the limo. That wants to give myself happiness and fun for maybe just one moment.

Loren tries to convince me again. "Willow would hate what we're about to do. You, on the other hand, will like what I have planned for my birthday. So I'm glad it's you and not her here." He flashes his iconic half-smile.

Okay.

Okay. *Okay.*

I breathe and then nod a few times.

A cameraman jogs closer, and Loren casts a scathing, threatening glare at him to stay back.

The guy cowers a few feet away, but he still shouts, "Where's Maximoff?!"

I glare now. Loren's kid is only *three*, and paparazzi harass him more in one week than I've been in my entire life. And anyway, I'm pretty sure that Maximoff and the rest of the Calloway sisters' kids are staying back with a babysitter. But like hell I'm telling this guy anything.

Loren ignores the cameraman like he's evaporated into thin air and his eyes ping to me.

"Let's go," I say.

Loren's lips curve upward and he slips around me to open the limo door.

What am I getting myself into?

OF COURSE, LOREN SURPRISES EVERYONE WITH A night at the Halloween Horror Fest, an annual October event at the nearest theme park. Mazes are decked out with decorations, and actors dressed as ghouls and zombies attempt to scare the guests.

Two out of ten on the "fright" factor. I swear I saw a vampire eating a pretzel on break. There's nothing terrifying about that.

Before we even make it to a maze, we stop at an iron café table in a safe zone where the actors aren't allowed to scare us.

Since I'm with the "core six"—as the internet affectionately calls Lily, Loren, Rose, Connor, Ryke and Daisy—bodyguards linger nearby in case they get a wave of unwanted attention. So far, only a few fans have stopped and asked for selfies and autographs. There'd probably be more if this place wasn't so disorienting with the fog, screams, and eerie music.

Mostly, I ignore everyone around me, including the automated cries that come from the nearby mazes.

Straw between my lips, I hold a soda with one hand and scroll through my phone. Willow should be asleep by now. She went to her first Wakefield Halloween party, and she texted me a bunch of drunk texts about an hour ago.

Willow: Garrrrisoon! Ur face is pretty. I miss ur face
Willow: ur my fav person ever
Me: Are you home?

PRESENT DAY

Willow: Not yet. Still at house. I'll text pics. The decorations are... interesting

Whoever hosted just put out a bunch of fake spider webs and then a bowl of punch. That was it.

Willow: Lo would have a stroke if he saw
Me: Good thing he's not there
Willow: I miss ur face. Did I say that alrdey?
Me: You did. But I'm pretty sure I miss your face more
Willow: not possible
Me: I'm going to see your face soon
Willow: Soon *sparkly heart emoji*
Me: *praising hands emoji*

That was the last text. She's coming home for Winter Break, and it may still be over a month away, but I'm starting the countdown. Fuck, I've been counting down since she left.

A shriller scream blasts from one of the foggy mazes nearby. Our current spot resides closer to the main entrance, and I've already been briefed how this table is "home base" in case anyone gets lost.

Which—if I had to bet would be Lily. Scratch that, she's clinging to her husband so tight, there's no way she'd drift away from the pack.

Maybe I'd say Daisy, but she's going to be chilling at home base all night. Daisy's white husky is sprawled across her lap as she digs into a bag of cinnamon rolls that Lily and Loren brought back from a Cinnabon run.

I was kind of surprised Daisy even came along to this, considering she has PTSD, and this place should be hell for anyone who gets triggered by sudden, piercing noises. But maybe she just didn't want to miss out.

The night is special enough that the Calloway sisters brought costumes for everyone. Albeit, *simple* costumes, but they thought about that shit.

A flower crown rests on Daisy's blonde hair, an identical one on Ryke's head. Lily and Loren sport glittery alien antenna headbands, while Rose and Connor wear these regal golden crowns. I don't even think they're plastic. Like, legit crowns. The Cobalts have to be the most extra people I know, and honestly, I can't believe I work for one of them.

I fix my backwards baseball hat. It lights up to spell out the word *boo*.

Maybe my costume is a literal flashing hat so that Loren makes sure I don't ditch them, but I kind of like that it's loud but not *too* loud. The flopping antennas would have annoyed the fuck out of me.

I glance up from my phone just to see Connor and Rose still arguing over the route. The park map is spread over the table, and they both brandish Sharpies like there'll be a test at the end of this. *Fastest Through the Mazes* isn't a thing.

"What are you doing?" Rose snaps at her husband. "That is the worst path. You can't go from Texas Chainsaw Massacre to Nightmare on Elm Street."

"Why not?" He grins like he knows what she's about to say but wants to hear it anyway.

"We're not doing gore back-to-back." She gathers her hair on one shoulder and traces a line on the map. "It's better if we do The Ring maze in between."

A chainsaw roars, pretty close. Girls run away from the masked actor as he chases them. Legally, he can't touch them, so running away is the wrong way to go. From experience, the actors prey on the people who look like they're about to piss their pants.

I'm about to return to my phone, but Rose's voice grabs my attention again.

"Gore does not frighten me," Rose retorts. "If you don't believe me, give me a fucking knife and I'll stab you myself and you'll see how frightened I'll be." She motions to him for a knife.

Connor's attraction to her threat is clear in his eyes, like he could go down on her on the fucking table right now. Jesus, they're weird. His grin expands, and he steps closer to his wife.

Loren interjects, "Careful of her talons."

"She won't harm me," Connor says easily. "But I appreciate the concern."

"I will gut you, Richard," Rose threatens. Her chin rises as he nears again, towering above her. Confidence mixed with dominance.

"And?" he questions in a deep breath.

"And I will remove all of your organs slowly and painfully."

"Painfully," he muses. "You exaggerate."

Lily is grinning from ear-to-ear. She's obsessed with everyone being happy *in love*. I should know. She's asked me how Willow and I are doing about a hundred-and-one times. To the point where I think she'll be as devastated as me if we end up not working out.

Rose glowers. "Fear. Me. Richard. I will annihilate you in a murderous, bloody..." Her breath hitches as he steps nearer, their legs thread. She reaches back, palms hitting the iron table. He almost has her pinned.

"Fear what, Rose?" he breathes against her lips.

She says one word in French, and he says two more in the same language.

Honestly, they look like they're about to kiss.

And this is where I'm definitely glancing back at my cell. Avoiding Instagram has been my mantra since I saw Salvatore Amadio. I don't need to look him up and have visuals of his entire life. So I'm not about to torture myself tonight with pics of his six pack abs or Porsche (not that I know he has either but with my luck, it's probable). Shit, stop thinking about Salvatore.

Tumblr, it is.

Willow hasn't reblogged anything in weeks. Her account is practically dead. Mine is almost the same, but I've got a couple gif sets from the latest season of *American Horror Story* on my feed. I haven't had time to make anything in a while.

No edits. No gifs. No videos spliced together. I want to blame it all on time, but deep down I know it's something else.

Something more.

Fuck it, I'm doing a questionnaire. I find the tag and click into the first one.

Current Location

I pop my head up just to see Daisy hoisting two cinnamon rolls in either hand. "My right bun is smaller than my left bun." She speaks to her husband.

Ryke is sitting beside her. Teetering back on the legs of his chair, he glances right at her boobs.

Her graphic tee says *boo-fucking-tastic*, and photographs of Daisy wearing that shirt have already spread over social media. To the point where the thing sold out on H&M in minutes.

Ryke focuses on Daisy's eyes. "Your buns look fucking perfect to me, Calloway."

PRESENT DAY

The intense flirting is something I'm used to seeing from them, and it used to make me super happy. I think because Willow loves Daisy and Ryke, and seeing them together is a good thing—but now I just see two people in love. Who get to spend time together.

And I don't have that. My stomach twists in horrible knots, my soda not settling well.

I'm bitter, I realize.

I hate being this bitter.

Daisy licks the icing off the right cinnamon roll and breaks into a huge laugh. "You'll like this one."

"Why's that?"

"It's really wet."

Ryke casually uses two fingers to swipe some icing off the dough. Then he sucks them while staring too deeply into his wife. When he drops his hand, he says, "Not wet enough, sweetheart."

I grimace.

I see Loren seriously cringing.

Current Location: pretty sure this is some circle of hell Dante hasn't invented yet

The kind made for bitter souls.

Daisy barely lowers her voice, teasing Ryke. "Will you still eat me?"

His *I want to fuck you* eyes answer her.

"Hey," Loren snaps.

Both of them casually turn their heads to him. Like this is just another day, and conversations about oral sex and cum are completely normal.

Lo adds, "Lily wants you to stop flirting."

Lily gapes. "I do not!"

Loren feigns surprise. "I could've sworn she said that you were making her nauseous."

Ryke raises his brows at me. "Sounds like you."

Mockingly, Loren touches his chest. "Never."

I almost snort.

Back to the questionnaire…

Height: 5'11''

Eye Color: I always thought they were bluish green.
My girlfriend calls them aquamarine sometimes. So
we'll go with that.

Why does every distraction I have make me think of her even more? Jesus…it's like running and hitting a brick wall and turning around and hitting another.

It's useless. I click out of Tumblr just as Loren is snapping his fingers in my face. "You. Garrison. Follow. Now."

I pocket my phone. "What, you forget how sentences work?"

Rose and Connor have already gathered their maps, Lily's hand is in Lo's, and Ryke walks away from the table, leaving Daisy in the safe zone.

Guess we really are heading out.

Loren drives a glare into me. "Says the guy who uses internet shorthand like brb and tbh." His half-smile meets me, but it doesn't scare me.

I just glare back.

He adds, "ICYM, I'm a sarcastic prick. Move your ass that way." He points in the direction of the first maze.

The Exorcist themed one.

Park security lets us discreetly skip to the front of the line. The perks of being around super famous people, I guess. It happens all without alerting the massive crowds that we've cut. Loren says it's for our safety. Waiting for hours in the roped off sections with park-goers is a sure way to cause stampedes and hysteria. They'll want autographs. Selfies.

We need to blend.

I'm not used to the constant scrutiny as much as them, but I can understand not wanting to be approached.

Ahead of Loren, I enter *The Exorcist* maze that's decorated like a little house. Pitch black. I can barely see in front of my face. Demonic cackling echoes around us, and the rest of our group walks in a single-file line.

"OhGodOhGod," Lily mutters.

I glance back to see her wide-eyed expression, and she's grabbing onto the back of Loren's shirt, so much that the collar is tight around Lo's neck.

Willow and I never went to one of these fright night things together. She's not into the scary shit as much as me, but I can imagine her here. I'd have my arms around her. She'd be pressed up to my side—

Shit, stop thinking.

Quickly, I look back ahead.

We enter the bedroom area, and a mechanical version of Regan MacNeil sits on the bed. Her head spins three-sixty degrees. It looks like whoever built the robot did a pretty damn good job.

"Cool," I say, impressed by the production quality. Even speakers are set up that narrate the exorcism from the movie.

"Lil," Loren says behind me. "Look up. It's not that bad."

I scan the area, trying to ignore them and focus on the rooms. There's so much detail, like how potted plants are overturned and furniture floats mid-air, as though a possessed being rattles the whole room.

Very cool.

"I'll have nightmares forever!" Lily shrieks.

From even further behind me, I hear Rose scream shortly in fright and then reprimand the actor, "You did that on purpose!"

I almost laugh. There's something about being with these people that make shitty days seem…I don't know. I shouldn't like their company.

I shouldn't want it.

Or ask for it. Or God forbid, *need* it. Because they've already done way too much for me, and they're not mine. They're Willow's.

I don't look behind me again, but I think I must be walking through the maze faster because Lily and Loren's voice drifts off. I enter one of the last rooms where fake puke flies onto the wall. I stand there for a couple long moments and literally the robot turns to me and grins. Wait…not a robot. This one is *definitely* an actress. She starts crawling on the bed towards me like she means to scare me.

I smile.

I don't know why.

Maybe because she thinks *this* is frightening. I've been afraid before—really scared—but not from green-puking demons. This is nothing.

She stops and tries to make another "freaky grin face" but I'm over it. I keep walking. Right on out of the maze. Cold air hits me just as I hear a shrill scream inside the maze.

I'm betting that's Lily. My lips lift into a bigger smile, just taking in the moment. I'm doing something on a random night, and it's not even bad. It's kind of fun.

PRESENT DAY

One of the bodyguards nears me and stations next to my side. Like I'm important or something, but I realize in less than a second that he's blocking my body from onlookers. Girls laugh loudly around the maze's exit and steal glances at me.

Maybe they want my autograph or for me to divulge details about the core six—the latter is most likely.

I shouldn't ask the bodyguard, but I do. "Hey, how do you know I don't want to be approached by people?"

The bodyguards don't block Lily all the time. Definitely not Ryke or Lo.

"Loren informed us that you don't want the attention," he says. "Has that changed, sir?"

I shake my head. No. It hasn't.

I'm smiling more now, and then I spot Lo. He exits the building, carrying Lily piggyback-style. She's burying her face in the crook of his neck like she can't even take a peek without pissing her pants.

My brows knot. "It wasn't even that scary."

Loren holds her thighs. "She's scared of her own shadow when I shut off the lights at night."

"That was one time!" Lily protests without lifting her head up.

Loren and I both laugh, and then he says to Lily, "We're out of the maze now. You want down, love?"

Slowly, she lifts her head up enough to rest her chin on his shoulder and then glances around the park. People are laughing or power-walking away from the maze's exit. No one is bloody or dying on the ground.

"Can I stay here for one more maze?" Lily asks. "Then I'll drop down."

Loren nods, and Rose suddenly exits with Connor, both undeterred by the horror element. Connor honestly looks like he just stepped out of his weekly phone conferences with oversea investors. Same casual *I own the world* confidence radiates off him…and his wife.

The golden crowns make this twice as noticeable.

I glance at Loren, and he looks upset. Like maybe the whole goal was to rattle the unshakeable. Nine mazes are left, and I know Connor well enough as my boss—and I'm pretty sure you could put him in a thousand mazes and he'd still exit each one with assuredness and ease.

Rose narrows her eyes at Loren. Probably understanding his ulterior motive.

Loren cringes. "Stop staring at me. I know you like my face, but my face doesn't like you."

Rose's yellow-green gaze pierces him. "You're a *child*, Loren."

They're bickering is non-stop whenever I'm around them. At first, I thought it was a fluke. Nope. It happens… All. The. Time. For no other reason than they just seem to not get along.

Loren mimes wiping a tear with his fist to his cheek, surprisingly able to hold Lily with one hand. "Go cry about it in your lair."

"Go dry hump a bed of nails." At this, she flips her hair over her shoulder and marches ahead in five-inch heels. Her husband is the only person that follows her, able to keep pace with his wife. Their fingers thread together, holding hands.

Don't think about Willow.

I'm not…

I'm *trying* not to.

I swallow a lump in my throat as we all follow the King and Queen— as the internet refers to them. With all the bodyguards trailing us, it's starting to feel like they're actually American royalty.

The more we walk, the more my mind circumnavigates back to Willow. Despite the skeleton-painted guys shrieking at the guests and chainsaws revving, I know she'd want to be here. She loves her family, and missing out on a group experience would bum her out.

There are pros and cons to being away, and this right now, is her con. Even if I'm having a decent…pretty good time.

So yeah, I feel kind of shitty about that.

I hate that we're on two separate continents. We're stretched thin for time as it is. And I'm not a mind reader. I don't know what she's thinking all the time, and especially now that she's around college guys like Salvatore Amadio, she has to be beginning to understand that I'm not a great person. Bottom barrel. I'm shit, and once she realizes that completely, she'll want it to be over. And how can I blame her?

I glance back at Ryke and Loren. Her brothers. They talk to her every week, and I wonder if she's brought me up. I'm not going to ask though.

Should I?

I feel like that's prying.

They're her brothers, not mine. They're not unbiased or anything. Not that I need someone on my side. I think everyone should be on Willow's.

Swiftly, I look back again. This time not discreet enough.

"If you have something to fucking say, just say it," Ryke says. His tone is softer than his words. "We don't bite."

"I do," Loren adds with a bitter smile. "But count yourself lucky, I won't bite you."

I don't believe that.

But I do believe that if he lashed out at me, I'd probably deserve it.

I slow down just to walk beside them. Taking a deep breath, I just let it all out. "You both talk to Willow a lot—I'm sure about me—and you can probably gauge her feelings, right? Honestly, I don't need a ten-page-long synopsis or diagram or anything, but I just want to know the *percentage* you two think Willow will want to break up with me in the next few years."

I must be a masochist to want to know. But I do.

Ryke's brows furrow. "Don't you two fucking talk to each other?"

"Yeah, but do you even know what it's like being in a long-distance relationship? I can only say *I love you* so fucking much. It's not the same as..." I take off the blinking baseball hat, hot all of a sudden. "It's just harder."

I want to hold her. I want to *be* with her. How do you do that if you're physically separated from someone? And that physical part of a relationship—she could get it so much easier from a guy like Salvatore.

But even thinking of my girl with another guy—*God, stop.*

I focus on the question I asked: *What percentage do they think Willow will want to break up with me?*

"Zero percent," Loren says, not even really hesitating.

I jerk back. "Zero percent?" I glance at Ryke. "Is he good at math?"

"Am I good at math," Loren repeats like I'm a toddler. "I can count to ten. One, two, my sister is too good for you, four, five, you both will survive."

I take that in, focusing on the important part. "You realize you didn't reach ten, right?"

Loren swings his head to Ryke.

Ryke flips me off. Two middle fingers.

It's his go-to move, and really, I earned it. I'm nearly smiling. "What percentage?" I ask Ryke.

"Zero," he says, "but I don't know what you'll fucking do." *Wait... what?*

I frown. "Why would you think that I'd want to break up with her? I'm *worried* about her breaking up with me."

"That broken heart fucking thing," Ryke says.

Shiiiiit.

My mouth falls in realization. I filled out that questionnaire months ago, but maybe it's been in the back of their minds. "You saw my Tumblr questionnaire?" Frustration surges. "How? You don't even *use* Tumblr. You're internet inept!"

"Fuck you."

Loren interjects, "It's true."

Ryke glowers at Lo. "I know how to use Facebook."

"Facebook is stupid, man," I say. "It's like the ugly stepchild of Tumblr." But right now, I'm not feeling great things about Tumblr either. It's easier liking the internet when it isn't cruel to you, and I've seen Willow and her family pressed underneath the weight of it. Like everything, I just think maybe there are good and bad parts of it.

Ryke wears a confused *I don't know what you're talking about* expression like I just spoke an intergalactic language. Loren laughs.

"Honestly," I say, "did you stumble on it or something?"

"Or something," Loren replies. *Fuuuuck.* That could only mean one thing.

I glare at the sky. "Daisy showed you?"

Ryke scowls. "Leave her fucking out of it."

"Whatever," I say into a big breath. "Look, it doesn't matter. I don't feel *great* about where I left things with Willow when she was in Philly."

Loren drills me with one of his iconic glares, a hell of a lot sharper than Ryke's. Which only confirms my suspicions.

"Great. She told you." *That we had sex.*

"Yep," Loren says.

Ryke adds, "And don't you dare fucking yell at her about it. We're her brothers."

That hurts. "I'd never...I wouldn't yell at Willow for anything..." I'm not that guy.

Ryke's eyes soften.

Loren is still glaring.

"If you're that fucking worried," Ryke says, "there's a solution right in front of your face."

"What?" I ask.

"Visit Willow," Ryke suggests. "Go to London. You don't have to fucking move there. Just see her for a week or two weeks."

Loren nods. "You'll both feel better."

They must not know that Willow and I have an agreement that I won't visit her until next semester. I worry about being the needy boyfriend, the one that doesn't give her space to succeed on her own. Anyway, she'll be back in Philly for Winter Break, so if I fly out before then, I will, one-hundred-percent, seem like the overbearing one.

So the best I can say is something noncommittal. Because that's how I feel right now.

"Yeah. Maybe."

TEN MINUTES LATER, WE'RE HEADED TOWARDS the second maze, up on a steep hill. The entrance arch is decorated with flashing bulbs like a carnival. Creepy music that I recognize echoes. It's *American Horror Story* themed. I'm not sure the others understand the references or if they've even seen season four, but excitement surges as we approach.

Suddenly, a rumble of chainsaws revs from the hill, and an abrupt wave of clowns rush towards us. But that's not the immediate threat. I turn around to see a taller, thinner clown with makeup stretching from cheek-to-cheek, gripping a fake sword, and approaching Ryke.

It's even faster than the chainsaws.

The clown screeches in Ryke's ear.

Ryke whips around, without even thinking or pausing or assessing the situation, he *slams* a fist into the clown's jaw.

Holy shit.

"Fuck," Ryke curses, realizing what he just did. He raises his hands like he comes in peace. But, kid you not, the clown stumbles back and falls on his ass.

Note to self: *do not get accidentally sucker punched by Ryke Meadows.*

I take out my phone. This needs to be recorded.

For Willow. Not for anyone else. Definitely not for the internet.

Connor and Rose start nearing us, probably to do damage control, but the damage is seriously already done. There is a rule about touching the actors. *Don't.*

A few clowns on the hill yell, "Security!" like their friend is dying on the cement. Another heavier-set clown charges Ryke for vengeance.

I'm near laughter.

I probably should be helping, but I consider my presence here helpful towards one person. Willow. She's not going to miss this.

Lily clutches onto Loren's back, and Connor increases his pace and *sprints* to Ryke.

Connor extends a hand to the heavier clown. "It was an accident," he says in a calm business-tone. "My friend reacts before he thinks."

The clown suddenly stops but his lip still curls, pissed at Ryke.

"The clowns look mad," Lily whispers to Lo, but I'm close enough to hear. "Like *real* anger."

Connor must hear, too, because he replies, "That's generally the sentiment that appears after someone is punched."

Ryke doesn't hear, since he's busy apologizing profusely. "I'm so fucking sorry."

The bodyguards surround us, and they take over, trying to deescalate the situation with the clowns. Creating barriers between us and them. Bystanders have their phones out like me.

Loren spins around like he's trying to count heads.

His eyes land on mine.

I nod. I'm here. I'm alive. Willow gets to see this. Tonight isn't so bad. Rose even holds a can of pepper spray, aimed like she's about to douse any clown that approaches her. *Classic* Rose. I make sure to get a video of that for Willow.

The security team talks with the park staff, and within minutes the verdict comes in.

Ryke is being banned from the *entire* park. Not just the scare zones and mazes. It's actually kind of hilarious.

A minute later, the clowns disperse, and Loren sets Lily on her feet. We all huddle together. I pull the strings on my hoodie.

Ryke removes his flower crown, just to run a hand through his hair. "I'll go wait in the fucking car. You all just go on without me." He sets his flower crown back.

It's tilted to the side. Off-center like it might fall.

Connor, standing closest to Ryke, is the one who straightens the crown for him. It's weird. Sometimes it seems like those two despise each other, and then there are moments like this. It confuses the hell out of me.

"No," Loren tells his brother. "You're not waiting in the car like you were cast out."

"It's fine, Lo."

"The park did technically banish him," Connor cuts in.

"Then the park banished *all* of us." Loren touches his chest theatrically. "I'm not leaving Ryke behind." Ryke opens his mouth to protest, but Loren says strongly, "It's Halloween. I call the shots, and I say we go to Queen Rose's place and watch *Poltergeist* on surround sound."

"Can we order pizza?" I ask suddenly, catching myself by surprise. I want this. To spend time with these people. They make me feel good.

"And there'll be *pizza*," Loren says certainly, his gaze latching onto Ryke, trying harder to convince him. Guilt crests Ryke's eyes, not wanting to crash Loren's birthday.

"And ding-dongs," Lily adds.

Lo tries not to smile. "And ding-dongs. And surly-faced brothers named Ryke Meadows. Yeah?"

Ryke hesitates. We've only been through one maze, but it was fun while it lasted, and the clown-fight might go down in history. I can't wait to show Willow the video. Hopefully, it won't make her miss home even more. But maybe she'll be glad I'm here to record it for her.

I hold onto that.

With a nod, Ryke concedes. "Okay."

I'm going to spend a night watching *Poltergeist* and eating pizza with Willow's family, and I'm finally starting not to feel guilty about it. Maybe it's because I want to be happy, even if I don't deserve it. *Just enjoy it.* I think I will.

Just today.

I tuck my white blouse into my navy-blue skirt, the Dalton Academy uniform as uncomfortable as I feel. I check the clock on my wooden desk. *7:23 a.m.*

Garrison said he'd be outside my apartment complex at 7:30, and since we didn't exchange numbers, I should probably just go now and wait for him.

I grab my tattered backpack, wondering if this will be violation of some dress code. I've never attended private school before, and I would've gone to public school but Lo refused.

He said, *I'll pay for it. Don't worry about it. It's one of the best schools in the city.*

I told Loren that I'd pay him back. Every cent, and that was that.

In the elevator, I update ryumastersxx's blog, restraining a smile at his username. Ken Masters is one of the most popular *Street Fighter* characters, and his rival and best friend is named Ryu. Every time I've refreshed his page, gifs and edits are the only new content.

This time though…it's different.

Rules: Complete the form by answering each section truthfully. Once you've finished, tag other users to complete the task. Begin by sourcing the person who tagged you.

He did it. "Oh my God," I whisper, so caught off-guard that I forget to push the lobby button. I do and then eagerly and yet tentatively read his answers.

What was your...

Last drink: lightning bolt! + vodka

I'm suddenly scared to read the rest, but like a fiend or junkie, I just can't stop. I have to know more.

Last phone call: can't remember. Everyone just texts now

Last text message: "Fuck you." - sent to my middle brother. He's a dick.

Have you ever...

Been cheated on: not yet. Give it time and I'm sure it'll happen

BACK THEN

Kissed someone and regretted it: I don't regret kissing

Drank hard liquor: no *sarcasm*

Been drunk and thrown up: only when drinking hunch punch that has too much fucking punch

Met someone who changed you: I guess one person. He's famous—so very few people would believe me if I said his name. He kind of gave me a hand when no one else did

Fallen out of love: I've fallen out of love with dill pickles. Fucking gross.

Found out who your true friends are: I think I just did

Lost glasses: don't wear them, but they look cute on this girl I just met.

I touch my cheeks that hurt from a smile that won't go away, but it disappears at the sight of the next topic.

Sex on the first date: do I really have to answer this? [w, if this makes you nervous, please skip over this]

W. I take a breath, wondering if I should glaze over his typed words, but if he's telling me to skip it, then maybe he knows the answer won't sit well with me. Or maybe he doesn't want to "come on strong"—it's not like he's hitting on me or anything.

This is just the start of a friendship, right?

I decide to look.

Already did it. It wasn't her first time either.

Either. Meaning he's had sex multiple times too.

And I haven't even been kissed...but it shouldn't matter. *Just the start of a friendship.*

Been arrested: not yet

Turned someone down: I don't know what this is implying. Turned someone down for a ride? For a smoke? What is this?

Fallen for a friend: sort of

Sort of. I don't know what *that* is implying!

More questions...

Do you have any pets: turtle named Abracadabra—it used to be my brother Mitchell's before he left for college.

What did you do for your last birthday party: smoked and watched Evil Dead with my friends - it was actually horrible (I had the spins all night and threw up)

Name something you cannot wait for: the end of senior year

What irritates you: being told what to do, what to wear, how to act

Nickname(s): Abbey

Relationship status: hiatus

Favorite TV show: Supernatural and American Horror Story

High School: sucks

College: probably sucks more

Hair Color + Length: brown, short but not that short idk

Height: 5'11''

Your crush: unknown entity ... not computable at this time

Tattoos: 2, one on the inside of my elbow, the other over my right shoulder blade (my mom started crying when she saw the first one, you destroyed your body!!) Right or left-handed: Right

Any surgeries: broke my wrist pretty bad and my leg once. I had to have a couple pins put in - I was only about seven and then nine.

Any piercings: no I didn't want anyone trying to tug that shit out

Favorite sport: lacrosse. All my brothers played, and I'm not the worst at it but I probably hate it the most

First vacation: France. I was nine-months-old and can remember absolutely nothing

Currently...

What are you eating: cold slice of pizza

What are you drinking: that energy drink + vodka

What are you waiting for: a certain someone's username

Do you want kids: I already feel bad for these kids

Marriage: if I love her enough

Career: who the fuck knows bc I don't

What do you like...

Hugs or kisses: definitely kissing but I'd take both

Shorter or taller: girls? I don't really have a preference

Older or younger: probably younger or same age

I'm not tagging anyone else, but if you feel like doing this, knock yourself out. It's not as bad as it seems. And someone out there owes me a username -- see you in the morning if I haven't already.

"Are you getting off?"

"Huh?" I peel my attention off my cellphone. A college student with a backpack is waiting in the lobby.

She motions to the elevator. "Are you getting off here?"

"Oh yeah." I quickly step off and check the time, still five minutes early. I pocket my cell, surprised at how much information I received and then in the same breath, all the conundrums that he presented me with too.

BACK THEN

I wonder if my questionnaire will read that way as well.

As soon as I walk outside, the September air cool, I notice a black Mustang parked on the curb. Garrison waits for me, leaning against the car with hands in his navy-blue slacks. His tie is loose around his neck, his white button-down fitting him perfectly.

In the Dalton Academy uniform, he looks more like a quintessential popular guy than the alternative black-hoodied one I'm used to seeing. He straightens up when he spots me, and I slow my pace a little.

No eggs are in his hand. I breathe easier. This is not a *Never Been Kissed* situation. He's just scanning me from head to toe like I did to him.

"Hey," he greets with a nod.

"You're early." I stop a couple feet away from him.

"So are you." His aqua-blue eyes land on my skirt and they never peel away.

"What...?" I wonder if I didn't iron the fabric enough.

"You're not wearing that right."

I pale. "What do you mean?" It's just a blue skirt, a belt attached with the same stiff canvas fabric and it forms a bow in the front.

"The bow is tied differently, and it shouldn't be lined in the middle of your body." He combs a hand through his hair.

I try to fix it, but I'm not exactly sure what it's supposed to look like. It's not like Dalton Academy gave me a manual on how to tie bows. I fumble with it, unsure and nervous.

Garrison takes *two* steps towards me, so close that his forehead almost brushes with mine when I look up. "Can I touch you?" he asks, his hands hovering by my hips.

My whole body heats, blazing from a moment in time. I'm barely able to nod. And then he takes the waistband of my skirt and shifts it to the right, the bow now resting on my hip and the zipper on my other one. It's not crazy to think the zipper was supposed to be in the back, is it?

He reties the bow, his knuckles brushing my waist more than once.

"Does the uniform matter a lot?" I ask.

"To most of the teachers, yeah. They'd make you stand up and retie the bow in the middle of the class."

I imagine all the eyes on me, and I wince, glad to be saved from that. When he finishes the bow, he tucks the edge of my blouse into my skirt, the corner astray. "I think you're good," he says with a couple nods. "I can take that." He gestures to my backpack.

I shake my head. "I'll hold onto it."

"Okay." He checks his watch—a charcoal-tinted one that appears expensive by the plate-size and band. "We'll make it on time."

About a minute later, we're in his Mustang and driving to Dalton Academy, back towards the ritzy neighborhoods and further away from Penn.

"My schedule is in the middle console if you want to compare," he tells me.

I open the middle console, take out a folded piece of paper, and then retrieve the crumpled one from my backpack.

I notice three similarities, which is a lot more than I expected.

"And?" he asks, glancing between the road and me.

"We're in the same British lit and Calculus class, and we have the same lunch period." I gauge his reaction, but he never smiles much, not even now.

He asks, "Are you good at British lit?"

"Sort of."

"Sort of…" He gives me a look. "What does that mean exactly? *Sort of.* Is it more of a yes or more of a no for you?"

"I guess…a yes."

He nods. "Good because I fucking suck at lit."

"I'm bad at Calculus."

He nearly smiles this time. "I'll help you if you help me."

I lean back. "You're good at math?"

"I like numbers more than words," he explains, "but I don't mind reading—just not classics. I fall asleep every time I flip a page." He fiddles with the windshield wipers as a sheet of rain suddenly falls from the sky.

"I like comic books mostly, but I pick up regular books from time to time." I hug my backpack closer, my skirt riding up a little. I try to tug that down. "Should I be worried…?"

He glances at me again, like he'd rather focus on me than the road, but the rain really steals his attention. "About what?"

"The people at Dalton. I know Loren called the cops on your… friends, and I'm just wondering if they're bitter towards him still."

Garrison tries to hide his expression, but I see him *cringe*.

"Oh God," I mutter, realizing it's bad.

"It's not just about that. Some of the guys there had brothers who went to school with Loren, and they hated him. That hate has passed down through siblings."

"Why'd they hate him?"

Garrison shrugs. "I don't know. It's probably just stupid shit, back and forth vandalism. My oldest brother killed a deer after hunting with his friends, and he put the head in some guy's pickup as a *joke*." He emphasizes the last word with more distaste.

My face contorts. People actually do that? "And they know I'm Loren's cousin?"

"Hey," he says, "if you're that worried, I can just tell some people you're with me."

I stiffen.

"Not like, with me, *with me*."

"So…you'll tell everyone that you're my friend?"

He shakes his head. "No, I have a lot of friends…" He stops short. "Or I *used* to. Anyway, that won't mean much to someone." He glances at me again. "I can just tell everyone you're my girl, and they'll probably back off."

"Your girl?" My brows jump.

He licks his lips and actually laughs into a small smile. "It's ambiguous. Not a girlfriend, but not just a friend. I don't own you or anything. It just lies somewhere between those two."

My shoulders loosen a little as I contemplate this. "It reminds me of the movie." I have to bite my tongue to keep from smiling. *My Girl.* A movie about best friends.

"What movie?" he asks.

"*My Girl*…you've never seen it?"

He shakes his head, and then he asks, "Are you okay with this? I can try to think of something else if you're not."

I contemplate it a little more. "So if someone asks you about me, you'll say to them…?"

"She's my girl." He says it with sincerity and threat, like *don't mess with her.* He takes a hand off the steering wheel and catches my gaze once. "Yeah?"

My arms heat, liking *my girl* more than I thought I would. Maybe because it's from him. "Yeah," I say, licking my lips. I realize they're a little cracked. "Are you sure they'll back off if I'm affiliated with you?"

"They'll probably just come harass me instead," he says with a dry smile. I don't think he's joking.

"Garrison—"

"I don't give a shit about any of the people at Dalton anymore, and I can take a few stupid comments and empty threats." He changes lanes and subjects. "I never asked where you're from."

"Maine," I say without thinking about my cover. *Willow Hale.*

"And you left your parents to be here?" He frowns.

I pick at a frayed strand on my backpack. "Yeah."

"How come?"

"I guess…" I start, trying to wrap my head around why I did this. Why I ultimately decided to plant roots here instead of return to Caribou. "I decided that I'd do whatever it takes to be the person I want to be and not what everyone else wants me to be, even if it means hurting some people I love along the way."

He stares far off as he drives. "Yeah…" He lets out a short breath. "I think I'm doing that too."

I relax more. "Willow bada boom thirty-three," I tell him.

He tilts his head at me. "Your username?"

"Yeah."

"I like it, Willow *bada boom*." He says it in *The Fifth Element* voice. My chest swells.

It's not every day you meet someone that understands the things you love, but somehow I've crossed paths with someone who really does.

"**R**eady?" I ask Willow.

"Ready."

I open the door.

We step into the school, halls congested like most mornings. Instead of rushing to classrooms, friends huddle in groups by lockers or wander around, searching for a familiar face.

Willow walks in a diagonal line, almost inwards towards me. She avoids bumping into a few passing students.

"What's your locker number?" I ask while she adjusts the strap of her backpack.

I almost set my hand on her shoulder, but instead I just let her hover close by. As soon as she unfurls her schedule, she hands the paper to me.

It's a little damp, like her palms are sweating.

I'm not going to be a dick and mention it though.

I glance at the locker number with the code written out. "You're over here, further down."

She nods mechanically.

I understand the kind of nerves that just completely eviscerate you. Only I don't feel them on the first day of school, or the second, or even the last. They hit me when I bike near my house. When I drive by. When I'm feet from the mailbox and then the front door.

When I step inside. Knowing my brothers are there.

They're gone. They're at college, I have to keep reminding myself.

Thank God.

"Sorry," Willow apologizes in a whisper. I think towards me, but I realize that someone barely brushed against Willow's arm on the way to a locker.

The girl shoots Willow a weird look, probably unsure of what she said.

We move along, out of her sight.

"So there are vending machines in the middle of each hall," I tell her. "We can grab some waters before first period." I'll see her in second period, Calculus. Our first periods are different.

She'll be okay.

She left Maine all by herself, didn't she? Bravery exists somewhere inside of her. She just needs to remember that.

Two guys crash against my right shoulder with complete disregard. It knocks me into Willow. I catch onto her waist so we don't both slam into the floor.

Shit.

She stiffens but holds onto me for support too. Once we're stabilized, I take my hands off her and try to find the two assholes.

I spin around.

"Really?" I snap, extending my arms at them, but as soon as they turn to face me, my arms drop immediately. One of the guys—he's a friend-of-a-friend who I've fallen out with.

He flips me off. "Watch it, Abbey," Pat Hayes snaps. Honestly, I expected worse than a shoulder-check and the middle finger.

"No thanks," I rebut and then walk forward, away from them. Willow keeps my pace. I glance at her. *You okay?*

She seems a little shaken.

The universe is basically saying: *Garrison Abbey, you're the shittiest welcome committee. Take a backseat and let someone who's actually well-liked show this sweet girl around.*

I don't want to hurt her.

Still, the thing I've always sucked at is leaving people when I should. I end up staying too long, too late. I'm not going to leave Willow alone, not now.

Maybe I should at least tell her I'm cursed.

I hear Pat huff angrily behind me, still enraged. He's captain of our crew team, an adversary of Dalton's lacrosse team. Our football team is shit, so all the country club sports are put on pedestals. Dalton's track, swimming, tennis, crew, lacrosse and equestrian teams are all top in the state.

Pat shouts, "You ran into me, Abbey!"

Bullshit.

I say loudly without turning around, "If that's what you think, then maybe don't have a fireside chat in the middle of the hall."

Pat shouts out a "fuck you" before a nearby teacher scolds him for his language. We're too far away from one another to keep combating. Thankfully.

Willow keeps muttering "sorry" every five seconds, and by the time we make it to her locker, I feel relieved for her. She wipes her forehead with the back of her arm. A strand of her hair is still stuck to her damp cheek.

I motion to her face. "Can I...you have something...?"

She's confused for a second and tentatively nods at me.

I pick the strand off and tuck it behind her ear.

She swallows once and stares at her feet and then her locker.

"Are you going to pass out on me?" I ask with concern, already trying to figure out the distance from her locker to the nurse's.

I think I could carry her there, no problem.

Willow shakes her head. "I'm not good at this...I forgot to warn you." Maybe she means that she's not good at being the new girl in a school full of strangers. Or maybe even more general: being surrounded by a lot of people at one time.

"You're doing alright."

She glances at her skirt. "How's the bow?"

My lips pull up a fraction. "Without a doubt, you have the best bow in the entire kingdom. If I were a princess, I'd even be jealous." I pass her schedule back as she begins to smile. "Fifteen, thirty-seven, twenty-seven."

I don't ask if she wants me to open it. I figure spinning the lock will be a nice distraction for a second.

While she turns the dial, I'm about to ask about her last school. I assume it was public and smaller than Dalton.

Just as I open my mouth, I spot someone familiar in the corner of my eye. Carly Jefferson. She whispers to a group of three girls, about fifteen lockers down from Willow's.

I'd like to think I'm more observant than paranoid. That this isn't all in my head. But I have this feeling. You know the feeling—the one where everything stills around you. Just for a moment. Where every crack and flaw that frames a photo suddenly magnifies ten *million* times over.

It's happening. Right now.

The hallway noises deaden in my mind. Leaving excruciating silence. Their furtive glances like sharp knives. Their smiles like snarls. Carly giggles and nudges her friend's side. A couple guys join the huddle of girls. They lean against lockers and smirk. Taking a front row seat to a show.

Wrong.

Everything is wrong.

"Willo—" I start and grab her arm to stop her from opening the locker.

The dial has already clicked, and the blue metal swings back.

It should be empty. But it's not.

Hundreds of tampons fall out, most in their wrapper. A handful have been torn open and soaked in what I hope is red dye.

She freezes.

I don't even know what to do. I go as still, as quiet as her.

And the hallway erupts in laughter.

Here's the truth: I've never been pranked at school. I've never been picked on by anyone but my brothers. I used to be well-liked. Even if I hated myself half the time.

I want to say something.

Do something.

Anything.

To stand up for the quieter person. For the first time in my life.

19

BACK THEN – September

Philadelphia, Pennsylvania

WILLOW MOORE
Age 17

My instinct is to run, but I have nowhere to actually go. I've already run away from Caribou, Maine. This is the place that I've run to.

My ribs tighten around my lungs with a hysteric thought and my new eulogy: *Willow Moore, that fool who ran away to have her locker filled with tampons and be publicly humiliated in a new school.*

It's not true. I can't let it be.

I ran away to build a relationship with my brother.

To become me without any apologies attached. None of these: "I'm sorry, Dad, I'm not as pretty or as popular as you hoped I'd be."

Garrison makes the first move. He kicks the tampons at a couple girls and guys, grouped several lockers away. When he swings his head to me, pieces of his hair fall to his eyelashes, and he says, "Blaze."

Blaze.

From *Streets of Rage,* an early nineties video game, she's one of the strongest female characters in a slew of men. While I don't have her judo skills or her physique, it's easy to pretend I'm her when someone pretends with me. And by saying her name, I know Garrison is trying to bolster my confidence.

On our trek from the parking lot to the school this morning, Garrison asked if I'd ever played *Streets of Rage.* When I said I did, he told me, *"So imagine you're Blaze and I'm Axel and this hallway—the one we're going to be walking down—is nothing we can't handle."*

"Axel," I whisper and brush the tampons out of my locker.

I remember the phone call from Rose Calloway—after I spilled tampons accidentally on the street. In front of the world.

I'm not going to be embarrassed. *Remember what Rose said.* I take a few deep breaths, my stomach twisting in knots.

It's harder than it sounds.

Garrison says, "Now I wish I had a crowbar." It's the go-to weapon in *Streets of Rage.*

My eyes widen behind my glasses.

"Kidding." He glares at the cluster of people, just now coming down from their laughing fit. "Sort of."

I quickly stuff my backpack into my now empty locker, slamming it shut. Just as I turn, I realize that Garrison has left my side. He's taken a few lengthy strides towards the group, all laughter faded.

I try to grip my backpack strap, only to meet air.

I stand stiffly, more in the middle of the hall. My uniform is as uncomfortable as I feel. I check the state of the bow, like a teacher will yell any second about its off-kilter state.

It looks okay though.

What doesn't look so great: the scene in front of me.

"That's not cool," Garrison tells the shorter girl with dirty blonde hair. I wonder if she'll have to take out her nose piercing before first period. This thought is trying to trounce the bolder, bigger one that screams, *these are his friends.*

He approaches them like he knows them. Like he's talked to them often. Like he's so familiar with who they are.

The shorter girl pushes out her chest and pulls back her shoulders to gain some height. "You know what's not cool? Betraying your best friends." Her eyes redden, and she takes an angrier step forward. The other girl clasps her shoulder. "You should be in there with John! You deserve jail time more than any one of them, and you know it!"

Her friend says, "Carly—"

"Leave me alone." She swats her hand off her shoulder and then points at Garrison again. I can't see his features, just the back of his head. He's unmoving. Even his fingers hang loosely, not curling into a fist. "You're a piece of shit, Abbey. You're a piece of shit—and you know it."

Garrison nears Carly a little more, and she goes still at his closeness. He hangs his head and whispers something to her. In seconds, she breaks down and bursts into tears.

"It's not fair!" she cries, sinking to the floor. I can only guess that she was close to John, maybe even in a relationship with him.

And I expect Garrison to swivel back towards me.

Am I being presumptuous? To assume that he'd come back?

Because he never does.

I watch him walk past his old friends. Away from me. I watch him disappear alone around a corner. I watch him vanish all together without another word. Without a goodbye.

The bell rings, and I'm left standing immobile in the middle of the hall. People pass around me like nothing occurred.

And I have two choices.

I can go to first period and forget about Garrison. I can act as though this intro to class never happened. Act like everyone else. *Forget about him, Willow Moore.*

Or I can go find him. I can step over my hurt feelings. The ones that say, *he left me,* and just make sure he's okay.

He approached them for me. To stand up for me.

That means something.

I make my decision.

I trace his footsteps down the hallway. I veer around the corner where I expect another hallway or a cluster of vending machines. Instead, I'm met with two bathrooms. Girls and boys.

"Oh God," I mutter.

I'm staring at the boy symbol. Just go in. This will be my first foray into this great unknown that is the boys' bathroom. I wish I didn't give a shit. I wish I could just push inside without a second thought or care.

It's just the boys' bathroom.

It's trivial, right?

Just go in.

I do this time.

I push the royal blue door with my shoulder. I'm met with one long row of sinks, two stalls, and three urinals. Not too shocking.

Garrison is sitting on the sink counter, a lit cigarette between his fingers. His head is hung, hair in his eyes, but as soon as I enter, he looks up. His bones seem to cement, joints unoiled. Frozen.

Maybe this wasn't a smart idea.

"I…" I gesture to the door I came from, as though that explains everything. It actually explains absolutely nothing.

Smoke wafts around his body, and it takes him a second to shift the hand that holds his cigarette. He casually sucks on it, quiet.

I like quiet.

I'm familiar with quiet more than I am loud. I walk further inside and rest my back on a locked, out-of-order stall.

He blows smoke up at the air vent. Then his aquamarine eyes study his cigarette, embers eating the paper. "Did you hear the bell?" He finally speaks.

"Yeah."

He nods a couple times, almost in realization, and then he takes another drag.

"Thanks for trying to help me," I say softly.

"I probably made it worse."

I cross my arms, feeling naked without my backpack. "They're your friends?"

"Were," he corrects. "They pretty much want nothing to do with me after…the thing." *The thing.* He takes a deeper drag of his cigarette. I know he must mean when his friends broke into Loren's house with gargoyle masks.

"What'd you say to Carly?"

He stares off past me, his gaze haunted. "I told her that she's right."

"What?" A weight bears down on me. And the room.

He puts out his cigarette in the sink basin. "I'm a piece of shit." He says it with such finality, as though he's accepted it for a long time.

I open my mouth to tell him that it's not true—that he's a great person. I pause.

I falter.

And I think. How much of Garrison Abbey do I really know? Not much.

Not yet.

I lick my dried lips and stare at the tiled floor. "You're better than your friends, you know?"

He says under his breath, "What an accomplishment." His pretty eyes land on me. "You don't have to cheer me up. It's a lost cause, honestly." He expels a deep breath and rubs his tired eyes with the heel of his palm. "You should go to class, Willow."

"Are you going?" I wonder.

"No." He pulls a carton of cigarettes out of his slacks. He undoes his navy tie and pops some of the buttons at the collar. Like the uniform has been slowly but surely choking him.

I unbutton some of mine at the collar and untuck my blouse. Feeling better. I don't brave a glance at him, but I do climb awkwardly onto the sink counter, right next to Garrison.

My legs are much shorter, and I push my glasses up before splaying my hands flat on my thighs.

"Do you smoke?" he asks me, staring down at my features. Our arms skim, and a thunderous sensation pounds inside of me, grasping tight of my lungs, reaching and stretching for my heart.

"Not a smoker," I tell him.

He doesn't offer me a cigarette, and I'm glad there's no pressure to join him. When he lights another one, he blows the smoke away from me.

We're utterly silent, but it's the kind that begins to slow my heartbeat. Silence and calmness, void of that aching loneliness.

After maybe five minutes or possibly ten or twenty, the door swings open, and in walks a five-foot-something student with short brown hair, expensive loafers and shock at the sight of me, a girl.

Garrison smiles in his next drag. He motions from the guy to me. "Barry, this is my girl, Willow."

My girl.

I begin to smile.

In context, it sounds just as Garrison described—somewhere between good friends and boyfriend-girlfriend.

Barry nods in recognition, at my name or the title Garrison has attached to it, I'm not sure. "Ohh…" He draws out the word, then he points at the cigarette. "Coach says you need to cut back for conditioning."

Garrison looks at me. "The lacrosse coach has this delusion that I can run a mile faster than my older brother. God forbid I fall behind Hunter Reagan Abbey." He spins the cigarette between his fingers. "Birthplace: Mt. Olympus. Age: Unidentifiable. Handsomest fucker there is." I can't tell if he's being sarcastic or just bitter.

Maybe both.

Before I can say something, Barry adds, "Cutting out cigarettes would help though."

Garrison gives him an irritated look. "Or I could just cut out lacrosse. How about that?"

Barry rolls his eyes. "Don't talk like that. You know we need you for state this year."

Garrison just takes another drag of his cigarette, more agitated. I remember his questionnaire answer about lacrosse being his favorite sport but hating it the most of his brothers. I wonder how deep that hate runs.

Barry briefly glances at me before disappearing into the stall.

Then Garrison hops off the counter and douses the cigarette in the faucet. "Calculus in ten."

Ten minutes? I check my watch, realizing it's almost time to go. I tuck in my blouse and button it higher while he fixes his tie.

I catch him glancing at me.

He catches me glancing at him.

His lips rise. I feel mine pull upward too. And I'm beginning to realize something.

I really like being in the company of Garrison Abbey.

20

BACK THEN – September
Philadelphia, Pennsylvania

GARRISON ABBEY
Age 17

slump down in the back storage room of Superheroes & Scones. I'm not on break. Not even fucking close. Unless this place gives breaks after only an hour stocking comics.

Unlikely.

I just needed to escape for a second. My fingers instinctively slip into my leather jacket for a cigarette, but I quickly ditch the attempt. I don't need to ruin the good thing I have going here by infusing Groot plushies with cigarette smoke.

I reach for my other pocket instead and slide out my phone.

A cardboard poster of Thor pokes my back. Pushing it away, I readjust and discover a bare patch of cement wall to lean against. Not like there's much. The fucking storage room is *crammed* with shelves of comics and merchandise, half of which is packed in boxes. It's easy to hide back here.

To get lost.

I log onto Tumblr and search for Willow's new username that she changed from *willowbadaboom33* and gave me ten minutes ago.

vegablaze33

It slightly matches mine. Vega is a character from *Street Fighter*. She told me that she usually dresses up as Vega for Halloween, so it has sentimental meaning.

What's terrible—what makes me hate myself more than she could even understand, more than she could know—is that I'm not even sure I would've befriended her if she came to Philly last year.

My group of friends—we'd been pretty tight since grade school. It would've been too hard to break away from that security. It's such bullshit.

I'm bullshit.

Because I already like her more than *any* shit friend I've ever had.

She dressed up as Vega, for Christ's sake.

I laugh and I smile. Just trying to picture it. I wish I'd been there. Right beside her, for every Halloween she had the balls to wear that costume. And I don't mean literal balls, but Vega is a dude.

What's worse: I think I'd return to my friends if it would be like it was. When I lost some of them to juvie and when the rest of my friends turned their backs on me, I lost *people*.

Not happiness. Just people. And that's what fucking hurts the most.

I'm not used to being alone. Having people near me, returning to what was, sounds comfortable and easier. Even if I wasn't really happy.

Willow's still a mystery to me. She's shy but brazen enough to enter a party where she knows absolutely no one, all to find her cousin. I can't even be without people that I don't really like and who don't really like me, and she could do that.

And she's wary of touch.

But she let me touch her.

I might be bad for Willow. I've been bad for everyone at some point, but I selfishly need something that will keep me riding down this road. I'm scared that Superheroes & Scones won't be enough over time, and I'll find a way to turn back around.

To return to people I've known practically all my life. To people who will never make me happy.

I'm just terrified. Of every single option in front of me. Even the good ones. Even the horrible ones.

To distract myself, I stick to Tumblr. Something I actually like. I scroll through her archive and find the questionnaire easily this time.

Here it goes.

What was your...

Last drink: Fizz Life

Last phone call: umm, my Grandma Ida. She wanted to crochet me a scarf for next winter and needed to know what color yarn. I told her blue.

Last text message: "I bought it! I bought it!" to Maggie, in relation to Understanding Comics by Scott McCloud—I've been saving up babysitting money to purchase the comic book. I read ANYTHING that Loren Hale recommends (my comic book guru), and he suggested this one not long ago on social media.

I didn't realize that she needed to save up money just for a comic book. I just figured her parents were loaded since she's related to Loren Hale.

My brows knot as I continue on.

Have you ever...

Been cheated on: never gave anyone the chance to

What does that mean? She's never dated? I don't know why that surprises me. I just thought…Maine. She probably knew some guy up there, right?

Kissed someone and regretted it: never been kissed (don't judge)

Willow…

I reread this part about five times, not able to move on yet. My hand is frozen to my mouth for a second. I drop it after the shock lessens. I'm not judging. (I promise.) I'm just confused.

Why hasn't any guy kissed her before?

Did she not want them to?

Did no guys want to? That pulls at me because it fucking sucks and I'm still just…confused. Then again, it's not like a person *has* to be kissed by a certain age, right?

Drank hard liquor: a couple times. I didn't like the taste.

I'll remember that.

Been drunk and thrown up: nope

Good for you. It's not fun.

Met someone who changed you: I met Loren Hale once (my only celebrity run-in). He was standing on my front doorstep (long story). Loren Hale left within like five minutes—but he actually spoke to me. He noticed my Mutants & Proud pin, and I mentioned liking X-Men Evolution (the cartoons). Then he made a comment about the comics and Lily Calloway. He called her his girlfriend, but they were and are still engaged if Celebrity Crush is right. It made me think that girls could read comics too—and the way he spoke, he presumed I already did. I never tried to read them until that moment, until he left and I thought yeah, I'm allowed to read these too.

I started New X-Men and related so much to Wallflower, a girl I really needed a year ago, when my dad divorced my mom. And I would've never read comic books and fallen in love with them if I didn't meet Loren Hale

There's a lot to take in there. She only met Loren Hale once before moving to Philly—which makes a lot more sense. The pieces click together. Why she was searching for his house that one night at the party. Why she didn't have any way to contact him. Why she doesn't have as much money. Their families must have been estranged.

She *really* loves comics then…

Wallflower. I make a note to look that character up.

Her parents divorced a year ago. That's got to be fucking hard. Unless, it was a good thing. One of my old friends, Jesse—his parents split and his mom seemed much happier afterwards. Divorce isn't always that great and terrible monster some people believe it to be.

But that line *a girl I really needed a year ago* makes it seem like it may not have been a good change.

Shit.

Should I stop reading this? I skim the next question instinctively.

I'm in way too deep.

Fallen out of love: I've never fallen in love to fall
out of it

Yeah well, in high school, love is for liars.

At least, that's how I feel.

Found out who your true friends are: this is why I
keep my circle small. Maggie is the truest friend
there ever could be.

How small is *small*? And Maggie must be the girl she tagged in this
questionnaire.

Lost glasses: multiple times. My little sis sometimes
takes them to be funny.

That's not funny.

Sex on the first date: ...idk maybe I'd do it? Thinking
about it makes me nervous...

The hairs on my neck bristle. I figured she was a virgin if she's
never been kissed, but this causes a wave of panic. I reread that line
over and over *idk maybe I'd do it?*

It makes *me* nervous that she'd even contemplate doing it if she's
nervous about it.

Like, why?

And I know why. I know how guys are. I know sex.

BACK THEN

I know what it feels like being pressured into something that you don't want to do. I mean, it's never happened to me with sex, but yeah...I know pressure.

idk maybe I'd do it. Thinking about it makes me nervous...
Shit.

Been arrested: in a nightmare

I actually laugh, my lips rising.

I glance at the storage room door to see if anyone heard, but it's just me here. No heavy footsteps or knocking yet.

Turned someone down: for what? Like dating?

Yeah, I didn't fucking get that question either.

Fallen for a friend: no. I don't like the guys at my school like that (you wouldn't either if you were me)

What the hell does that mean? I shift my weight on the ground, uncomfortable all of a sudden. And it takes me a moment to realize that I'm uncomfortable for *her*. Were they pricks? Were they aggressive? I'm just picturing assholes running around her school like uncaged gorillas.

More questions...

Do you have any pets: my dad hates pets, but when he moved out a year ago, my mom let Ellie get a hamster. It smells really bad

Hamsters are gross.

What did you do for your last birthday party: ate
out at the Noodle House with just my mom, sister and
Maggie. I don't like big parties, especially not ones
about me

This one rips at me a little bit. Last time I had a small party—with
only three people attending—was, well, never. I'd usually invite most
everyone in my grade. Even when I was three and four and five, it'd be
huge. I didn't want to be alone on that day—though I'd always sneak
out early midway through.

Name something you cannot wait for: A REBOOT OF NEW
X-MEN (PLEASE HAPPEN!!! I'LL TAKE ANYTHING!!!) Also,
for Maggie to meet Scarlet Witch (aka Elizabeth Olsen)
one day.

Again, she *really* likes comics.

What irritates you: being forced to speak up in large
crowds

Yeah, that's not fun.

Nickname(s): none (I'm not that cool)

I shake my head. She doesn't even know how cool she really is.

Relationship status: single

I'm smiling, a full-blown smile that I haven't felt in years, honestly.
I shake my head at myself. *You're in way too fucking deep, Abbey.*
I know.

Favorite TV show: tie between Gravity Falls & X-Men:
Evolution. I love them

Never heard of either of them. I actually pop up the notepad on
my phone and write down *Wallflower, Gravity Falls, X-Men: Evolution* so
this all makes more sense.

High School: ready for it to expire

College: wish I could go. I'm working on it

Hair Color + Length: light brown, straight, and about
to my chest?

Height: 5'5''

Your crush: TOM HIDDLESTON!!! (aka Loki)

Loki? Really, with the long black hair? I touch my forehead. My
hair is a medium-whatever. I mess my hand through the strands as I
continue reading.

Tattoos: my dad says no

Strict Dad? Why'd he let her move here then? She's not even out
of high school.

Right or left-handed: Right

Any surgeries: nothing that serious

Any piercings: double lobe piercings on both ears,
just four little studs, two bats and two stars

Yeah, I saw those.

Favorite sport: `sports? *runs and hides*`

Sometimes I feel like that too. At least with lacrosse.

First vacation: `never left Maine before, but when I was really little, we used to go to the coast, about 4+ hours from Caribou, and we went sailing one time. I can't really remember it, but my mom has pictures. Everyone seems happy`

What...

My knees fall, and my foot knocks over a cardboard cutout of Hawkeye. I pause for a second, but nothing else stirs, no one coming in here. I glance back at Tumblr.

She had never left Maine before.

Without having ever really traveled, she moved *here*. Away from her parents and sister.

These thoughts just crash into me, trying to process. Trying to understand. Because I see myself trying to do the same fucking thing, and I'm not sure I'd have the courage to step one foot out the door.

I stare at the wall, for about three minutes total. Just staring and *imagining* that giant leap into the unknown.

I don't know how...I can only feel fear.

Currently...

What are you eating: `vanilla birthday cake that I made for my sister. I snuck downstairs for a slice & brought it back up`

What the fuck. Why is she sneaking downstairs in her own house? Did they lock her up there? You know what, I don't like her family. It's a declaration I make in my head with limited facts from a Tumblr questionnaire. I get that. But I don't give two shits. I'm sticking by it.

What are you drinking: a flat can of Fizz Life

What are you waiting for: this birthday party to end

Seriously. What happened?

Do you want kids: idk I don't think about that

Marriage: I don't mind either way

Career: too soon to tell

What do you like...

Hugs or kisses: hugs for now

Has a guy ever even hugged her? It's my only thought. One that I'm sure will be plaguing me all night.

Shorter or taller: taller than me. Even if it's only a little taller. That works too.

Older or younger: older but not too old—I couldn't do what Daisy Calloway does with her boyfriend, who's like seven or eight years older (I can't remember).

And that concludes the questionnaire. She meant it when she said it was personal. I pull my knees up and rest my elbows on them, staring off at the ground.

Shit.

I thought the point of reading that was to get answers, but now I have a thousand more questions. My heart pounds harder, my pulse fast. My body has responded like I chugged a Lightning Bolt!

The door to the break room opens, and I immediately freeze, only now realizing that my legs have been jostling.

"Garrison? Are you in here?"

Lily Calloway.

Great. I'm about to get fired. I rub my temple and run my hands up to my hair, aggressively pulling at it for a second before taking a breath. And then, I slowly stand.

"Yeah?"

She keeps the door propped open, not edging further towards me. "The *Avengers vs. X-Men* issues need restocking, and they need more hands behind the counter."

She's not firing me?

I stare at her blankly for a second before nodding. "Yeah, fine."

She squints a little. "Are you okay?"

"Fine." I motion towards the door. "You going?"

She opens her mouth like she might say something, but then someone calls her from the break room. She turns back to me quickly. "Forget about the comics. Just go help up front." Her words drift as she rushes out to take care of something else.

I let out a breath of relief.

I still have this job.

And that has to count for something.

21

WILLOW HALE
Age 20

As soon as my plane lands on the tarmac, a text from Garrison pings my phone. Nervous, giddy butterflies invade my belly. Countdown to seeing my boyfriend: *minutes away.* It somehow doesn't even feel real.

I click into my cell, the plane rumbling to a halt and the other passengers grabbing suitcases from overhead.

Garrison: Waiting at baggage for you.

He's waiting for me. I take a deep breath, excitement trouncing nerves.

And then my phone rings.

But it's not Garrison.

"Hey?" I answer quietly, crammed in a window seat and hugging my backpack on my lap.

"Did you land yet?" Ryke asks.

In the background, I hear Lo retort, "She already did. I'm telling you the flight tracker says so."

Ryke growls back to him, "Let me ask our fucking sister, Lo."

Our sister.

It still rings through me like a soft padded hammer to a bell, even after two years of knowing Ryke is also my brother.

I can feel a smile on my lips. Palm sweaty, I adjust my grip on my phone and stare out at the tarmac. "Yep, I've landed."

I'm back.

"We're waiting in the car," Ryke tells me.

Lo chimes in, "Paparazzi won't hound you that way. Garrison should be at baggage."

"Yeah, he texted already."

"Great," Lo says. "Can't wait to see you." He mumbles something to Ryke about a honking asshole nearby, and after a few *see you soons*, we hang up.

I'm thankful there'll be less chaos when I reach baggage claim. Lo and Ryke would definitely bring a stampede of adoring fans.

They wanted me to fly on the family private jet, but I chose commercial, wedged in the back near the growling engines.

I still have a difficult time accepting the perks of being a Hale. Garrison says it's because I only learned that Jonathan Hale is my birth father two years ago—when I was eighteen.

It means that Lo is my full sibling. Same mom and same dad. And Ryke is my half-brother.

But my relationship with Jonathan Hale is new. Fresh. And it comes with a load of baggage.

Ryke hates Jonathan.

Lo loves Jonathan.

I'm caught in the middle. Not knowing how I should feel about a man who was rumored to have molested Loren. A rumor that was false and caused Lo to relapse years ago. What I do know: Jonathan isn't all good, even if that rumor was wrong.

But Jonathan is kind to me. He makes an effort to get to know me and my interests. We talk on the phone sometimes about comics, and he asks how my school is going. Rob Moore, the man I grew up thinking was my birth father, never even pretended to care about me. And he was right all along—I was never his daughter.

Not really.

So maybe he had a right to hate my existence.

It'd be so easy just to put all my hate into Rob, while putting all my love and trust into Jonathan. But Ryke says our dad is manipulative.

He says to not trust him.

To not fully love him.

I don't know what to think.

I'm paying for my first semester of college on my own, but I'm also taking some of Jonathan's money for the rest of the tuition. That's all I want to take.

So I don't fly private. I budget. I'm not going to pretend that I'm wealthy because it's not my money, and I don't want to be so far indebted to him that I can't find my way out.

"Thank you for flying with us," a flight attendant tells me as I exit the plane. I shake off all thoughts of my dad, each step towards baggage claim reminding me of the man on the other side.

Garrison.

Do I even remember what he smells like? I wonder if he changed shampoos while I've been gone. If he will look more tired and gaunt in person, or if that was just the trick of the cellphone screen.

Maybe the circles under his eyes aren't as dark. Maybe he's better…I hope so.

I follow the signs and descend two different escalators. My palms sweat and my heartbeat thumps wildly with each passing second. But then the baggage carousels come into view.

Whipping my head around, I try to find him in the crowds.

And then I freeze.

People move around me, passing to the nearest carousel, but my eyes are on *him*.

Garrison stands near carousel four, his gaze already pinned to me, a bundle of pink orchids in his hand. But he's just as frozen and rooted to place. Unmoving.

We just stare at one another like we're processing the fact that we're here.

In the same room.

Almost in breathing distance.

"Hi," I say, but he's too far away to hear me. But he sees me.

He sees.

Hi, he mouths back. I read his lips.

Tears prick my eyes, and I walk.

I jog.

I run.

My backpack almost slips off my shoulder, but I catch it at my elbow. He meets me halfway. We practically collide into one another, but it's like reuniting a missing puzzle piece. Arms fitting around bodies. Heads leaning to the correct side on instinct. His chest against my body, warmth blazes through me—a hug so powerful that I tremble from his touch.

Our lips meet like they can't stand to be away for a second longer. And I forget where I am. In public. In an *airport*. The only thing that matters is him.

My fingers slide up the back of his neck, threading his soft hair. His hand cups my cheek strongly, protectively. My head is lighter than air. Urges pulse through me, hungry for so much more. Touch. Talking. I want everything all at once.

I break from his lips first, lightheaded.

"Garrison," I say in slight disbelief.

He's here. I'm here. *We're together.*

He hugs me again, tighter this time. My forehead presses into his chest. His shirt smells like fresh laundry detergent and orchids. Different but the same.

Our chests are flush together. His heartbeat thumps and thumps, the embrace like a comforting return home.

But he feels thinner than I remember, yet still bigger than me.

"Willow," Garrison says quietly and tenderly as if we're the only people in the airport. We break apart a little, his eyes flitting around me like he doesn't want to stop staring. "You still look twenty." He tilts his head, longer pieces of his hair falling over his brows. He pushes it back. "I could have sworn that fifty years passed since you left."

I laugh and brush tears from my eyes. "You don't look twenty anymore," I say.

He's twenty-one now, and I wasn't here for his November birthday. Guilt tries to crash against me.

He shrugs. "How does twenty-one look on me? Gray hair. Wrinkles. I'm practically Gandalf, right?" I missed hearing his dry wit out loud. In person.

My cheeks hurt from smiling. "Gandalf is two-thousand years old. Maybe dock some years on that one."

He smiles. "Okay, yeah. Dumbledore, then."

"One-hundred-and-fifty years old," I say.

"Look at that." He grins. "I'm already a hundred. I'm in my prime."

"You're too pretty to be anyone other than you," I murmur.

But the dark circles weren't a trick of the screen. And his hoodie looks baggier on his body. Has he even been eating? Worry infiltrates, but neither of us stops touching.

My hands are still hooked around his neck. His still on my waist. Like if we completely break apart, some magical force may rip us away again.

Garrison takes a deep breath. "You're prettier than me," he says. "But also..." His eyes sweep my body. "Have you been eating Willow?"

I almost laugh, we're both worried about each other. I think it's been that way since I left. "I could say the same about you."

"I asked you first."

"I've just been busy and stressed with school." *And being away.* But I don't add that part.

He opens his mouth to reply but a man with a professional-quality Canon camera skirts over to us. "Willow!" he yells. "Where are your brothers?!"

Garrison slides his hand into mine, and he exchanges a look with me like *yeah, nothing has changed.* "Welcome back to Philly." Sarcasm drips from his voice.

Can't say I missed this part.

Garrison reaches into his hoodie pocket and pulls out a balled up baseball cap. He passes it to me along with the bundle of orchids. I gratefully put the cap on and shield my eyes.

PRESENT DAY

"Willow!" Paparazzi approaches as we start walking towards carousel six. "Look here!"

There's only one person I want to look at.

One person I can't take my eyes off of.

Garrison glances back at me, and then he squeezes my hand. I feel it. Palm against palm. That simple pressure lights up my world. It's strange—how something so simple can mean so much.

His hand in mine.

I will never take that for granted again.

22

GARRISON ABBEY
Age 21

After a long car ride, Willow and I are dropped off at my apartment. Alone again. Tomorrow we'll be back surrounded by her family.

We're spending the holidays at their lake house in the mountains, which will be filled with a lot of screaming babies and crazy antics. But I'm honest-to-God looking forward to it. Because Willow is here.

I'm not going to be the seventh-fucking-wheel in the core six anymore, and I won't have to video-record anything. We can whisper to each other. We can laugh together.

Willow wheels her suitcase into my apartment as I flick on the lights. She never saw it in person. I moved in after she left, so she's soaking up the surroundings.

"It's strange," she says. "I feel like I've been here before, even though…I haven't. Obviously."

I get it. I've never been to her dorm in London. But I can picture every piece of furniture there. Mostly because I watched the videos she sent me about a million times.

"You're here now," I tell her. "Want anything to drink?" I pop open my fridge.

Only Lightning Bolt!, Fizz Life, a bottle of vodka and a couple six packs on the shelves. I do have a tub of hummus.

Willow notices the contents—or lack thereof. Her brows furrow. "What have you been eating?"

"The food of gods." I swing open my freezer, packed with five frozen pizzas.

She laughs.

"Also Cobalt Inc. has a pretty awesome cafeteria. They have every-thing: prime rib, sushi, and a thousand different vegan options." I nod to the fridge. "Pick your poison."

"The vodka, definitely," she says, which causes a chill to rake my skin. That would have been the very *last* thing I would have thought she'd choose. How much has she changed in four months?

My hand solidifies on the top of the fridge door.

Willow's lips slowly rise. "Garrison, that was a joke." She points to the soda. "I'll take the Fizz Life…or the beer. Either is good." That's what I thought she'd say but…

"Are you sure?" I question. I don't want her to feel like she can't change or grow. Like I'm stifling her. "If you want vodka—"

She puts her hands to my chest and electricity practically shoots through my veins. "Garrison." Her eyes fill mine, and whatever she was going to say, it just gets lost from her gaze to mine.

The air stills.

She curls her fingers over my jeans' waistband. I hold her cheek and lean down, our lips connecting. I kiss her strongly, pulling her closer. Heating my blood. We stumble out of the kitchen, never breaking apart.

Willow fumbles with the button to my pants, her chest rising and falling in quickened breath. I run my hand up underneath her shirt. Bare skin warm under my touch, but she still shivers.

Like this is the first time all over again.

"Willow," I breathe.

She slowly unzips my pants, so fucking slowly. Like it's a metaphor for how slow we've always been *physically* together. It almost makes me smile, but I nod her on like it's okay.

She inhales, trying to rid anxiety, I think. While we're lip-locked again, my hands roaming up her shirt, the backs of her calves hit my couch. I spin her towards my bed, and I walk her backwards and meet her eyes.

"You sure you want to do this tonight?" I whisper, cupping her cheek. "You can say *no—*"

"I *really* want to," she says and then stops unzipping me. "Don't you?" Fear springs in her eyes. Like maybe I wouldn't want to touch her.

Like maybe I've grown less interested.

Never. Impossible.

"No question. Of course I do." I kiss her again, fully and deeply. Reminding Willow that she's all I want. Her limbs seem to slacken in relief.

And I back my girlfriend up to my mattress. She plops on the edge just as she tugs my pants down, also slowly. I can practically hear her thoughts: *is this the right thing to do right now? Should I be taking off my shirt first or...*

I help her tug down my pants, showing that there's not a right or wrong way. There's just our way.

Willow smiles up at me, but as soon as my jeans bunch to my knees, her breath catches in *shock*.

She gawks at my thigh, then reaches out to trace the new ink. "When did you get this?" she asks softly.

I step out of my jeans. "Two months ago." I couldn't muster the nerve to tell Willow about it, so I figured she'd see the tattoo in person. It'd be better that way.

Willow seems to hold her breath. Unblinking, her gaze bears on the tattoo. An inked skeleton hand brushes fingers with a smaller hand like they're trying to hold on. Hang on. I didn't really plan on getting a tattoo, but I walked into a shop and sat down and came out with this.

"You don't like it," I assume.

She shakes her head. "It's beautiful but...also really sad." Her brown eyes rise to mine. "You're not dead yet, you know that, right?"

Do I?

How many skeletons will I tattoo on my body before I agree with her? Don't know.

I hold my wrist out to her, palm up. We've done this enough that she gets it. She places two fingers to my pulse.

Our eyes don't break. "Garrison Abbey, you are definitely *alive.*"

Only around you.

"It's a miracle," I say into a bigger smile. "Fire off the cannons. Light the torches. Let's celebrate." I lean close to kiss Willow.

Her mouth soft against mine.

I hold her face and gently urge apart her lips, my tongue slowly meeting hers while we both crawl onto the bed. Carefully, I rest my knee between her legs, and I grip the hem of her shirt, pulling the fabric off her head.

Her light brown hair messy around her face. Flush staining her cheeks.

PRESENT DAY

After I shed my hoodie and tee, I dip my head back down. Returning to her lips. Willow hangs onto my shoulders, and I feel her heart quickening against my chest.

I know the more assertive I am, the more she sinks into the moment, and I easily take charge and unbutton her jeans, snap off her bra—desire and craving coats her eyes.

I yank her pants off her ankles and toss the clothes to the floor. Gray sheets beneath our bodies, our legs thread again. My waist aligned with her hips as I hover over her frame.

"Garrison," she whispers, *wanting*. Her fingers skate down my biceps like they skim the surface of a lake. Light touch that annihilates my senses and fists my dick.

Fuck. I knead her small breast, nipples hard beneath my thumb.

Her hips instinctively rise into me.

A guttural noise rumbles in my lungs. *Holy fuck.* My knees push apart her legs so I fit between them, and I suck the nape of her neck, finding a sensitive spot that shakes her limbs.

She quakes and lets out an aroused cry.

Blood pumps in my veins. *I want inside her.* Closer. We both claw at each other for *closer*. Her fingertips gripping my ribs, and my hand descending to her panties.

I cup her warm heat, the fabric already soaked.

She trembles. "*Garrison.*"

My dick throbs.

Her palm travels down. She lightly touches the outline of my erection that presses against my black boxer-briefs.

I groan against her lips, "*Fuck.*"

She smiles, and with a heavy breath, I smile back. We stare at one another for a second, and very gently, I slip off her fogged glasses.

Willow breathes in, watching me reach over and place them on the nightstand. She holds onto me, and I lean back and whisper what I feel balled up in me. "I love you, Willow."

Tears well up in her eyes. "I love you too."

I brush the wet corners of her eyes, and then I pull off my boxer-briefs. Her hand goes back to my erection, and I slip aside the cotton fabric of her panties. Not removing them, just pushing them out of the way.

While we look at one another, I slide two fingers into her tight warmth.

Her smile vanishes to make room for a pleasured *O*. She half-gasps, half-moans, like she can't figure out how to inhale.

I soak up her arousal, my muscles tightening. Sweat already building. Her hand is still on my length. Not moving.

It brings me back to the past. To us together—how her hands always freeze in place—it's still the same. It hasn't changed. She focuses more on where my hands roam, the pleasure that wraps around her, and she forgets to move altogether.

It's the cutest thing, but I know it's also what makes her nervous. Thinking she's not getting me off, but whenever she remembers to shift her hands, she moves her palms in tiny increments. So light and teasing—the start-stop-start-stop drives my body to a fucking edge.

The best kind.

I pulse my fingers in Willow and rub her clit. My other hand gliding down her leg to her ass. Soft noises eject between her parted lips, sweat glistening on her bare body. She drinks in my naked form, the way my muscles flex above her—I'm not grinding my dick into Willow.

Not yet.

PRESENT DAY

I'm not sure if she wants to go there tonight. I don't want to assume, even if I'd *love* nothing more than to thrust into her. But I've only had sex one time with Willow.

A cry breaches her, and she turns her head into the pillow. "Garrison. *Garrison*, oh my God," she cries, as I hit a point and I pulse faster. Her legs twitch, and she clenches around my fingers.

God.

Her hand reanimates, rubbing my dick again. *Fuuuck*. I grit my teeth, arousal spinning my head. The blistering, soul-affirming feeling mounts pleasure upon pleasure.

I force myself not to rock against her heat.

She turns her head, her hand paused again, and her eyes find mine. "Can we…can you…will you…" Her breath staggers like she's been on a ten-mile race. Sheepishly, she glances down at my rock-solid erection.

She contracts around my fingers again. *Fuuck*.

I tense with desire. "You want me inside you?"

Willow nods strongly, cheeks flushed. "Right now."

It takes a lot of energy to remove my hand and not get her off again. But I want my length inside her, too. I want everything with my girlfriend.

I reach for the nightstand drawer. For a condom, and she cranes her neck, feeling my movements.

"You don't need to…" she tells me.

She isn't wearing glasses, so she can't see much. "I'm getting a condom," I explain.

"We don't need one." Her voice is so soft that I dip my head closer to hear her next words. "I'm on birth control."

I frown. Okay, she wasn't on birth control when she boarded a plane to London. I'm trying not to think dumbass things. Like why she'd take birth control once we were split apart.

Lots of girls take birth control for more reasons than just to prevent pregnancy. Like acne and stuff, right? Maybe to help with cramps, I don't know.

Willow can't see my complete confusion. But maybe she can feel my body tense, because she rushes to clarify, "I asked Daisy if it was a good idea since you and I had sex before we left and it would probably happen again, and she said, *totally.* So I thought…I thought it'd be good to prepare for next time."

I'm an idiot.

I let out a breath. Easing a lot more. "That makes sense." I come back fully to Willow. "It is good." My hand encases her cheek. "No condom then?"

She nods.

I place another kiss against her lips and spread her legs wider around my waist. My pelvis aligned with hers.

She pants some and clutches my biceps.

I have her in my grasp. "Tell me if it hurts," I say, my voice low.

This is only the second time she's had sex.

The second time a man has been inside her.

Me.

"I will," she murmurs, instinctively touching her nose. To push up glasses that aren't there.

I peel a sweaty piece of hair off her forehead, tucking the strand behind her ear. And then I grip my shaft, and slowly, I press the head near her entry. Watching her reaction.

She clasps my arms tighter.

I slide inside Willow—*fucking*…she's so tight and wet, the pressure and warmth sending a rush through me. Head spinning. Nerves firing.

Willow shudders a little, but she hangs onto me. I hold her hip and sink deeper and *deeper.*

PRESENT DAY

She lets out a strangled moan, head tilting back. "God," she cries softly.

I fill her completely, and I rock between her legs, slowly at first. Long movements, until the friction flames, and my body blisters for more. Ravenous, hungry—ready to eke out every ounce of pleasure from her and drive it into me. Months apart. Months without a single touch.

I thrust deeper, my ass flexing. Gasps escape her parted lips that can't close, struggling for breath, and my muscles contract—*fuck*.

Fuck.

I fuck Willow. Veins igniting, muscles on fire. My hands on her hips, I sit up some on my knees and pound into her—and her palms fall off my shoulders and find my wrists, clutching me for support.

"*Garrison*," she cries in a sharp moan, her eyelids fluttering.

I lower back, our mouths meeting. I kiss her as deeply as I rock in, and she pulls at my hair. I lift her leg higher on my waist.

Every thrust is filled with an emotional current that ravishes both of us. Like we've both been asleep and we're slowly recharging, coming back to life.

My forehead presses to hers. "I love you." I breathe it out a few more times. Rocking, *rocking*, and her love swims inside her eyes.

I lose time. I lose sense of space. It's just her and me. The world around us is gone until we both ride into pure bliss.

"Ahhh," she cries into my shoulder, and I hold her while her toes curl, her back arches. A groan barrels through me, and I milk out a climax that seizes my tendons in a vice.

We kiss and kiss, my lips stinging against hers—it's going to take heaven and Earth to pull me away from Willow.

I just want this to last. Longer.

Much longer.

How much time is left?

SITTING SIDE-BY-SIDE IN BED, NAKED, WRAPPED
up in the sheets, and eating semi-warm pizza, I stroke her head while
she picks off the mushrooms and puts them on my plate.

"I could have made the cheese," I tell her.

"Supreme is better." She licks her finger. "I like the olives."

This, right here, feels normal. Pizza in bed, like the degenerate I am.
Can't even eat at a table. Being together at night should be happening
all the time, not just once every four months.

Okay, so maybe it's *not* normal, I guess.

This, right here, is rare. I hate that.

"How do you think we're doing?" She hands me the plate with the
mushrooms. "With this whole long distance thing?"

Terrible.

I shrug. "I miss you, but I think that's supposed to happen. Right?"

Her knees knock into mine. "Is it supposed to hurt this badly?"
Her voice cracks.

I kiss the top of her head. "I don't know."

She leans her cheek against my shoulder. "Maybe I should…should
I just…I could transfer to Pe—"

"No." I stop her before she says *Penn.* "You'll be harassed every
day by paparazzi."

"Then NYU, it's not too far a commute from Cobalt Inc.," she
mutters.

"No," I say, my chest on fire. I'd love to agree with her. To say *sure.
Yes. Please fucking come home.* But I couldn't live with myself. I couldn't
wake up with her in my bed, knowing she's sacrificed something for
my shitty existence.

I'm not meant to be fully happy. I've known that since I was little and my brothers were shoving me to the ground.

I'm cursed. It's just the way it is. She doesn't need to share in this damn thing.

Willow pushes her glasses up with her wrist.

"Wakefield is your dream," I say. "You have friends there. You have a life. Don't start over for me. That's the *last* thing I want, Willow."

"Okay." She breathes heavily. "But you'll come out next semester like you promised? I want you to meet my friends and see my dorm and the campus."

"I promise. I'm there."

She exhales and takes a small bite from her pizza. "Something cool kind of happened."

"That's perfect because I'm in need of some cool. Working at Cobalt Inc. is literally the antithesis of cool. Most of those guys are pencil-pushing pricks."

Her lips rise. "Well, it's probably not *that* cool. Your expectations should lower a smidge."

"Lowered." I wave her on.

"Okay, so you know how second-year students usually room *off-*campus?" Willow sits up a bit more to meet my gaze. "I didn't think anyone would ever ask me to be their roommate. But Sheetal, Tess, and Salvatore *asked*." She smiles, almost blushing. "They're getting this four-bedroom flat in the city and needed to find a fourth. Pretty cool, right?"

Happiness radiates off her. She has real friends in London, and that's big for Willow. I want to be the kind of person that's happy for her happiness.

But I hear the name *Salvatore* and my blood turns to tar. She's going to be living with him next year. The guy with the awesome accent and *Vampire-Diaries*-adjacent name and stylish haircut. The one who could've raided my brothers' closet.

He's going to be living with my girlfriend while I'm thousands of miles away.

Great.

Awesome.

So fucking happy about it.

I want to mention my feelings, but they're insignificant. Because Salvatore is *just* her friend, and she's going to say that to me. And I'm not about to ruin this good, *happy* thing in her life because I'm the paranoid motherfucker.

So I layer on a smile. "That sounds awesome. A lot of fun."

I must do a shit job because she's shaking her head like she can hear the sarcasm that I seriously can't control.

"I shouldn't have brought it up. I'm sorry." She sets her plate on her lap and winces, her head hanging. "I wasn't thinking. It's anything but cool. You're living alone, and I didn't mean to rub it in that I'm…"

Shit.

"Hey." I lift her chin, so she'll look at me. "I'm not upset that you have friends and I don't. I'm happy you feel included in London and not ostracized or whatever."

"You have friends," she argues with tears in her eyes.

I'm saying all the wrong things.

"You're right. I have you," I say quickly. She is my only friend.

My words don't help. She's shaking her head.

I cup her cheek in my hand. "You can't worry about me. You have to just live your life in London, Willow." Am I pushing her away? I don't know. I don't know what the fuck I'm doing. My insides twist, and speaking is starting to hurt.

Her tears spill over my fingers, but I don't stop holding her. She says, "You know what I learned in the four months we've been apart?"

A lump lodges in my throat.

"I'm unable to not worry about you," she says in a tight breath.

Something sits on my chest. Heavy. I want it off. *Off.* "I love you," I say. "But you have to, Willow. Because you're not going to be happy if you're just constantly worried that I'm not having a good time here in Philly." I want to say that I'll make friends, but I'm not planning on reaching out to random people and accidentally grabbing a fame-leeching parasite.

I want to say that I don't need any friends, but I don't want to lie. I hate being alone.

Hell, I also hate having friends.

Like I said, I'm cursed.

She sniffs. "Lo told me something like that."

Of course he did. "What'd he say?"

"That I have to let you get used to the long-distance. That I can't do anything to make you feel better."

Loren Hale. *Jesus.* I wonder if he even knows how much he gets me. Like he's taken a road trip in my head and come out the other side. I don't understand it.

"He's right," I say. "You sacrificing shit for me isn't going to make me happy or feel better."

"Then what will make you happy?"

I don't know.

I should have a better answer to that question. But there's one thing I know. She can't suppress her happiness because she feels guilty. I can't be poison in her life.

And then I hear her brother's worry in my head. *I don't know what you'll fucking do.* Lo and Ryke thought I'd break up with her. Now I understand why.

But I won't.

I won't.

I still believe we're good for one another, even a continent away. She *is* the thing that makes me happy. But it's on me—because I need to find something else that can push me through a day. Not someone. Some*thing*.

I desperately need something to get me through the next three-and-a-half years.

23

PRESENT DAY – December
Philadelphia, Pennsylvania

GARRISON ABBEY
Age 21

What the fuck was I thinking?

I must be out of my mind. Watching Willow leave to board a plane and fly back to London must have really fucked with my head.

Because there's no other explanation as to why I accepted the invitation to return home.

It's the weekend before New Years, and I should have hung up when I heard my mom's voice, but instead, I listened to her pleas, *begging* me to just come home.

For a second. For a minute. To spend time with family. The family that I keep distancing myself from like the miscreant troublemaker that I am.

So I went home.

And during a ham dinner, I've been listening to stories about Mitchell's grad school. How Hunter is coaching lacrosse at Penn, and Davis has put his MBA to use, snagging a six-figure promotion at our father's loaded tech company.

"Garrison." Dad diverts the attention to me. He scoops the last portion of potatoes onto his plate. "How's Cobalt Inc. going?"

Davis wears a look of surprise. "You haven't quit yet?"

"Nope." I bite back a harsher retort.

Hunter laughs. "They haven't fired you?"

"Nope." But no one is more surprised about that than me.

"Connor Cobalt wouldn't fire him," Davis adds. "Not as long as he's dating Willow Hale, right?" He nods to me. "Keep that on lock, man."

I'm not dating Willow for my job. My skin crawls even letting that thought cross my mind. Sitting here turns my stomach. I stab at a piece of ham on my plate, not planning to force the thing down.

Our mom stands. "Garrison, stop playing with your food." She waits for me to set my fork down and hand her the plate, so she can clear the table. She doesn't always do the dishes. Most of the time we have *staff* wash them.

Did I mention my family is rich? Yeah, I think I did.

My brows scrunch at my mom. "It's already dead," I say dryly.

She sighs out like I'm being unreasonably difficult. "Please, Garrison."

I'm about to do as told, but Hunter kicks my shins from underneath the table. *Hard.* I drop my fork, the utensil clattering on the lip of the plate.

Fuck.

Dull plain plumes, and Hunter gives me a harsh look like *don't be a shit.*

My jaw clenches, my pulse starting to race.

Mom places a hand on my shoulder. "It's fine, sweetheart." Yeah, she knows my brother kicked me, but all she does is smile at Hunter with the shake of her head.

Boys will be boys, she used to tell me as a kid, blowing on my cut knee-caps after being shoved in asphalt. *You have to pick yourself up and fight back.*

Right.

She collects the dirty plates around the table. Including mine.

Hunter narrows his assholish eyes on me. He jerks his head from me to our mom like, *help her.*

I glare.

He has two feet.

I haven't stepped into this house for months. They're lucky I'm here right now.

"Garrison," Davis snaps out loud. "Help Mom."

Our mom waves me off. "No, you boys go relax and catch up. It's been so long since you've all seen each other."

Shit.

My heart rate ratchets up. "I'm actually going to head out," I say. "I've got an early morning."

Our dad makes a noise of disapproval. "Connor Cobalt surely isn't making you work during the holiday." True—I do have off—but that doesn't mean I'm actually going to take it. I still planned to go into the office. Because I love my job.

Because it's keeping me going.

Hunter pushes out of his chair and treks over to mine. "Come on, Garrison."

Relax, I tell myself, and I stand up. Hunter slings an arm around my shoulder and pats my chest. Once he starts pulling me to the door, he tightens his arm into a fucking *headlock*.

"Stop, man," I choke. I'm stumbling to catch up with my own goddamn head, and I try to pry off his stupid arm.

"That's all you've got?" Hunter goads.

I attempt to elbow his ribs—he slams a fist in my kidney. I cough.

Davis laughs. "Still can't get out of it?"

Acid drips down my throat. I didn't realize I was supposed to become a fucking wrestler.

Hunter laughs with our older brother, then he looks over at Mitchell, who's busy grabbing his Columbia coat from the hook. Acting like he sees nothing.

Hunter messes my hair with his knuckles, digging hard. Burning my scalp.

Davis snatches his coat while I'm still struggling to remove Hunter's bicep from my windpipe.

I don't have time to reach for mine. Because Hunter forgoes his own winter jacket. Front door open, he exits into the cold night in a preppy sweater and collared shirt—forcing me outside with him.

I almost slip on the fucking icy steps, and he's *still* crushing my windpipe. So by the time Hunter lets go and pushes me into the two-inches of snow with only my thin hoodie—I'm livid.

I land on my knees and hand. Body shaking, anger barely warming me in the chill. Picking myself up, my chest rises and falls heavily and my breath smokes the air.

"Come on," Hunter says like I'm a three-year-old kid crying over spilled milk.

I'm not crying.

"Fuck you," I sneer.

Davis tosses a football in the air. "He's just playing around, Garrison. Lighten up. It's the holiday."

PRESENT DAY

I swallow hard. *Cool.* "I'm grabbing my coat—"

Hunter blocks me, his chest puffed out against mine. "What do you call this?" He fists my hoodie.

I slap his hand off me. "Don't touch me." My heartbeat hammers my ribcage.

He laughs. "Come on." When he sees I'm serious, he shakes his head. "Don't be such a pussy. You don't need a fucking coat." He spreads his arms out to illustrate that it's not cold, and how he's also without a winter jacket.

My speeding pulse is now in my throat. I tear my eyes off him, and I lift my gaze to Mitchell, who zips up his teal Columbia jacket—he looks away from me.

Not doing a fucking thing, per usual. It's hard to blame him, but it's easy to hate him.

Davis pats my back.

I tense more. We're adults, and I still can't figure out a good exit strategy from "bro time" with my brothers.

"Boundaries are the edge of the property." Davis points the football between all of us, his younger brothers. "Two-on-two. Mitch and Hunter versus Garrison and me. Tackling is fair game. You okay with that Garrison?"

Hunter smirks. "Or are you going to pussy out like you always do?"

I stare at my brothers. Davis. Hunter. Mitchell. All in their mid-to-late twenties now. And I'm not seventeen anymore.

I'm not a kid.

But they're still bigger and taller than me. Still treating me like the rope in a game of tug-of-war. Something to pull to achieve whatever the fuck they're after.

I rub my frozen hands. "No tackling."

Hunter rolls his eyes. "Seriously?"

"Yeah, he asked." I point at Davis. "I'm telling you *no* fucking tackling."

Davis gestures to me with the football. "How about light tackling?"

Really. "How about none?"

"Learn to compromise, man," Davis tells me like he's the wise older brother here. "It'll solve a lot of problems for you in life." He squeezes my shoulder. "Light tackling is fair game."

Hunter jumps up and down and cracks his knuckles.

Bile rises in my esophagus. Being here. Outside. Alone with them. Why did I put myself in this situation?

It's on me.

They're my family.

It's still on me.

I don't want to see them again… But they're my family.

It's still on me.

I war with my thoughts, unable to decide where to place blame other than myself. It's all I can think, even as Davis tosses me the football.

Run, I think. Move your fucking feet or drop the ball—something. Anything. But I'm frozen, and Hunter sprints towards me. He goes in for the tackle.

His full weight rams into my chest, his elbow driving in my ribcage, and I land with a violent *thump* on my ass. *God, motherfucker!*

I wince through my teeth, my tailbone searing, the snow not bracing impact with the hard ground. Tears sting my eyes—but I refuse to fucking cry in front of them.

Hunter pushes his knee in my stomach on his way to a stance. I cough hoarsely, and he grabs the ball from my loosened clutch. Far too easily for his liking.

PRESENT DAY

Anger surges in his eyes. "Why do you have to give up? It *sucks* playing with you, man. You're worse than a fucking girl."

Say hello to my misogynistic brother. I try to catch my breath and glare up at him. "Then don't play with me." I cough again. "I'm fine with that."

He growls in frustration and swings his head to Davis.

Davis gives me a look. "You're too sensitive. Stop being weak shit. Get up." He gestures for me to rise.

I am weak shit. I feel it.

Sucking in a pained breath, I rise off my shrieking body that screams for me to *run away.* Flee. Flee.

Flee.

My hands are numb from the snow. My stomach is in knots. Like I might actually puke in a second. I stare right at Mitchell.

My twenty-three-year-old brother hangs back. Behind both Hunter and Davis, and I think, *can you please…*

Help me.

Mitchell stuffs his hands in his jacket. And he drops his gaze to the snow.

Right.

I rub my nose that drips from the cold.

"We'll be defense," Hunter says, tossing the ball to Davis.

Not again. "Look, as fun as this was," I say sarcastically, still trying to catch my breath, "I have work tomorrow—"

"Don't be like that," Davis says.

"Like what?" I snap, my pulse accelerating again.

He shakes his head, pissed.

Hunter cuts in, "You're such a little bitch."

"I'm not doing anything!"

"Exactly!" Hunter yells. "Just be a fucking *man*, you cocksucker. Stop pitching these tantrums."

I let out a short, bitter laugh. "I'm pitching a tantrum? Look in the mirror."

Hunter fumes, his jaw locking. He breathes hard, literal smoke coming out of his nose thanks to the cold air.

I glare back, against better judgment.

Davis pats the football. "Let's just play. Garrison sprint."

I have no choice. Because Hunter charges for me—already planning on tackling and Davis hasn't even thrown the ball for me to catch yet.

I run towards the neighboring house. Feeling the weight of my brother on my heels. Encroaching my space. Closer, and closer. Coming for me.

The ball soars through the crisp night air, and I don't care about it. I don't want it. Yet, I'm reaching up for the stupid fucking thing.

My fault.

Hunter tackles me from behind. My chest meets a blanket of hard snow, wind knocking right out of my lungs. I inhale but can't exhale.

He laughs, happy that I finally gave in. "Barely better." He messes my hair.

I'm about to stand, and he playfully pushes my head.

I shove his hand away as he tries again. "Stop, man."

He shoves harder.

"Hunter—"

He forces my face into the ground. Making me eat snow. Cold burns my lips, and I shut my eyes.

Davis laughs.

I struggle out from Hunter's hold, trying to rip his hand off my fucking head.

PRESENT DAY

Mitchell just stays quiet. Just stands there.

I manage to turn over on my back, my face stinging raw. Hunter pins my shoulders and pulls my right arm in a lock. Like we've suddenly switched from football to wrestling. "Come on, get out of my hold."

Davis stands over us. "You got this, Garrison. Just try."

Just try. Why didn't I think of that? What a genius. "He has a million pounds on me."

"Don't make excuses," Davis says. "Or else you'll always be flat on your ass."

Hunter laughs, wrenching my arm harder. *Motherfuc*—I wince again, the brittle air drying my lungs.

I writhe under my brother. Trying to escape. He's cement. I'm being crushed to death, breath comes shorter. "Get off," I say, panicked.

He slaps my face. "Fight me, man." He slaps harder. "Come on, grow some balls."

My cheek sears. I push at his chest and scream between my teeth to force him off.

Unable to move him.

I can't move him.

I picture myself easily sliding out from under Hunter. I picture myself straddling him. I picture two of my fists repeatedly slamming into his face. Until my brother is bloodied beneath me—but my fight or flight response is screaming *fly the hell out of here.*

"Take a breath," Davis coaches. "Think about your next move. Stop flailing."

Hunter looks over at Davis, and they laugh like this is all in good fun. Always at my expense.

"I'm done," I choke out.

Hunter eases up some, enough that I gain control of my left arm.

"Swing," Davis says.

I stupidly try to sit up and swing.

Hunter clasps my fist and shoves me down. The back of my head hits snow. His knuckles land in my stomach. In my ribs, over and over. I heave for breath and try to curl into a fetal position.

Fuck.

"Stop," I gasp, clawing at the snow to get the fuck out.

Hunter drags me back, about to put me in another hold, and I kick his chest.

"GET THE FUCK OFF ME!" I yell into the deadened air. Somewhere down the street, I think I hear Christmas music.

I don't want to hear it.

I don't want to hear it.

Please don't let these bastards ruin Christmas music for me. Please let me keep something. I thrash and must connect with Hunter's dick because he backs off a little, clutching his crotch. Davis kicks snow in my face before I can get up.

I cough and wipe it out of my eyes. My whole face scalds painfully. My throat feels raw, but I can't tell if that's from screaming or the cold.

Staggering to my feet, I rise without another blow. Mitchell picks up the football off the snow and throws the thing in a clean arch to Davis. He catches the ball like we're still playing.

While they're distracted, I do what I've done since I was a teenager.

I stumble to my feet and I bolt.

"GARRISON!" Davis yells.

I don't look back, my feet carrying me to my car in the driveway. I'm shaking, and I fumble with the keys before I unlock the door.

Slipping inside the Mustang, I turn on the ignition. Heat almost immediately blasts from the vents. Great car, thank you. Exhaust gurgles from the pipes.

PRESENT DAY

My hands are still quaking. My teeth clanking together, but I glance through my rearview and start to back out.

I almost think Hunter might stand at the end of the driveaway just to fuck with me and block me in. But the three of them don't move off the yard. And I start to get it.

Why they always let me go…

Because when I run away, I seem like the petulant child. Like the overly sensitive son who can't handle playing rough with his brothers.

Fuck that.

Fuck them.

I leave anyway.

SHE CAN TELL SOMETHING IS WRONG.

I never told Willow that I was having dinner at my parent's mansion. Even now, I don't tell her about what just happened with my brothers—how Hunter repeatedly nailed me in the ribs.

Part of me is ashamed. Shame is strong, even years later when I know my brothers are complete shit and it can't be all my fault. Right?

But she can sense that something's off—just over the phone. Elevators to my apartment complex are out of order, so I take the stairs. Slowly, one of my arms hovering around my battered ribs.

With the other hand, I press my cell to my ear, my boots making wet puddles on the concrete steps.

"Garrison." Worry coats her voice. "Can you please talk to me?"

"I'm talking," I say tightly, pain in every movement.

"No, you're *breathing*," she refutes. "Really weirdly."

"Then I don't want to talk." It hurts to breathe, and my fingers itch for a cigarette. Which makes no sense—I can barely breathe but I want to smoke. Sounds like me.

I reach for a pack in my jacket. I started smoking again a couple weeks ago. Just to stay awake during the later hours at work. Now, I light a cigarette because it calms my nerves.

My fingers shake while I put the cigarette between my lips. I stop in the stairwell, my shoulder bracing my phone to my ear.

Willow stops talking, but I hear the familiar pounding of a keypad like she's typing on a computer. She's back in her dorm room in London. She flew out there a couple days ago so that she could celebrate New Years with her friends from school. She invited me.

But I declined because I feel like that's her world.

Not mine.

Mine is here.

Apparently getting ragged on by my brothers. Oh, and I got this special text from my dad five minutes ago.

Dad: your brothers are just trying to make a man out of you. You're lucky to have them. I only had a sister. If you'd just stop and listen maybe you'd learn a thing or two.

Thanks, Dad.

I suck on my cigarette, and one more level up the stairs, I reach my floor. Slowly pushing through the heavy door and into the hallway.

"Do you have your passport ready?" Willow suddenly asks.

I cough on the smoke. "What?"

"Your passport," Willow says.

"I heard you—"

"Garrison!" Jared yells at me, just as the heavy door clanks shut behind me. He's leaning against the wall next to my door. He's been waiting for me?

PRESENT DAY

"Shit," I curse. My hand hangs, cigarette burning between my fingers.

"Jared?" Willow guesses.

"Can I call you back?"

"No," she says. "I'll stay on the line. Don't hang up on me."

I clutch the phone, almost about to break down because *that* gets me for a second. Someone cares. She cares. Okay. *Okay.*

I take a deeper breath and walk forward to confront my asshole of a neighbor. "Jared," I say. "I don't have time." I put the cigarette back between my lips, and with my free hand, I fish out my keys from my pocket. Trying not to shake.

"Hey, man, yeah." Jared nods and scratches his neck. "I just wanted to invite you to—"

"Just fuck off," I growl out, my words mumbled through my cigarette.

"Look, this party is going to be lit. Maybe you can invite some of your friends, too. Promise, they won't want to miss this."

My anger surges like a geyser. My door clicks, unlocked. I pluck my cigarette from lips and turn on Jared. "How do you not understand this? I don't want to go to your party. I don't want you standing beside my fucking door."

"Come on." Jared reaches out to put a hand on my shoulder.

I jerk back. "Don't touch me."

He raises his hands in surrender. "Dude, I'm just trying to be a friend."

My nose flares. "We're not friends. Read my lips when I say *we'll never be fucking friends.* Ever. You know why I disconnected my smoke detector? So you couldn't offer your stupid broom again. You want to get down on your knees and suck me off, as your girlfriend propositioned?"

He turns red. "I…" He scratches his head. "She was joking." Jared reads my features. "You're really that pissed? Come on, man. You're famous. I'd *kill* to have what you have." He lets out a short laugh. "You know how easy you've got it?"

I glare, unblinking.

Rage and resentment infiltrates his eyes. He thinks he knows me, and I wonder if that jealous bitterness towards me has been there all along, hidden somehow.

"Stay the fuck away from me." I unlock my door and slam it closed. That felt good.

That shouldn't have felt that good. I take a larger drag and blow smoke upwards. My hand trembles.

"Garrison." Willow's voice comes from the cell in my other fist. I press it back to my ear.

"Sorry," I mutter, involuntary tears squeeze out of my eyes. *Fuck.* I wipe my wet face with the heel of my palm.

"How soon can you make it to the airport?" she asks. "Because I can get you on the next flight to London."

I'm already heading to my closet. Grabbing a duffel bag. "Book it."

"**Y**ou're not dressing up?" I ask Garrison.

Seated on my fuzzy blue rug, he plays *Street Fighter II* on an old Sega Genesis that he brought over in September. My dorm-sized room has more personality than just the bare built-in desk, wooden dresser, and short single bed from when I first moved in.

Daisy Calloway helped me decorate. She said she'd be my labor force, and I could direct her where to go, but I liked hearing what she thought. We both agreed to string lights over the ceiling, nail a yellow poster that says *Mutant & Proud* in the wall, and arrange my collection of comic books on my desk.

When I tucked in my white bedding, she tossed pale blue pillows on the mattress. The last one was a blue cupcake. It wasn't something we picked out in the store together. She said that she stitched it in her spare time—with Rose's assistance who's "the better sewer"—but it's my favorite pillow. Because Daisy made it just for me.

Sitting on my bed, I watch as Ryu (Garrison's character) attacks Blanka.

Ryu lands a punch, pushing Blanka back a couple inches.

"I don't know yet," Garrison says. His fingers nimbly fly over buttons, and as Blanka lies flat on his back, he pauses the game and rotates to face me.

A blonde wig is already tight on my head. I twist the hair in a single braid, the strands so long the braid reaches my thighs. This Halloween, I'm going with my staple costume, Vega from *Street Fighter*.

Garrison scrutinizes my hair and then his eyes fall to mine. "Are you sure you want me to come?"

My brother (it's actually starting to feel normal calling Loren Hale that) is hosting a Halloween party for the neighborhood. Garrison is technically already invited since he lives in the same neighborhood, but I asked him to come with me anyway.

This past month has been…difficult at Dalton Academy.

No one harasses me or stuffs my locker with things anymore, but I haven't made any friends either. Lots of behind-the-back whispers.

If someone even tries to talk to me, they only ever ask about Loren Hale. I always shut down at the start of those questions. If I discuss my time with Lo and Lily or any of her sisters, I feel like I'm betraying them.

But I finally have a nickname.

Wordless Willow.

Apparently not responding to someone paints a target on you. Though, my whole body was practically painted red before I even arrived at Dalton.

I haven't exactly told Lo any of this. I also don't plan to tell him today or tomorrow. Some things, I have to deal with on my own.

My current plan: focus on my classwork and not the *people* in my classes. I only have one semester after this one ends. I can make it.

"I want you there," I tell Garrison. *I'm not going to know many people besides Lo, Lily, her sisters, and their significant others.* "But if you don't want to go—"

"I do." He twirls a cigarette in his fingers. He won't smoke in my room. I've never told him, but he's the only reason school isn't unbearable. He's the reason there aren't more tampons in my locker— or worse. He made sure his old friends left me alone.

I've needed him.

If he wasn't here, I'm not sure I'd have the strength to stay.

Maybe I'd find it somewhere else, but he's kept me looking forward. At a better future. At a better place.

In our quiet, I hear the front door to the apartment opening, audible from my cracked bedroom door. Voices emanate from the hallway, and I'm sure my roommate (the only other person with a key) has stepped inside the living room.

Seconds later, my door swings further open, until Maya sticks her head inside. She wears a pink wig and plastic body armor. Her costume: Lightning from *Final Fantasy*.

"Hey," she says. "I'm heading out. You sure you don't want to come?" A smile creeps on her lips. "Your first college party could be a cosplay Halloween."

At seventeen, I might be living in an off-campus apartment near the University of Pennsylvania, but I've successfully avoided the college parties so far. Thinking about them brings on this whole new wave of anxiety that I didn't even know existed.

"It's tempting, but I have to go to Loren's neighborhood thing." *It's Lo, Willow.* Right. *Lo. Lo. Lo.*

"Yeah, I heard about that on Yik-Yak."

Garrison snorts from my rug. "Someone yakked about it?" He returns to the video game, eyes glued to the screen as he plays.

Maya squeezes a little further into my room but stays in the doorway. "I think the yak was something like 'my dream is to party with Loren Hale on his birthday'—not at all detailed." She casts sly glances from Garrison to me, back and forth, but she's not as worried as when I first brought him over.

As the Superheroes & Scones manager, she finds his attitude *troubling.* She was worried he'd steal the comics and sell them online.

The fact that I brought him to our apartment—that he's grown closer to me—made her a bit more protective and apprehensive too. I think she thought maybe this all might be a trick. Get close to the geek for other reasons.

Burn her. Make fun of her. Humiliate her.

Like classic teen movies. He'd try to change me, so that I'd become popular like him. Or he'd pull some cruel prank in the very end.

Neither has happened.

Outside of lacrosse, he spends nearly all his free time with me. He'll message me on Tumblr first. (We still haven't exchanged phone numbers.) Sometimes, he's already in the parking lot before he asks if he can come up. Sometimes I wonder if a tree was outside my apartment complex, if he'd climb it and knock on the window.

I think he would.

Garrison might not be up-to-date on comics like the other Superhero & Scones employees, but he has a geeky side that he's repressed and hidden from his friends.

He loves computers.

He *loves* video games. Retro things like Lion King on Sega and Pokémon. We spent three whole days playing Mario Party on N64, and if he asked, I'd waste another three weeks doing the same thing with him.

That doesn't *feel* like someone tricking me.

And so far, he's proven trustworthy at the store. No theft. No vandalism.

"Garrison," Maya says, catching his attention from the video game. "Just a heads up, I'll be quizzing you about Cable's history on your next shift. Two wrong answers"—she holds up two fingers—"and you have toilet duty."

"Shit," he mutters and mouths to me, *who's Cable?*

I try to restrain a smile. "I'll help you." Cable is in *X-Men* and has a complex history, tangled with Scott Summers, so it might go over his head at first, but he's caught on with other superheroes before.

Garrison swings his head back to Maya. "Should I take this *heads up* as you partially liking me?"

Maya wears a great poker face and then says something in Korean, knowing he can't understand. She grips the door, about to leave.

"One day I'm going to learn Korean!" Garrison calls after her. "And then what are you going to do about it?"

She pops her head back in. "That'll be the day." She slips out, just as quickly. Then she pops her head in one more time. "Friendly reminder: I'm to report back to Loren if anything R-rated is happening in Willow's room. I don't like being a spy, so don't make me be one."

I go rigid. "We're *just friends*," I emphasize for probably the millionth time to Maya, to Lily, to even Lo.

I haven't even hugged Garrison. I don't want to ruin what we have by turning it into something more. I can't imagine...I can't imagine losing his friendship.

Garrison nods in agreement. "She's just my girl."

I pale and then begin to smile impulsively. I hide it by busying myself with my hair.

Maya's eyes dart between us again, but they land on me. "Be sure to lock up after you leave. A lot of bodies will be roaming the halls tonight."

"I will."

She gives me the Vulcan Salute, and I return it before she disappears for good this time.

Garrison sets down his controller, pausing the game one more time. He rises from the rug, and I situate a mirror on my mattress. When it's settled, I remove my glasses, grab my eyeliner and mascara and tuck my legs under my butt.

I don't wear much makeup, except for costumes.

Garrison paces in front of my bed, running his fingers through his brown hair. At least that's what I think he's doing. Without my glasses, he appears mostly blurry. I can't see him all that well, and I'm debating about wearing contacts tonight. I don't like them, but my character for Halloween doesn't wear glasses like me.

"So..." Garrison draws the word out. "I have a question, and you don't have to answer if you don't want to."

I freeze, the mascara wand only halfway out of its tube. "What is it?"

"You know that questionnaire you made me take a month ago? I mean, you didn't *make me* take it. But you know...that one?"

How could I forget? It's what kind of started our friendship. When he told me that he read mine, he only mentioned how he was surprised that I hadn't traveled. He never explained his other feelings on it or if he had any.

And I didn't ask.

Maybe because I never probed him about his own questionnaire.

About why his relationship status was *hiatus*.

About what his tattoo looks like, the mysterious one over his right shoulder blade. He never takes off his shirt in front of me, so I've never spotted it.

Or what it meant when he answered *fallen for a friend* as "sort of"—a two-word combination that he's pointed out I use more than him.

We've both been sitting on these things. It's been easier to live without the full meanings; though I realize we're both curious about them. I'm just as interested in the reasoning behind the answer as much as Garrison.

It doesn't mean I'm not scared to find out.

"Yeah?" I say, unsure of the direction he's about to take us.

"In your questionnaire, you said that you didn't like any of the guys at your school and that people wouldn't either if they knew them." He faces me. "Why?"

I frown. "Have you been thinking about this for that long?" I drop my mascara on my bed.

He shrugs. "On and off, I guess." He turns his head like he's staring at the wall. I squint, but I can't make out anything else. "I didn't want to ask back then. I didn't want to pry or whatever. We were just getting to know one another. It's different…now."

We're better friends.

I pat my bed for my glasses. I can apply mascara if I put my face really close up to the mirror, if you're wondering. Garrison suddenly nudges my hand, my glasses in his clutch.

"Thanks." I put them on, the world ten thousand times clearer.

I also notice his downturned lips and worry creases in the corners of his eyes.

"They're just not the guys you would want to date," I try to explain. "Nothing terrible. Just…not my type."

He contemplates this and then rests his back against my dresser. "What's your type?"

"Not douchebags or guys who'd make fun of me…that's for sure."

His brows jump. "Did someone make fun of you?"

I stare at my hands. "I was mostly invisible. I don't even think they noticed that I left."

"I'd notice," he says, full of conviction, enough that I believe him.

"It's okay. I didn't want them to notice me anyway."

"Because they're not your type?"

"Exactly." It makes sense in my head. I've explained it to Maggie before, and she understood. Maybe you have to be there. In that school. Around those people. In my shoes. To truly feel what I feel. I let out a tense breath and ask, "What's your type?"

He shakes his head once. "I'm not sure." His eyes flit all over my room. Every time he's in here, he skims every item, every *thing*. Like the stuff propped on the back of my dresser: a copy of *Understanding Comics*, a Loki bobble head, ticket stubs to *Harry Potter and the Deathly Hallows Part 1 and 2*.

I wonder what his room looks like, but he says that he'd rather be here, away from home. I once asked him why and he said, *"My brothers are dicks. And they sometimes stop by the house so our maid can do their laundry."*

I didn't pry further, and I never beg to see his place, even if it's tempting to ask. He learns a little more about me when he steps foot in here. I don't see more of him.

Garrison plucks one of my old photographs off the dresser. It's of my thirteenth birthday at the mall, the photo taken right after I got my ears pierced for the first time. My mom is there, holding a tiny Ellie.

My dad couldn't make it.

Work stuff, he said.

"You also wrote about your little sister's birthday party." Garrison rests the frame back. "Why couldn't you go downstairs?" He sets his grave expression on me.

"It's not what you think," I say quickly, though I'm not sure exactly *what* he's thinking. "It's actually kind of funny."

"I hope so." He walks to my desk and sinks down in the chair. In all the times he's been in my room, he won't ever sit on my bed. Not once.

I've offered a couple times. Just to be nice. There's not a lot of comfortable seating in this cramped space. But he always chooses either the desk chair or the floor.

"It was a princess party," I start to explain. His brows knot the more I talk. "And Ellie wanted a real princess downstairs. She sees me as her kind of geeky older sister, so she asked if I could stay upstairs, and my mom hired another girl to be the elder princess."

A long wave of silence passes.

"So you couldn't go downstairs?" he asks like he's still confused.

"I wasn't...a princess..." I say slowly. "It makes more sense if you know my sister." I push up my glasses and stretch my mind to that vivid memory. "She took the theme of her party really seriously."

"Sounds like she was channeling a character from Cinderella."

I smile weakly. "She's six-years-old. She doesn't know any better."

"What about your mom? Does she know better?"

A sharp pang punctures my heart. I must wear a pained expression because he says, "Sorry"—and I shake my head like *it's alright.*

I haven't talked to my mom as much as I would like. Our conversations are so stilted anyway. She won't open up to me. She just says, *it's not your place. You're the child.* It's about *us*—doesn't she realize this?

I'd like to know why she goes quiet every time I utter Lo's name. Not just facts—I have some of those—but her feelings. He's her child. Why wouldn't she want to know him? Just a little more. And is she sad that I'm gone? Is she happy?

But I'm just the child.

"My mom," I say casually, "sided with the birthday girl. Which is only fair, it was her birthday."

Garrison does this thing where he groans without even opening his mouth, and I can hear the deep rumble in his throat.

"You don't agree?"

He shakes his head and retrieves a cigarette again. "It seems kind of fucked up."

I try to view the situation from his stance, and I think I can. I just don't want to.

"Can I ask you something now?" I wonder.

Garrison nods.

I open my mouth but struggle to broach *his* questionnaire. I actually pale again, and my neck heats. "Um…it's about one of your answers."

"Which one?" He doesn't sound surprised.

"Hiatus?" I quickly add, "Not that I care. I mean, I care out of… curiosity, but your relationship status can be whatever you want it to be." When I look up, the corners of his lips are lifting.

"I know what you meant." Still sitting, he rolls on the desk chair. Until he's positioned right across from me. "I've been on-and-off with this girl at Dalton who wants absolutely nothing to do with me now, so…" He shrugs like it is what it is. "There's my hiatus."

"Do you miss her?"

"Not like I probably should. And for the record, at the time, I thought—maybe if Frankie and my friends forgave me, I'd think about…"

"Going back to them?" *Leaving me.*

Would it be that easy for him? My heart sinks more, a pit in my stomach. This is why I never asked.

I can feel him watching me, and I turn towards my mirror, about to take off my glasses. His voice stops me. "It's different now. I'm different."

I can't imagine the person who he's described to me. The one who'd drink alcohol at playgrounds and destroy public property, just because he could. Who'd graffiti houses and knock over mailboxes with baseball bats.

He's said that he's always liked Sega, Pokémon, the Sims—and part of me believes that he was always *this person* on this desk chair, right in front of me. He just felt too much pressure to be a different guy in front of other people. He was too scared to be himself. With his friends gone, he has nothing to lose by being the real Garrison Abbey.

So he's let him free.

All I ask is, "What kind of name is Frankie?"

He almost smiles, glad that I'm not mad at him. "Nickname for Francesca."

"Of course, she has a cool nickname," I mumble. I don't know if he hears or not because I ask speedily, "What about your tattoo?"

He pulls off his hoodie, splaying it on the chair. Now just in a black tee. He stretches out his arm, about to show me the tattoo on his forearm, but I've seen that one before. It's a skull with lyrics to an Interpol song. I had to Google it.

"The one on your shoulder blade, I mean."

He goes a little rigid and then his arms fall to his sides. "That one is kind of an intense tattoo." He pauses. "My mom hasn't even seen it."

"Not even when you go swimming?"

"Honestly, I can't remember the last time I went swimming in my pool."

More silence spreads in a long moment. Neither of us moves or speaks.

We look at each other. We wonder. His brown eyelashes flit up, each time he peeks at me. Strands of his hair fall over his forehead, and he rests his forearms on his thighs, thinking.

I wait, just as calmly. Inspecting my mascara brush. Glancing at him.

He's never pushed me, and I won't push him to do anything or reveal more.

He licks his pink lips and then nods to himself once or twice. "How about"—he retrieves his phone from his pocket and then flips the cell in his hand a couple of times—"we make a trade. I don't know your Twitter username yet. You give me yours, I'll show you my tattoo."

As he processes his own declaration, his eyes flit to the wall, the ground and the window, more than a few times—almost nervously. His joints even stiffen more than usual.

"Are you sure?" I ask.

He raises his gaze and nods. "Yeah." He adds, "I want to see what Willow Hale tweets about."

Willow Hale.

He still has no idea that I'm not Lo's cousin. *I'm his half-sister.* Willow Moore. And I have no idea when I'll be able to trust Garrison enough to tell him the truth. It's not just my secret to keep. It involves *everyone.*

I know that I can't jump the gun on this, even if he's my friend.

BACK THEN

"They're not that great of tweets," I warn him. "Mostly fandom stuff." I reach for my phone on my bed and then pause before logging into Twitter. "I was thinking about changing my username though."

"Oh no." He points at me. "You're one of those people who changes their usernames every day, aren't you?" He's nearly smiling as he says it, and he tilts his head at me. "How am I going to find my girl if you're *willowkicksass* one day and *vegalover* the next?"

"Ha ha." My cheeks hurt from my own smile. In the mirror, I notice an actual blush rising. "And you'd find me. It'd just take you a couple seconds...maybe even less." Not because he's good at computers.

But because he knows what I like.

"Probably." His knee brushes against mine, on accident. We both go still. My heavy breath is more audible than his.

So he scoots back his chair, giving me more room.

I clear my throat, my neck burning again. "The next username I make, I want to go public with it and promote Superheroes & Scones. Lily also keeps asking for my u.n. so she can tweet me." I hold my phone flat on my lap. "I won't change this one all the time like the others."

He sees the Twitter login screen. "Have you already picked it out?"

"Yeah, I wanted to do something like Lo. He has his name paired with his favorite mutant." His username: *lorenhellion*. "The problem is that *willowallflower* is already taken."

Garrison doesn't seem surprised when I say the word *wallflower*—instead he just points at my phone screen. "Make the double L's in 'wallflower' capital I's and it'll look the same on Twitter."

I type in the changes, and he's right. The I's show up more like L's, and this username is available. Before I accept the new username, I ask, "You know Wallflower?" She's not a well-known mutant, and she's not around for long in the comics.

"You mentioned her in your questionnaire."

I did?

"I looked her up," he explains off my confusion, "figured it couldn't hurt with Maya grilling me every shift." He spins some in his chair, pretty casual. "Do you like Wallflower with the blond guy or the brown-haired one?" He leans back.

I'm trying so hard not to smile like he's put his hands on my cheeks. Like he's kissed me. I just—this is surreal. That he's here, talking to me about my favorite mutants. He's not laughing. He's not calling me a little girl. He's not calling me dumb or silly. He's respecting the things I love.

He stares at the ceiling, trying to recall something. "I remember looking up their names." He swivels. "Shit." He thinks a second longer. "Elixir…and Wither?"

"Yeah, that's them. They're in a love triangle with Wallflower." I don't mention how their romances don't end very well, in case he wants to read the comics. "I like her with Wither, even if they're doomed from the start."

"Why are they doomed?"

I intake a breath as I say, "He can't touch her."

Garrison's chair goes still.

"Whatever or whoever he touches decays to dust." He also wears only black, but I don't mention this either.

Garrison blinks a few times, processing Wither's superpower. I think he mutters something about *being cursed* and then he asks, "What about Elixir?"

"He can heal people. He's an Omega-level, so his powers are even extraordinary among mutants." I pause. "He's also mean."

Garrison begins to smile. "I already hate him if you think he's mean." He suddenly brings his phone up to his chest, and he lifts his brows at me like he's doing something secret.

I take the time to log into my new username, and within the second, I get a new notification.

@garrisonwither: @willowallflower looks like it was time for a change for me too *gasp* we're matching

I look up at him, my mouth ajar. "…is…is this your real account?" He could've made a fake one just to tweet me.

Garrison nods, slipping his phone in his jeans pocket before he stands. "Yeah. It's my primary account. Favorite one." His voice is so honest that I trust him.

I have a matching Twitter account.

With a guy.

Maggie wouldn't believe me, even if I told her.

"So…" Garrison towers above me, his hands on the hem of his black shirt. He looks beyond hesitant.

He looks scared.

"You don't have to—"

"It's fine. Just don't freak about the bruises. Lacrosse gets rough and…" he trails off. "I tripped over some guy during last practice."

I swallow hard and just nod, but I wonder if this was the reason why he didn't want to take off his shirt. Or why he doesn't want to dress as Ryu or even Ken Masters for Halloween.

As he peels the fabric off his head, my eyes trace the lines of his lean, toned muscles. In a sharp inhale, his ribs are apparent, along with his tightened abs. Most of the bruises appear faded, but the dark, *dark* purple welt by his right ribcage seems brand new.

When he tosses his shirt aside, I say, "That looks bad."

He glances at the welt. "It's nothing."

"Garrison—"

"Don't!" Panic spikes his voice, and he raises his hands like I sprung up from the bed and tried to touch his ribs. I haven't even shifted.

He shuffles back, breathing heavily. Then he freezes and stares off for a second, attempting to calm down.

I hold up my hands to show him that I'm not coming at him.

He mutters a *sorry* but stays still.

My stomach twists. I'm just scared for him, of whoever did this to him. I'm not sure it's just lacrosse. "You said…you don't like your brothers, right?"

"It's nothing," he repeats, but he pauses and adds, "They play rough, but it's just brother stuff. Football. Wrestling. They don't mean it."

"What if your ribs are broken?"

"They aren't." I don't ask if he went to a doctor, and I can tell he wants to drop the subject. Especially as he turns his back to me. To show me the tattoo on his right shoulder blade.

It's another gothic skull, only its jaw is wide open, screaming. It's also inside the mouth of a wolf's head, which looks violent, saliva dripping off its teeth as it roars too.

You can't hear ink, and something about a silent scream guts me.

Everything about the tattoo is haunting. Everything about Garrison Abbey feels just the same. Like a boy you'd find lying on a tombstone, smoking a cigarette, a bundle of flowers on his chest. It makes no sense, but something deeper, something hidden, wants to crawl out. So I keep staring. I keep looking.

I'm not sure what I'm supposed to find. I'm not sure if I'll ever truly *see* what he's expressing, but I don't leave. Maybe later, I'll know. The pieces will add up and I'll see what he wants me to see.

Some things can't be forced out of people. I wouldn't want him to force things out of me.

BACK THEN

Without even spinning back around, he picks up his shirt and tugs it on. He doesn't want me to see the welt again. When he plops down on the chair, he shrugs on his hoodie, and then our eyes meet.

"Have you ever been hugged by a guy?" he asks me, so suddenly.

I shake my head. "No."

"Will you stand up for a second?" He adds, "If you want to."

I slowly rise, dressed in pants and a white blouse for my Vega costume. Then he stands from the chair, pushing it back into the dresser, away from us. He takes a step closer to me, until his chest is an inch from mine.

He mostly smells like citrus, spearmint and his pine car freshener. I once asked why he keeps his Mustang so clean. He never smokes inside, and the interior is always spotless, like a brand new car.

I don't like the smell of smoke lingering around all the time, he told me. *And I can't think straight if my car is dirty.*

Garrison, more than just a few inches taller than me, stares down at my features. I look up, my pulse quickening.

And he asks, "Can I hug you, Willow?"

I breathe deeply, pushing up my glasses. "I'm not that good at hugging."

"You don't have to be good at hugging. I'd still want to hug you."

"Why?" I whisper.

His aquamarine eyes skim my cheek, my neck, descending. "…because I think you may be the best friend I've ever had, and I've had a lot and spent a shit ton more days and months and years with them than the short time I've spent with you." His hand wavers by my hip, but he doesn't touch me. "I've never wanted to bolt out of your door. I've never wanted to leave you. This—it's a first for me." He nods to himself a couple times. "So you're the best—and I want to hug you, if you'll let me."

My lips part, speechless. Inside, I'm blown over.

Outside, I'm frozen in place.

When my brain functions again, I rewind and all I can wonder is whether this *feeling* of not wanting to leave my room—of not wanting to leave me—surprised him after he revealed his tattoo. After he was vulnerable in front of me.

Yes, my brain says. *Most likely.*

Can I drop my guard just the same? Can I express more emotion than I usually do? I don't think he's testing me, but maybe I need to test myself.

He watches me, waiting for a vocal response.

I open my mouth to say *you can hug me* but my tongue is dry and my throat closes.

His brows scrunch. "You nervous?"

I nod. "This would be a first…for me." *He knows that, Willow.* I cringe a little but try to wipe it away with a weak smile. "I'm not touchy-feely or anything like that."

Garrison's eyes soften like he's trying to understand me. "Would it be bad if I touched you?"

I can hardly look up at him, my gaze dropping to the floor. "Um…" I swallow. "I don't think so. It'll just be new, and sometimes new things are frightening." My heart thuds so hard and so fast.

"Willow," he murmurs.

I look up, our eyes lock, and he sets his hands on my shoulders. I hold in a breath. His palms—they slide *slowly* to my biceps, his skin heating my skin, and then they slip around me, to my back. He draws me tenderly to his chest.

My feet just barely cooperate and step closer.

Garrison leans his head down, his jaw skimming my cheek, his arms wrapped around me, and mine hang uncertainly.

He helps me. He lifts one of my hands and places it on his waist. I follow with the other. My touch is feather-light, but he doesn't seem to care.

Garrison pulls me tighter, his body warm and comforting. In comparison, mine is awkward and stiff. He holds the back of my head, and his breath tingles my ear as he whispers, "This okay?"

"Yeah," I breathe, so softly.

"You're shaking." He draws his head back, just a fraction, and I realize my arms and legs are trembling, out of anxiety.

"It's just a lot…not bad." I wish I could express my feelings better, but maybe that's the problem. So much has suddenly poured through me, so many foreign sentiments, that my system is basically overloading.

Willow Moore at approximately 115% capacity. Delete or reboot.

I don't want to delete anything with him.

Before he speaks, I ask, "Am I hurting you?" My hands are barely pressing on his ribs, but I just want to make sure.

"No." He pauses. "Am I hurting you?"

"No."

He nods a couple times again. Then he lets me go, his arms falling—then mine do too, but he never takes a step back. I worry about the second hug, now that the first has ended. I wonder if I'll grow used to this embrace in time.

"Will you alert me?" I ask him. "Next time you hug me again?"

"By plane banner and smoke in the sky."

"I don't think I'll be looking up."

He nearly smiles but feigns surprise. "You'd miss an aerial ad? No way."

His sarcasm isn't the mean kind. It pulls my lips higher.

Garrison never takes his eyes off me. "Willow," he says in a quiet, calm moment, "can I hug you again?"

My chest swells. "Yeah."

Garrison wraps his arms around me once more, and my arms almost stop trembling. His lips to my ear, he whispers, "How was that alert?"

"Perfect." I try to relax a little more.

He rubs my back, his hand soothing as it travels in a short up and down wave. And he says, "Thanks for inviting me."

I look up at him. "You were already invited to the party."

"Not by you."

This is the day, the very moment, that I realize how much Garrison Abbey is glad to be in my company. Mine.

Willow Moore from Maine.

You may not be such a fool after all.

25

PRESENT DAY – December
London, England

WILLOW HALE
Age 20

It's been almost a full 24-hours since I booked Garrison's flight to London. A delay from a snowstorm held up the plane in Philly all night, and he didn't actually leave the airport until noon today. The sun has already set, and my nerves have gone from worry to catastrophic levels.

Thank God for the flight tracker app. I've been obsessively watching the plane cross the ocean, and now it's only a couple minutes from landing.

Sitting on the steps to Bishop Hall, the wind picks up and howls. Music blasts from speakers on the snowy quad. A party starts to gain momentum, people dancing and passing around cans of cheap beer. Most of the parties here have been at houses or pubs, but apparently

Wakefield always has one themed party on the quad at the end of every year.

Tonight, the theme is "celestial" and everyone is wearing white, but I'm in a green puffer jacket and jeans. I don't even care that I stick out like a neon sign. My stomach knots, unable to join in the festivities.

I don't know what happened last night, but Garrison doesn't sound that upset unless something is going on with his family or the paparazzi or maybe his ex-high-school friends paid him a visit. My mind has been racing through the horrible possibilities.

I was even tempted to text Connor about Garrison's job to make sure he wasn't fired. But unless it's a group text, I don't really have a texting friendship with Connor Cobalt. And anyway, I'd much rather learn what's going on from Garrison, not run around him for information.

So I'm waiting.

"Willow!" Tess plops down on the stair beside me, beer in hand. She wears this fluffy, white fur coat that contrasts her rich brown skin. Glitter dots her cheeks. She looks gorgeous, truly fitting the celestial theme. Tess frowns when she sees my green jacket. "Do you have nothing white to wear? We can go to my closet."

I tuck a flyaway strand of hair behind my ear. "Thanks, but I'm not doing the party tonight. I'm actually waiting for Garrison to get here."

Tess's grin lights up her face. "Wait, we're going to meet the boyfriend tonight!" Her knees bounce in excitement and she claps her hands, even with a beer in one.

"I mean…maybe," I say.

At this point, I'm not sure what will happen. Garrison could arrive in London and then just hop on a plane back to Philly. He didn't want me going to the airport to pick him up. His words: *I'm already inconveniencing you enough. Please just let me get a cab, Willow.*

PRESENT DAY

Normally, I would have argued with him, but his voice was so… broken. I don't want to push him.

Tess sips her beer. "Well, I'll be excited to see him even from a distance. I can tell you love him a lot, and I may be biased, but I think you have great taste in people."

I match her smile.

Sheetal steps over in furry boots and a sleek white jumpsuit. "What are you two grinning about?"

"Tess was just saying that I have great taste in people," I say.

Sheetal narrows her eyes at her girlfriend. "I love how you find a proper way to compliment yourself inside a compliment to someone else. Bloody brilliant."

Tess smiles wider. "Say that again, but…" She tugs Sheetal onto her lap. "Now."

Sheetal's eyes fall into Tess's. "You're bloody brilliant." Their lips meet in a tender kiss, and I look away as the music changes to an EDM song that I recognize. It's one of Lo's favorites.

I let out a tense breath.

Sheetal breaks from Tess and frowns. "What's wrong, Willow?"

"Nothing, really," I mutter.

They both exchange concerned glances, and then Sheetal says, "You should be celebratin' like the boss champ you are. We all made the highest marks on our project. And second semester will be even better. Nowhere to go but up."

We did *very* well on our marketing project. It was a strange coincidence that we chose an umbrella for our marketing project, and then a month later Netflix dropped the trailer to their new show *The Umbrella Academy*. I'd already read the comics that the show's based on, and it seemed like a great opportunity to capitalize on the timing.

So we tied in some of our marketing around the show—and put in a budget of what it would cost to cross-promote with the studio and the actors. Of course, it was all a theoretical scenario. But I was able to put my old teenage skills in editing fan videos to good use, splicing the trailer into an ad. It was fun.

And it worked. The professor was impressed that we thought about our demographic: the superhero-obsessed generation.

Garrison and I already celebrated over Christmas. We read the comics together side-by-side while drinking champagne straight from the bottle.

Cold slices my exposed cheeks, and I zip my jacket higher, trying to block the wind. I shake my head. "I am excited about school," I tell Sheetal. "I'm just worried about my boyfriend."

Tess wraps an arm around Sheetal and explains, "Garrison is coming in tonight."

"Tonight?" Sheetal's brows rise.

I shrug. "It was a spontaneous thing."

"I'll say." Sheetal smiles, her excitement just as palpable as her girlfriend's. "We're finally meeting *the* boyfriend."

Tess nods. "That's what I said."

"Great minds—" Sheetal can't get the rest of the words out because Tess kisses her again.

My phone pings with a text. My stomach has butterflies, drunk on concern. Flapping around in my belly with an intoxicated, sluggish rhythm.

Garrison: Just got in the cab. Be there in twenty.

I just need him to be okay. *Please* be okay.
That's all I can hope.

PRESENT DAY

26

GARRISON ABBEY
Age 21

An excruciating delay, an eight-hour flight, and twenty-minute cab ride later, I've finally arrived at Wakefield. The snow-blanketed quad in front of Bishop Hall is filled with inflatable jumping houses that little kids have for birthday parties. Music thumps the cobblestone path.

Willow warned me that since this is the one and only party on the quad it's a bit extravagant, but it feels more like some strange carnival. People dressed in all white, some have angel wings on their backs.

College is weird, man.

I tip back a small travel bottle of vodka to my mouth. The liquor slides easy down my throat. In first class, they were handing me these almost every fucking hour.

Okay, I asked for them.

It's been a shitty day. A shitty year.

A shitty life.

Each step towards the brick building is heavy. A couple of people shoot me weird looks, eyeing my clothes. Red T-shirt. Black hoodie jacket. Dark pants. If I came here to blend, I'm failing at critical levels.

My small duffel is slung on my shoulder. Cold wind bites my face, and I press my phone to my ear. No gloves. Forgot those on my hurried course to the airport. My fingers sear from the chill.

Willow picks up on the first ring. "Are you here?" she asks, urgency to her words.

"Yeah, present." I spin around, trying to find her. But everything suddenly blurs. My head tilts. Sickness rises in my throat. Shit.

"I'm waiting in front of the building," she says. "You can't miss me. I'm in green."

She didn't dress up for this party. She's been waiting for me. I don't know why that makes me feel like worse shit.

I rub my eyes. An angel passes me, laughing shrilly with her friends. I blink hard. *Jesus.* Where am I? I down the rest of the vodka and toss the little bottle off to the side. It lands in a deeper patch of snow.

"Garrison," Willow says, still on the other line. "I think I see you. Turn to your left."

I turn in a circle again.

"Your left," Willow repeats.

I stop, close my eyes, take a breath. Open them, but as I follow her instructions, she says, "I'm coming to you. Don't move."

Finally, I see her. Green puffy winter jacket. Glasses perched on her nose. Hair blowing in the wind. She's pocketing her cell so she can walk faster.

PRESENT DAY

People wave to her like they know her. And I realize…she's popular here. Has a bunch of friends. Is loved and wanted. She brushes them off with a perfunctory smile, her course on me.

What the fuck am I doing here?

What the fuck am I doing to her?

My chest blazes in pain. I stumble back, almost falling onto my ass, but someone catches me by the arm.

I jolt, the touch pushing me to panic, and I shove at the person on instinct.

"Whoa!" The guy steps back, eyes confused and angry. "Just trying to help, man."

His voice. His accent is so familiar. And then I really look at him. Windswept hair and wide jaw. White sports coat, white pants and angel wings on his back. *You've got to be shitting me.*

"Salvatore." Willow jogs over, out of breath as she lands next to her friend. She waves to me. "This is—"

"Her boyfriend," I say. It doesn't come out right, though. I feel like a jerk.

Salvatore looks between us and he nods slowly, connecting the dots. I don't know what she's told him about me, but the way he's appraising me like I'm *exactly* what he pictured has me on edge.

"What are you looking at?" I snap at him.

"Garrison," Willow says and reaches for my hand, but I pull away. My focus is on Salvatore. All my rage pooling into this one goddamn thing.

Salvatore narrows his eyes at me. "Are you drunk?"

I wave my arms around. "Look around, *Salvatore.* We're at a college party. Everyone is drunk." I hate his name. It's cooler than mine. It still reminds me of that vampire TV show that Willow and I used to watch together. Gif sets that we'd send to each other.

It's like the universe is mocking me.

Here he is.

In fucking angel wings.

I mean, come on.

"Garrison," Willow says, but she doesn't try to reach for me again. "Let's just go inside." She hugs her arms to her chest.

Salvatore shakes his head and under his breath, but loud enough for me to hear, he says, "I don't think you should be alone with him, Willow."

"Fuck you, man," I growl. "I'm her boyfriend. Who are you again?" My voice accidentally grows louder, and people close by stop their conversations to watch us. Willow takes a step back as if she can physically avoid the attention.

My whole body tenses like my brother just slammed a fist into my gut again.

The world around me spins. I touch my pocket, hoping for a cigarette, but I think I ran out in the cab.

"I'm her friend," Salvatore refutes.

"Salvatore, you don't understand," Willow says quickly, sticking up for me.

"I understand that he's drunk and obviously angry and you shouldn't be near him right now," he says. That really rubs me the wrong way. Him dictating who she can even talk to. I don't care if it comes from a place of concern. Willow and I have been through more together than he'll ever know.

"Hey, she can make her own decisions," I snap and move towards my girl. She lets out a breath of relief.

But then Salvatore says something. I think *hold on*. He puts his hands on my shoulders to stop me from walking to Willow. It's a light touch, but it feels like someone descended fifty tons onto me. And I just swing.

My fist connects with Salvatore's cheek. Hard enough that he goes down on the ground.

Some other guy with jet-black hair is pushing me back like I might go in for a kick to the stomach. I wouldn't. I don't…I don't even know why I punched him.

My head throbs now.

My knuckles burn.

"Garrison!" Willow yells, but I can't see her.

"Get off!" I say to the guy trying to push me back. "Get the fuck off!" I hold up my hands, showing him I'm not going to start in on Salvatore.

He steps back.

People begin to clear a path, and I notice Salvatore rising to his feet, his angel wings bent from the fall. Willow stands near but her eyes flit around the crowds, searching for me. Two girls flank her sides and whisper to her. Their lips move hurriedly. I recognize them instantly: Sheetal and Tess.

Sheetal's hands gesticulate angrily and she waves them in my direction.

I can imagine what they're saying to Willow. *Don't go with Garrison. He's jealous, dangerous.*

Willow's gaze finally finds mine. Her brown eyes sink with pure concern. She's not scared or hurt or mad at me.

She should be.

I'm not a good guy.

Hasn't tonight proven that?

I take a step back and glance towards the street. Maybe I can catch a cab…

"Garrison." Willow's voice draws me in; she's already moving towards me, despite her friends' protests. She reaches my side and almost tries to touch my hand again, but she stops herself short. In a whisper, she breathes, "Can I hold your hand?"

"No." My answer is quick and caustic.

It knocks her back. But she blinks and nods. "Okay." She crosses her arms over her chest like she's cold.

"I'm going to go," I tell her.

She shakes her head adamantly. Hurt and confusion bunching her brows. "No. You're not leaving."

I can feel the cellphones whipped out, recording us. I don't even know if they realize who we are, or if they're just doing it for the internet. People are cruel like that.

One of the worst nights of my life will be out there for public consumption. For their entertainment. Hell, I used to be one of them. Feeding the gluttonous, cannibalistic internet at someone else's expense.

I can't tell if it's the cold, but it's harder to breathe all of a sudden. The wind stabs my lungs.

I lean closer to her.

The music picks up near the party.

"Willow," I whisper. "I think we should…" *Break up.* I can't even force out those words without my eyes reddening. Pain searing. It's selfish of me not to end this.

I know that.

She glares as tears run down her cheek. "Don't you dare. I *love* you, Garrison."

"I love you, too." I'll always love her. I stuff my chilled, burning hands into my pockets. "It's why I have to go."

PRESENT DAY

We stand in the middle of her college campus. Phones pointed at us. And I feel like I've grabbed a shovel and buried us both under.

"You're not breaking up with me," Willow says in defiance. Like it can't be done. "I won't let you."

I don't deserve her. *I don't deserve her.* God, I don't. But I'm ruining her. My eyes sear, cold stinging the water that threatens to spill. "Willow—"

"You want to go," she says. "I heard you. So we're going to get in a cab and drive to the airport and you're going to fly home. But I'm coming with you to the airport. You don't have to talk. We can just *sit*. And then when you're back in Philly and sober, you'll call me. You'll tell me what's wrong."

I don't know if I will.

But I nod.

"I love you," she says again. Wrapping her arms around herself because I won't let her touch me. If she touches me, she'll know I bruised…or broke my ribs. Or rather, my brother broke them.

Maybe she already knows. It's probably on her list of possibilities. Still I can't bring myself to mention what happened. It doesn't excuse me punching her friend. It doesn't excuse how I ruined tonight.

Yeah, I should let her go. Reject her offer. But I feel like the inked skeleton, fingers slipping from the one thing still alive in its hand.

And I hold on.

I'm holding on.

But I don't know where we go from here.

CONTINUE THE STORY. . .

Garrison & Willow's story continues and concludes in Book 2

of the Bad Reputatuon Duet, which still follows

both past and present storylines!

It's all going down in _Wherever You Are_!

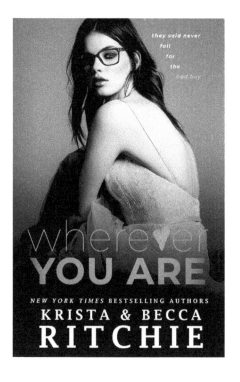

CONNECT WITH KRISTA & BECCA

www.kbritchie.com

www.facebook.com/KBRitchie

www.instagram.com/kbmritchie

ACKNOWLEDGEMENTS

Pizza, comic books, video games, pop culture references (hello, *Gilmore Girls* and *One Tree Hill*)—this book is a bowl of nostalgia that we've absolutely *loved* writing and experiencing together. Whatever It Takes has always been this overwhelming passion project of ours, and to be able to return to Willow & Garrison's love story (as they were first side characters in the Addicted series) and give them *more* is what dreams are made of.

Their romance and journey isn't over yet, but we have amazing people to thank for making Whatever It Takes possible.

To our superhero mom, thank you for being our Rose Calloway, our fierce supporter when we're doubting ourselves. You always come in the clutch when we need you, and this book wouldn't be nearly as sparkly without your touch. We love you like Garrison loves pizza!

To our agent Kimberly Brower, thank you for helping Garrison & Willow's story become audiobooks! It's a dream to be able to hear their romance come to life.

To Jenn, Lanie, and Shea, thank you so much for believing in us and helping us shout about Willow & Garrison from the rooftops of the world. We're the luckiest twins to be able to know you three and that you still love our books and characters after all these years. We love you like family.

To patrons, this book wouldn't have been possible without you. *Thankyouthankyouthankyou.* We're able to keep writing full-time because of you, and you're a huge reason why we were able to return to side characters like Willow & Garrison and take time to write their stories.

And finally, thank you to the Fizzle Force and to you, dear reader, for finishing this book in its entirety. We're incredibly grateful that you've taken the time to read our words when so many books exist, and we hope that you've enjoyed spending your day with comic-book-loving, video game and TV-obsessed geeks.

More is on the way! Next up is *Wherever You Are*, the conclusion to the duet, and hold onto your pizza slices, it might be a bumpy ride!

CPSIA information can be obtained
at www.ICGtesting.com
Printed in the USA
LVHW041730170322
713685LV00001B/55